fallingoverstandingstill

John Jantunen

Vocamus Press
Guelph, Ontario

Cover art by Francisco Goya
Public Domain

ISBN 13: 978-0-9880176-9-6 (pbk)
ISBN 13: 978-0-9880176-6-5 (ebk)

Vocamus Press
130 Dublin Street, North
Guelph, Ontario, Canada
N1H 4N4

www.vocamus.net

2012

To Tanja

Freedom

The word was scratched in six inch high letters on the wall over the bed in René's room. Underneath: a series of hash marks, the kind prisoners in movies make on the walls of their cells. Six groups of five and four on the side. Thirty-four days of freedom.

For thirteen of those days René had been living in Larry and Heather's basement. Leather and Harry. That's what he called them, or sometimes The Good King Larry and His Wonderful Wife Heather. He'd scratched the word into the wall using a pocket knife on his first night. It was late. They'd stayed up talking and listening to music, old stuff like Muddy Waters and Jethro Tull, all the while drinking a full case of beer and smoking forty dollars worth of weed. He'd been buzzed all right but it was a clear buzz. After a while even Heather had joined in. She'd finished the dishes and swept then sat at the kitchen table and asked for a hit. When Larry passed her the joint she held it for a moment.

"Sorry Mike," she said then took a taster. Her next inhale was deep and long, the kind you take when you're a kid doing knives to impress friends.

"Who's Mike?" René asked when she finally blew the smoke out in a long, carefully measured stream.

"Mike's my brother. And he's also–"

Larry reached out and put his hand on hers. She looked shyly at René then shook her head.

"He's also?"

But the joint had already come back to her. She took another drag and by the time she'd exhaled she'd either forgotten what she was going to say or wanted to move on.

"Hey, let's play cards," she exclaimed. "I love getting stoned and playing cards. Do you know how to play three-handed euchre?"

"Sure."

They played until three in the morning when Larry fell off his chair trying to decide whether two aces were enough to back up a king and a nine. Heather ushered René into the bathroom first and after he'd pissed up a six pack's worth, Larry saw him to the top of the basement stairs.

"See you tomorrow," he said.

"Yeah, shit."

René went downstairs with an armload of blankets, a pillow and a pocketful of toilet paper he'd nicked from the bathroom. He made his bed and stripped off his pants then paced the room, not much bigger than a prison cell. He wanted to scream and laugh and run out into the night. He wanted above all to be with a woman. He wanted to get laid and afterwards whisper into her ear, "Freedom." She wouldn't have understood, or maybe she would have, it didn't matter. It would have made her smile. Or frown. Or ask, "What do you mean?" And all those words bottled up inside him would have come out in a flood. He would cry and she, this imagined woman, would run her hand through his hair and tell him that no man had ever had the courage to cry in front of her. "You're the bravest man I've ever met," she'd say and they'd fuck again, desperate like it was the end of the world. One last screw for all time.

Above him, the house grew silent. Lying in bed, he unfurled the ball of toilet paper and quietly jerked off. Afterwards, he craned to reach his jeans crumpled on the floor, to get the knife out of his pocket, then scratched the word into the wall.

Freedom

The sight of it spelled out two feet from his pillow made him want to cry.

heather&winnie

Four hours after Larry and René had left for work, Heather came downstairs to look for a roach in the small black iron woodstove that she suspected René was using as a garbage can. Before he came, before she began referring to it as René's Room, the room had been a mystery to her. It had all the charm of a root cellar – four bare concrete walls, uneven with splinters of wood stuck to the cement where the forms had been ripped off, and in place of a ceiling, exposed rows of ten by ones with strips of blackened, peeling bark trailing from their edges. Someone had laid a bright orange carpet the texture of Astroturf on the floor. A fold-up bed and a wooden desk had been added, the latter's steel-grey paint speckled with nicks as if its final resting place had come after a lifetime of searching. Beside the door, hollow and made of cheap plywood – a closet door – sat the small woodstove.

Three years ago, when she and Larry first moved into the house, Heather had thought of using the room for storage but Larry'd warned her against it.

—There's no ventilation. Anything you put down there will just rot.

Larry was in construction so Heather took his word for it and the room remained exactly as it was until René had left his mark on the wall.

Freedom

When she flicked on the light the word was a shock to her, as if it had said Satan Rules or For A Good Blow Job Call Heather 645 - 18-, and she stood staring at it thinking, I was right, Larry. She could have stood there all day and when Larry saw her she wouldn't have to say a damn thing because he'd know, seeing her standing there like a statue, that she'd been right.

—I was goddamned right, Larry.

Mumbling it to herself broke the spell. She glanced at the wood-stove and saw that its door was wide open. The terror she had felt evaporated, replaced by a mild revulsion. Several crumpled-up wads of toilet paper were visible amongst assorted chip bags and apple cores. She'd have to dig for a roach and God knows what he'd picked up in jail.

□□□

Noon News
The Moose, 100.9 FM
July 1, 20—

Police are speculating that alcohol may have been a factor in a hit and run that killed a thirty-five year-old man and sent a nine month old girl to hospital. At approximately 3:30 pm on Friday, Charles Frick was driving on Highway 35 with his infant daughter in the back seat when his Mustang convertible was struck head on by a white Ford pick-up truck that swerved into his lane. Both vehicles sustained heavy damage though the pick-up was still able to drive away from the scene of the accident. A search of the area located it in an abandoned sand pit several kilometres away. Its plates had been removed before it was set on fire. Police are asking anyone who has information regarding the white pick-up or the person driving it to call Crimestoppers at 1-800-222-8477.

□□□

On the drive to work the news was horrendous. The two lead stories were about a suicide bombing and a pedophile ring, and midway through the latter Heather switched the radio from the CBC to the local station, The Moose, where Kim Mitchell was singing about patio lanterns. She sang the first few lines of his other song, the one with guitars, before giving up and turning the stereo down low.

It had been three weeks since they'd met that couple at the falls, whatever their names were, and she'd told Larry that she'd wanted René out. Is it because he's an Indian, he'd spat at her.

—How dare you ask me that? When my brother- How dare you? It's because he just got out of prison. It's because he almost killed a woman.

—That's not the way it happened.

—How can you be sure?

—I can't, but I take his word on faith.

Faith. When her brother used the word it came out full of hope, like it was a challenge to the world. When Larry used it, it felt like an accusation.

—And what about last night?

—What about it?

—I can't live this way, Larry.

Something tickled her nose and she looked at the ashtray. Smoke trailed out from amongst the butts, jumbled like a game of pick-up sticks. She poked at the pile with her thumb, trying to extinguish the embers that had spread from her most recent cigarette to the three or four surrounding it. A horn honked from behind and she looked at the green light suspended over the intersection in downtown Bracebridge.

—Shit.

She applied the gas and the Sunfire lurched forward.

How long did I sit there? Fuck. What if it was a cop behind me? This is why you promised you weren't going to get stoned before going to work. It's fine when you get there, but you always forget about the drive. And with the new laws. They can take a blood sample. And how does that work anyway? Do they stab you right there on the road or do you have to go to the station?

Heather took a deep breath. Thirty seconds from work and she was freaking out. Get it together girl, she scolded herself, doing her best to keep her eyes alert to the road. On the radio, the song had ended and a news announcer was saying something alarming. Heather pulled to a stop at the four-way before the bridge and turned up the volume.

—Police have issued a warning to people in the Bracebridge area to be on the lookout for the two pit bulls responsible for this early morning attack. One is brown with white spots and the other is white with a brown eye patch. Police urge extreme caution when dealing with these two dogs and advise anyone who spots them to call 911 immediately.

The car bumped onto the bridge spanning the falls and Heather's eyes drifted to the Canadian and American flags given equal weight on either side.

Did he say one of them killed a three year-old? Jesus. How many three year-olds do I know?

□□□

From An Interview with Morgan Reilly
July 2, 20–
O.P.P, Bracebridge Detachment
Attending Officers, B.P & S.T.

Yeah, it was my dog that attacked the kid. I don't know why you're fucking asking. You already know it was. But it never would have happened if you fucking cops hadn't come busting in the way you did. I hear your buddy lost a finger. Serves him right. It's a fucking duplex. Seems like the kind of thing you'd have uncovered in your, uh, investigation. Why do you think I have the dogs? Living underneath that...fuck. It's him you should be talking to. He's the fuck who stole my car. What car? The blue piece of shit Cavalier that was parked in the driveway beside my house. My car. He's driving a blue piece of shit Cavalier leaking oil so bad you could light a match and follow the trail of fire. Why aren't you writing this down? Huh? Ah, fuck it then, don't. So what about the kid? How is he? Dead? Well I hope you're real fucking proud of yourselves.

□□□

—What's with the Christmas tree?

It was sitting in the front lobby of The Riverside Inn, twelve feet tall and covered with tinsel. Derek, a bus boy from the restaurant, was perched on a ladder sawing off the top so that he could get a glass star to fit.

—It's Christmas in July.

Lorraine looked up from behind the reception desk, saw who it was and went back to her computer.

—That's this week?

Hustling up the stairs, Heather flung open the heavy, steel door leading to the west hallway. Pearl and Mavis were already pushing their carts towards the elevator. She hung her purse on the hook below her name in the supply room and pulled her cart into the hallway. The stock sheet was hanging from her clipboard and she navigated the series of boxes without fault, expertly checking them off down the line. A few minutes later, scanning the shelves in the supply room, she heard Mr. Crane calling her name from the hall.

She ducked her head out and gave her boss a quick glance. Lips upturned, perhaps a smile, wearing his glasses, not cleaning them, chewing gum. The latter threw her off because whenever Mr. Crane bawled her out for being late he liked to chew gum.

—Good morning Mr. Crane.

—Ian, please.

Heather nodded.

—You know where the chocolate Santas are?

—Should be in a box marked X-mas in July.

Mr. Crane took a step closer, trying his best, Heather could see, to not look at the shelf she'd been staring at for the past two minutes.

—The box was empty. Pearl and Mavis must have got the last ones.

—I'll have Derek check the store room.

—Thanks.

Heather smiled and Mr. Crane turned slightly, drawing her attention to the woman standing behind him. She was young, late teens or early twenties, and black, the colour of ground coffee. Her hair was pulled into a ponytail so tight that her face looked like a mask. She'd been working in the kitchen, as far as Heather knew, for a couple months. Her name was Wendy or—

—Winnie.

Mr. Crane had been talking but the woman's name was all Heather managed to catch.

—I need you to train her today.

Mr. Crane squinted his eyes sharply, stressing the urgency of the matter, then looked to Winnie.

—Just listen to Heather, and you'll do fine.

—Thank you, Mr. Crane.

—Ian.

—Yes, Ian. Sorry.

Mr. Crane rubbed his hands together.

—Well, carry on.

Heather didn't look at Winnie again until they were alone in room 203. Heather had opened the door with her pass card and, handing Winnie two sets of sheets, told her to set one on each of the doubles. She followed her in carrying two neatly folded blankets and scanned the younger woman's behind. Skinny, she thought, telling herself right after that she didn't mean anything by it. She made the first bed then got Winnie to practise on the other. It was kind of tricky and Mr. Crane was very particular. Some trainees took a couple of hours before they got it right. Winnie's first try was almost perfect and her second was as good as Heather's. By break she was doing her own rooms unsupervised and the only time Heather had to add anything was when she stood at the door of a single watching her arrange the bouquet of flowers on the dresser. After three breaths, Heather interrupted her by saying that they didn't have to be perfect. Winnie startled, recovering with a big, toothy grin.

—They are lovely.

—Yes.

—What are they called?

—Um, they're Christmas flowers.

—Christmas flowers?

—Yes.

—They are very lovely.

The name of the flowers came to Heather during lunch break. She was sitting beside Winnie on one of two benches overlooking the pier that Mr. Crane said the staff could use. They were the only two that didn't have a roof over them so they were exposed to the elements and were disintegrating quicker than the ones reserved for guests. The wood was frosted with mildew; white swirls that reminded Heather of snow even though it was the heat and rain that made them. She scratched at the surface with a fingernail, trying to distract herself from the grumbling in her stomach. The surface peeled back as easily as the skin of an apple. Inside the wood was dark and spongy. Scraping at the wood lodged under a fingernail with her car key the name had popped into her head.

—They're called poinsettias.

—Excuse me?

—The Christmas flowers.

—Oh.

—I remembered, like, two minutes later.

Winnie smiled and took a bite from her sandwich. Tuna fish. Plain with a little mayonnaise. Heather'd left her lunch on the counter at home. Flies would be buzzing around it in the July heat. She drank two cups of coffee instead, along with a handful of saltine packets she'd swiped when she was cleaning the Continental Room and three cigarettes. Smoke from the last one had settled around the bench. Heather waved at it, trying to ward it away from Winnie and looked over at Pearl and Mavis.

They were talking about the three year-old who'd been killed by the dogs. For most of the morning, it had been stuck in Heather's head, this not knowing for sure. Same feeling that made her always read to the last page of the mysteries she bought from the quarter bin in front of the bookstore downtown. She'd have asked Lorraine but Lorraine would have told her that she didn't know anything about it because Lorraine didn't talk to cleaning ladies in front of the guests.

—Pearl will know.

She muttered it when she was restocking her cart and also when she was sitting on the toilet in 219, flipping through a fashion magazine left by a guest. Hush now, she told herself each time, and when that didn't help she frowned at her reflection in the mirror to show she meant it. Pearl was cleaning the east wing. After she disappeared into the elevator Heather hadn't seen her until break, two hours later. By then Heather already knew as much as she needed to about what had happened to the three year-old. The radio playing in the Continental Room had filled her in between wiping down the sink and swiping the saltines.

—It's terrible.

Mavis patted her arm and told her again that she should go home. Pearl shook her head.

—I bounced him on my knee three days ago.

—It's horrible.

—I can't stop thinking of his mother.

—Poor thing.

—I'm going to make her a lasagne.

—You make the best lasagne.

Pearl let out a staggered sigh and Mavis speared a crisp of lettuce from the Tupperware container in her lap. Stubbing her cigarette,

Heather pulled the last cracker from its pack and stared at the Lady Muskoka, the sightseeing ship moored a few feet from where she sat. Winnie folded the crusts of her sandwich into the square of tin foil in her lap and set it on the bench, then took an apple from her brown paper lunch bag. She turned it over in her hand, inspecting every inch of it before taking a bite. Heather'd picked up a few things about her over the past two months, things that she'd overheard, she couldn't exactly say when or from whom, but there they were, little tidbits that didn't make the person anymore or any less than what she looked like sitting there beside her, eating an apple and squinting against the sun, smelling vaguely of cleaning solution and something sweet that Heather couldn't place. Cinnamon maybe.

—Africa.

Heather garbled it between chews, not meaning to but there it was.

—Pardon?

—So you're from Africa.

—Yes. Uganda.

—It must be exciting coming to another country-

—Yes.

—Meeting new people.

—It is very exciting.

—I'll bet your parents miss you.

Winnie smiled, lowering her eyes, and cast a discreet look at her watch.

—We should be getting back.

—Right.

Winnie reached for her folded square of tinfoil then brushed the crumbs from her slacks with her free hand and stood.

—See you inside.

Salt from the cracker stung a crack in Heather's lip. She licked at it as she watched Winnie walk in a straight line towards the building, veering only at the last minute so she could drop her garbage in the can beside the back door.

☐☐☐

From Comments Issued By O.P.P Sergeant D. Ball,
O.P.P. Press Conference, Bracebridge
July 4, 20–

First off I want to express my deepest, deepest sympathies to the Allen family over the loss of their son. It's horrible what happened. I really can't express how dreadful everyone involved in the investigation is feeling...We um, we-we had received several tips about the location of Darren Bourque, the individual alleged to be responsible for the crash that killed Mr. Charles Frick on July 1, 20–, and sent his infant daughter to the hospital where I have, uh, I have just been told that she is in stable condition. Um, on July 3rd, at approximately 8:05 am, several officers were dispatched to 240 Hiram Street as per the information we had received. They followed standard protocol for issuing an arrest warrant. Two officers knocked on the front door while a team of officers positioned themselves in the rear of the building in case the suspect fled. Ahem. An individual, later identified as the resident of the ground floor apartment, was observed exiting the house through the rear sliding doors. He stepped to the edge of the deck and proceeded to urinate. The officer's positioned in the rear of the house, um, mistook this individual for Mr. Bourque and executed the warrant. Two officers remained to secure this individual while two other officers entered the house through the rear sliding doors. Upon announcing their presence they observed an individual, a woman, attempting to flee through a side door and intercepted her. She resisted, both physically and verbally, and it was while the officers were struggling with her that Officer Dumoulin was attacked by the resident's two dogs. The male, we believe it was the male, bit Officer Dumoulin in the hand, severing two of his fingers, and the female latched onto his leg. Officer Dumoulin fired a single shot which struck the female dog in or around the head. She immediately released and ran out through the rear sliding doors. The male dog followed her and they were observed running from the yard and, um, disappearing through the row of trees that separated the property from the Allen's, uh, backyard. We have time for a few questions ...Yes, um, well, as you can imagine there was a great deal of confusion, given the circumstances. We had one officer requiring medical attention and two individuals who were uncooperative and in the case of the woman, combative. And um, of course there was the matter of Mr. Bourque, who was, uh, determined to be residing in the top portion of the house but was not at home ... Yes, I agree that it would have been ideal had the officers at 240 Hiram, given their proximity to the Allen residence, been the ones to have responded to the 911 call from Mrs. Allen but as I said there was a great deal of confusion ... No, the response time was well within official guidelines ... I don't have the times that the two calls were made to 911 ... I don't know why an ambulance was dispatched to 240 Hiram Street in advance of the Allen residence ... Um, that's a question for the coroner's office ... Sorry, I can't comment on an ongoing investigation ... We haven't located the two dogs yet ... Officer Dumoulin is recovering ... No, his fingers have not been recovered. That's all the time I have. Thank you.

□□□

Heather sat in her car after work and smoked a cigarette. Afterwards, she lit another from the cherry of the first and smoked half of that before she saw Winnie come out of The Riverside Inn's front doors. She finished it while she waited for Winnie to cross the parking lot then started her car and drove after her.

Winnie had traded her uniform for a floral-print dress. She'd taken off her running shoes and was carrying them as she walked along the shoulder of the road. Heather thought her feet were bare and that she must have developed thick soles walking around Africa. When she got closer though, she saw that she was wearing yellow flip-flops, the same kind that Heather had bought at the dollar store for when she went to the beach. She drew the car up alongside her and leaned over to roll the passenger window down.

—You need a lift?

Winnie smiled and opened the door.

—Where do you live?

Winnie snapped the buckle into place and tested it to make sure it was tight.

—By the school.

—Which school?

—The one with the machines.

—The machines? Oh, you must mean Monk.

—Yes, that is it. Monk.

Heather turned right at the lights and drove across the bridge. Both she and Winnie looked down at the tourists piling into the Lady Muskoka for the evening cruise.

—That's a long walk.

—It is not so bad.

Heather nodded and snuck a quick peek sideways at her. Hands folded in her lap, eyes wandering back from the river unsure of what to latch onto next.

—So, how do you like The Riverside?

—It is nice. Ian is very nice.

—Mr. Crane.

—He said-

—I know what he said but he hates it when the cleaning ladies call him Ian.

—Oh. Then why-

—You got me.

Heather laughed and looked to Winnie. She wore a puzzled expression.

—You'll get used to it.

The car accelerated through a yellow light at Dill Street. Heather took her foot off the pedal and it coasted, losing speed, and was back at sixty by the time it'd passed the old community centre that had sat derelict ever since they'd built a swimming pool into the new high school. On the left, the houses along Wellington Street broke for Monk Field, a square of grass big enough to play six soccer games on at once. On the far side, an excavator dug out the foundation for the school's expansion, and a dozen men stood around watching and smoking cigarettes in between whatever it was that they were yelling at each other above the noise.

—They're working late.

—Yes, every night.

A man stepped into the middle of the road holding a stop sign. Heather applied the gas and swerved around him. The dump truck pulling out of Monk's parking lot honked and Heather waved. Just another ditzy blonde, don't mind me, it seemed to say, although fuck-you-get-out-of-my-way was closer to what she was thinking.

—It is the next right.

The next right was actually straight, as the main road curved around towards the mall. On the sidewalk, a child lay underneath a tricycle screaming while a fat woman sat on the steps of a row house, yelling for him to get up.

—It is the last house.

Heather pulled the stick out of gear and let the car drift to the curb. Winnie unbuckled her belt.

—Thank you.

—Hey, no problem.

Opening the door, Winnie stretched one leg out then turned back to Heather.

—Can I show you something?

—What's that?

—Come, I will show.

Heather shrugged. Unstrapping her belt she slipped out of her seat and followed Winnie up her front walkway. She waited at the bottom of the steps while Winnie pulled a long strand of shoelace from her purse. Tied to the end of it was a key. She used it to open the door.

—It is in here.

Winnie strode across the kitchen floor, not bothering to turn the light on. She pulled a towel from underneath the bedroom door, opened it and stepped quickly inside. Heather hurried in behind. Light from the bare window revealed a starkness to the room that Heather found unnerving, as if it being so empty meant that there must be something terrible hiding in there. A bed with neatly made maroon blankets, same as the ones at The Riverside, was wedged in the far corner and a plain white dresser sat beside it. A hole in the wall, at fist level, was the only ornament and there was a faint odour of cat piss.

Winnie gathered the hem of her dress in one hand and knelt down in the middle of the room. She bent her cheek to the floor, craning her head to look under the bed, and immediately yelped then scurried backwards towards the door. Her hand shot out and she pointed to where she had been looking.

—It is there.

Heather, standing by the door, took an involuntary step forward then checked herself.

—What?

—A snake.

—A snake?

—Yes.

Heather walked to the middle of the room and imitated Winnie's caution as she bent to have a look. Pin pricks of light shone off the snake's eyes, staring straight at Heather.

—It's just a little garter. Do you have a broom?

Winnie hurried from the room and Heather eased to her feet. Pain shot through her lower back and she thought about the kid trapped under the tricycle while his mother sat on the steps unwilling, or unable, to get up and help.

□□□

From anonymous comments posted in July 20–,
on the message board of bracebridgegazette.ca.

—This is in response to the letter to the editor written by L. Waverly in today's paper. She wrote, "They shouldn't have just muzzled and neutered the dogs they should have muzzled and neutered the owners too.' I would just like to say that I have a pit bull, Smiley. We got him just before my son was born and he's been William's best friend and sleeping buddy for his entire life. He loves that dog more than anything but when he got home from daycare today he wouldn't go near him. I asked him what was wrong and he said he's afraid Smiley was going to kill him like he killed that other boy. So L. Waverly, why don't you come over and explain to my four year-old how cutting his dad's balls off is going to give him his best friend back.
—Right on, man. Pit bull owner. 17 years. 3 dogs. That law is bullshit. Those fucking muzzles make them look like Hannibal Lector. Who wouldn't be afraid?
—Here's a question? What breed is responsible for the most attacks on people? Golden retrievers, that's what. You buy your dog from a puppy mill and beat him when pisses on the rug he's going to turn mean. You can't legislate personal responsibility.
—What about cars? How many people die in car accidents every year. A helluva lot more than are killed by pit bulls but we don't make cars illegal.
—God, if I have to hear that argument about cars one more time. Cars have killed more people than smokers. Cars have killed more people than trans fat. Cars have also killed more people than nuclear bombs but I don't think it should be legal to bring one into your home.
—And cars weren't designed to kill people.
—And neither were pit bulls. Look it up. They were used for centuries in England as farm dogs, working dogs, to bring in the cattle and to

kill vermin that attacked the crops. It's just another example of how the working man, and his dog, gets screwed.

—Actually it is true that the 'pit bull' was originally bred to kill - other dogs. However the dogs lived at home as a family pet in the late 1800s. They lived in the house with the wives and children of the men who fought their dogs for sport, so they needed to be absolutely reliable around people. Dogs that showed human aggression were culled - that means they were euthanized and never bred from. These actions have evolved a unique dog personality where animal aggression has absolutely no correlation to human aggression.

—There's not even such a thing as a pit bull. There's like a half dozen breeds that all get called that. I have a Staffordshire Bull Terrier not a goddamn pit bull. I'm sick and tired of always having to explain that.

—Then why do you have a pit bull?

—Staffordshire Bull Terrier.

—A pit bull by any other name is still a pit bull.

—And a fucking retard is still a fucking retard.

—Just what I'd expect from a pit bull owner.

—I have an American Staffordshire Terrier, pit bull, whatever. And you better be afraid. You come into my house and I don't want you there, you're going to lose an arm.

◻◻◻

Heather sat at the kitchen table with one hand resting on the shoe box. She could feel the snake batting its head against the sides and the lid. Every bump sent a little thrill through her like putting her hand on her sister's belly had when she was pregnant. Then, she had mumbled an agreement when Lara had asked her if it made her want to have one too, but the truth was she'd just as soon have this snake inside her as a baby. She'd said as much to Larry on the first night they'd spent together. His reply had been the last word they'd had on the subject. Too fucked up, he'd said. Whether he was talking about himself or the world Heather couldn't tell. They'd both had a lot to drink.

In the kitchenette, Winnie cut lemon slices while she waited for the kettle to boil on the stove. She'd been talking about her uncle getting bitten by a snake and dying.

—That's terrible.

—Yes. It was very bad for my aunt.

Winnie poured water from the kettle into two cups and pinched a lemon slice over the rim of each.

—We will drink outside, I think.

—Sounds good.

The sliding door in the living room led to a small patio that resembled a swim raft, the kind that every lake in Muskoka was littered with. Peels of paint crunched under foot and the shards stuck to Heather's socks. There were no chairs. Winnie sat on the edge and Heather sat beside her. She was still wearing her uniform, a maroon golf shirt and black slacks, and felt hot and sticky. She pulled off her socks and shook them out onto the lawn then laid them flat on the deck. She stretched her feet into the grass, clenching the blades between her toes. The grass felt like hairs and she pulled upwards until she could feel the blades ripping then released. Closing her eyes, she took a deep breath then exhaled slowly between parted teeth.

Cars could be heard beyond the hedge separating the small backyard from the street. Little snatches of music drifted in and out with them - quick flares of electric guitar and deep rolling bass lines that blotted out everything else - nothing that Heather recognised as a song. Beside her, Winnie sipped at her tea. She opened her eyes and took up her cup. She dropped the lemon into the hot water then squeezed the brown out of the tea bag and set it on the deck. It was seven o'clock, the sky was just beginning to lose its light, and she hadn't eaten anything but crackers and chocolate Santas since breakfast.

—I like your place.

—John Williams, from the church, he lets me stay. Rent free.

—Can't beat that.

—No.

—Do you plan on staying long?

—I will stay until John Williams tells me to leave.

—No I mean, do you plan on staying in town long or–

—Oh. I am here until I get my education. I will become a doctor. Then I will return to Uganda.

—You're going back? Why?

—My country needs many doctors.

Heather sipped her tea.

—Where will you go to school?

—I do not know. Toronto, maybe. John Williams said the church would pay.

A note of uncertainly crept into her voice and Heather wondered what else John Williams had promised. She licked her teeth. They were aching for a cigarette but she'd left her pack in the car. Winnie stood and looked towards the house. She held her empty cup in her hands, her fingers crossed through its handle.

—The snake.

—Yes.

—You will kill it?

—It's bad luck to kill a snake.

—I see.

—We'll set it free.

—Far away?

—Far enough.

—I will use the bathroom first.

—Okay.

Heather waited by her car. She lit a smoke and held the box balanced against her hip. The door to the unit beside Winnie's was open and through it came the angry voices of a man and woman fighting.

—I don't give a flying fuck what he said. I want you out. Get out. Get the fuck out!

—This is the last time. I ain't coming back.

—Good.

The door slammed open and a skinny man-boy wearing loose fitting gym shorts and a pair of basketball shoes, his shirt clenched in his hand, skipped the middle of three steps on his way to the stone walkway. He let out an exasperated, Fuck!, and cut across the lawn heading for the sidewalk on an intercept course with the overturned trike. It looked to Heather like he was in search of something to kick but when he got to the trike, he righted it without missing a beat and gave it a gentle push towards home. A car on Wellington honked, jamming on its breaks, and the man-boy set off at a jog, his sneakers flap-slapping the pavement behind him. Ministry at max volume bled out of the neighbour's house, the singer screaming about thieves and liars.

Winnie locked the door behind her and wrapped the shoe string around her wrist as she walked towards Heather leaning against the Sunfire. Both watched the man-boy slide into the passenger seat of his friend's car, laughing at something the driver had said.

They set the snake free in the vacant lot behind Monk. It was wild with neglect and had a dirt road running through it, barricaded at either end with cement blocks. The snake made almost no sound as it disappeared into the tall grass. Heather chucked the shoe box in after it.

—I guess that's that.

—What is over there?

Heather turned to where Winnie was pointing.

—Christmas in July.

Heather lit a smoke and rubbed her tongue over her gums.

—You want to check it out?

—No. I am–

—Come on, it'll be fun.

—I have work to do.

—We won't be long.

—Okay.

—Perfect.

Heather led the way through the fringe of grass between the Monk playground and the dirt road. Winnie stayed close. She scoured the ground as if she was worried about running into the snake again.

—It's the dogs you should be worried about.

—Pardon?

—Watch out for the log.

—Oh yes, thank you.

Winnie stepped high over the fallen tree branch and hurried to catch up with Heather. The gravel crunched under their feet as they made their way towards the midway that had taken up most of the mall parking lot in view and, Heather suspected, a good chunk of the one around the corner. Halfway to where the road broke onto the driveway leading to the grocery store Heather stopped, listened then started again and stopped a few feet further along.

—What is wrong?

—Nothing.

—Do you hear something?

Heather shook her head and pitched her butt into the field.

—So what do people do for fun in Uganda?

—I think, the same as here. We visit friends and family. We play games. We watch TV. Sometimes we dance.

—I love to dance.

—I am not so good, but my little brother, he was a very good dancer. I used to watch him. Sometimes he would ask me to dance with him. It made me very happy.

They circled the cement barrier and stepped onto the asphalt. Heather glanced back at the field. The grass rustled though she could feel no breeze.

—He still there? In Uganda?

—No. He died. When I was at school. My whole family, they were killed.

—I'm sorry.

—Thank you.

—I didn't-

—It is okay.

□□□

From An Interview With Ronald Currie
Recorded by Deacon Riis, *Bracebridge Gazette*
July 15th, 20-

I saw the dogs, like I told the police. They was in the ravine behind the house. I'd show you exactly where but you ain't wearin' boots. It's a touch muddy down there. I go to collect the golf balls, you see. The golf course is on the other side of the ravine. Winds along half the back nine. Maybe find two, three dozen whenever I look, which is once or twice a week. I sell them at the end of the driveway. Clean 'em up first, of course. Built a special box with a lock on it so they could leave their money when they take the balls. Cemented the post four feet down. Ain't no one going to take that box. They can have the damn balls if they want 'em. Most often they pay though. Four dollars a dozen. I make enough for beer on Fridays. Used to go to The Albion, you know, to watch the peelers. They closed it years ago. Now I sit at the end of the driveway. I wash the balls that need it. Gives me something to do. The dogs, they come up from behind me. This was when I was down in the ravine, like I said, just behind the 12th green. A lot of golfers lose their balls on the 12th so I always start there. I didn't hear a sound until the one growled. They were on the other side of the creek. Ain't more than two or three feet of water across at this time of year, even with the rain we've been having which is a damn sight more than we used to get in June. The one could have jumped it, had at me or whatnot, no problem. The other, I could see it was hurt, and that's putting it lightly. Half its head was missing. Just the one good eye. The cop I talked to said that the officer who lost his fingers had shot it. I couldn't hardly believe it was standing, but there it was. It stood there just staring at me. Don't know for how long. Ten minutes, maybe more. The whole time the other one was growling, showing its teeth. I ain't afraid to say that it scared me something fierce. Nothing like facing a set of teeth that was meant for snapping bones to give the heart a tap. Then, all of a sudden, the one that was hurt just walked on. Just like that. The other one followed. I got out of there pretty quick. Found 17 balls already. Figured that was enough.

□□□

The midway was just as Heather expected it would be: loud and bright with the sickly sweet smell of candy floss not quite sickly sweet enough to cover the smell of the fumes generating all that loudness and brightness. Christmas music rang from the speakers, blaring a different song from every booth broken only by the Guns & Roses cranked on the stereo of a car parked behind the ring toss. Heather and Winnie walked past the games and stopped a moment to look at the rides. Parents stood around the metal fence of one called The Twirler. Some took photos and all waved to their kids when they whooshed by.

—I used to love that ride. When I was a kid. Except it was called The Scrambler.

—The Scrambler?

—Yeah.

A group of teenagers stepped off The Salt and Pepper Shaker and one of the boys made an elaborate play of stumbling over to the nearest garbage can and puking. One of the girls broke free from the pack to chastise him for being so immature. She skulked away and he trailed after her, already reaching for the wallet hanging by a chain from his jeans.

—Do you want to go on a ride?

Winnie shook her head.

—They make me-

Holding her belly she leant forward and made a retching sound.

—Yeah, me too. Hey, they have candy apples.

Heather joined the line behind a man with a toddler sleeping on his shoulder.

—I want the one in the back. No, not that one. The fresh one. What is it? Four bucks?

The man shifted the toddler to his other shoulder and the boy stirred. He blinked and raised his head slightly. The man's shirt came with it, stuck to his son's cheek by candy floss. The boy set his head back down and closed his eyes, already asleep before the man could pry a ten from his wallet.

—Four bucks for a goddamn candy apple.

Heather waited until he'd stomped past then leaned into the window, scanning the three remaining apples in the glass display case. Winnie stood a few feet behind, fidgeting with her dress.

—You want one?

—I didn't bring my money.

—It's on me.

—I couldn't.

—Sure you could.

—I will pay you back.

—It's not necessary. Two candy apples. I'll take two.

Heather passed the first one to Winnie then took a bite out of the other.

—I love candy apples.

The flesh of hers was brown beneath the skin but juicy and she was already thinking about getting another.

—It is very loud.

—Yeah.

Winnie took her first bite, a nip that barely penetrated the hard red shell.

—Good huh?

—Yes. I was wondering.

—Uh huh.

—Why Christmas in July?

A chunk of the candy coating broke off Heather's apple and clung to her shirt. She plucked it off and popped it in her mouth.

—It's for the tourists. You know-

—Yes, the tourists.

—Because of Santa's Village. It's kind of what we're famous for. Forty-fifth parallel. Half way to the North Pole and all that. Do you have tourists in Uganda?

—Yes. My grandfather's village was near a mission. They came all the time. They would go to the lake. Victoria. Do you know it?

—No. I mean, I've heard of it.

—It is very big. A man sold chickens. The tourists would buy the chickens and feed them to the crocodiles.

—Live chickens.

—Yes. They would feed them right out of their hands.

—Did you ever do this?

—No. I think it was not very smart.

□□□

From An Interview With Virginia Laughton
Recorded by Deacon Riis, *Bracebridge Gazette*
July 15th, 20-

I was sitting right here on George's bench when I saw the dogs. George was my husband and when he died, oh five years ago now, the grandkids, I have thirteen of them spread across the country, they had such fond memories of going down to the river with him that they pooled their money and put the bench here. They chose this spot because this is where George taught every one of our dogs to swim. There's a ledge at the bank there. It's only a few feet drop but the water is deep below it. George would carry the pup to the edge there and, he always made sure one of the kids was with him, he'd make a big deal out of holding the pup over the water. What do you think, he'd say, sink or swim? I remember Laura, who was there one time, came running back into the house crying, Daddy's trying to drown Koko. I told him to stop it after that but he never did. He thought it was a big joke. I was down there when he did it to poor Charlie. He was our last dog. A Golden Retriever. Michael was with us, he's our Philip's youngest. Sink or swim? George asks. What happens if he sinks? Michael says. He was only three or four but smart as a whip. Then I'll have to get a new dog, George tells him. Michael thought about it for a moment and then, dead serious, he says, Swim. George drops him off the ledge and Charlie goes down. Almost stopped my heart to see him disappear under the water, but sure enough, a second later, up he pops. Couldn't hardly get him out of the water after that. Now that George is gone it's nice to come down here and sit on the bench. And that's what I was doing when

I saw those two dogs. They were swimming across the river. Must have started at Bass Rock, which is just on the other side. At first I thought it was only one dog because the injured one, I understand it was the bitch, was riding on the other one's back. She was holding onto his dog collar and he was pulling her across. I've never seen the like of it. The current wasn't too strong, even though there's been a lot of rain lately, but he was having a devil of a time. There was one moment when they got caught in middle, there was a thin strip of current there, it looked like a twisted ribbon if you know what I mean, and I didn't think they were going to make it. They seemed to be stuck there, paddling like mad, not moving an inch for I don't know how long. My heart went out to them, it did. I thought about going to get someone to help but I knew it would take me a half hour to get back home, what with the stairs and all, so I just sat there and watched and prayed. They were making progress and then for a little while I couldn't see them because of the bank. A few minutes passed and I had the worst feeling. It's terrible when you get so old you can't do anything but watch and hope. Suddenly, I saw his head pop up and it was such a feeling of relief, I can't tell you. I think I may have even given a little cheer. He climbed up there then bent back down and dragged her up and for the longest time they just lay in the grass, panting. Finally, I don't know how much later this was, he got up, gave her a little nudge with his nose and the two of them trotted down the path toward the falls. It never occurred to me to call the police. I feel horrible about it now, knowing what happened afterwards. Horrible. I-I had heard about the young boy that they'd-they'd mauled on the radio but seeing those two dogs swimming across the river, it was such a beautiful moment, and exciting, my heart was racing all the way home. I never would have thought, never, never in a million years could have thought...

□□□

Wellington Street was clogged with cars trapped behind Santa's sleigh, being pulled by two horses. Hooves clopped on the asphalt and jingle bells rang in an even jangle. Engines revved and a group of teenagers in the back of a pick-up truck hollered at another group on the sidewalk. When they turned, the ones in the truck unleashed a barrage of water balloons on them. They scattered but quickly regrouped in a gravel parking lot and collected pocketfuls of stones.

Heather and Winnie skirted through the space between cars and crossed to the sidewalk leading towards Winnie's house. Heather could hear the little boy ringing the bell on his trike and see the cherry of his mother's cigarette suspended in the dark above the stairs. The light at the end of the street winked off and for a moment it looked like it had taken the Sunfire with it. She stopped and took her time finding her smokes in her purse.

—Is there something wrong?

Heather shook her head. The high beams of a passing car shimmered briefly in the sweat on Winnie's forehead and Heather couldn't help staring.

God, she's beautiful. I didn't see it before, but there it is. And young. I wonder how old she is? Not more than twenty, I'd bet.

—You want to go somewhere? For a walk?

—I have work.

—Just around the block?

—I can't. Really. Thank you for helping me with the snake.

Winnie unwound the loop of shoe lace with the key tied to it from her wrist.

—What kind of work is it?

—Math and science.

—Book work?

—Yes.

Heather lit her cigarette. Her tongue wiggled at the cement-like patch where the candy from her apple had filled a hole in one of her molars.

—Too hot to be sitting in front of a book. Little while, the sun'll be down...

Winnie looked at her feet.

—A quick walk around the block. We'll be back before dark. I promise.

—Okay.

Heather led her back to Wellington Street, checking her pace to keep Winnie from falling behind. Cars and pick-up trucks made a play at jostling each other in the line-up stretching to where the road ducked out of sight before the bridge. A couple of kids on BMX bikes wove in and around the traffic, eliciting a blast from a horn for coming too close to the front bumper of a Hummer. One of the bikers raised his middle finger and the Hummer's door opened so its driver could respond in person only to have the car ahead of him jolt forward a few feet. The driver slammed the door shut again and the Hummer pulled up in line behind it.

Heather watched with a gentle grin as she and Winnie walked past. The scene made her think of Toronto, the only city she could claim to know even a little. She'd lived on campus there for four months before dropping out of Seneca. Her roommate, Naomi, was a fine arts major who'd grown up in New York. Heather had helped shave her head after she'd tried to give herself dreadlocks during frosh week and Naomi repaid her by letting her tag along on her forays into the east end of the city. Stoned and drunk, they searched out what she called disposable people, anyone good for a laugh or a toke, lost souls whom Naomi treated like road signs and whose names she never asked. Alert to every sound, every gesture, every smell that the city threw at her, a scene like the one between the BMXers and the Hummer would have had Naomi's juices flowing, setting her off on any number of tangents. Maybe she would have flirted with the guy in the Hummer, or flashed him her tits, like she often did to guys passing in cars who yelled catcalls at her. Or she might have chased down the boys on the bikes to see if they were holding, talking to them like they weren't fourteen so they'd take her to see an older brother who always had something.

On their first expedition Naomi had gone off about small towns.

—By twenty-five everyone's got the same hair, same opinions, same fat fucking ass. There's no resistance; no one pushing back, everyone's so disengaged. They've all settled into middle age, nothing better to do than flip the channels and yell at the kids. In the city there's always someone pushing back. You have to define who you are and keep defining yourself every minute of every day of every fucking year until you drop and the street sweeper pushes you into the gutter with the rest of the dying and the dead. That's the city and that's why I love it. So choose your identity girl, cause it's war, and sweats and pigtails ain't going to cut it.

It all sounded so true and Heather did her best to keep up; to wear the right clothes, to listen to the right music and engage, always engage (which to Naomi meant snarling at everyone who walked by and if they snarled back, and were cute, taking them back to their dorm and fucking them). By Christmas, Heather was failing every one of her courses. She returned home at break and, without telling anyone what she was planning, she dropped out of school.

Spring was clogging the streets with ice flows, the drains sealed with leaves left over from the fall, and Heather had snagged a job waitressing at one of the more modest resorts on Muskoka Lake when a post card with a picture of the CN Tower on it arrived. All it said was: chickenshit. There was no signature but she recognised it as he ex-roommate's printing; she more carved the words into the page than wrote. chickenshit. The word – for that's how it was written as if two words would allow the possibility of a reprieve, a gap, a way of seeing herself through it – became her summer. She muttered it as she cleaned the tables of dirty plates in the dining room; she whispered it at night when she thought her co-workers were asleep in the girl's cabin; she screamed it at the gulls on the rare occasion she borrowed one of the resort's canoes and paddled her way into the middle of the lake; she carved it into the willow tree behind the tennis courts where she sat reading, hoping the act would exorcise it and when it didn't, she let the word run freely in her mind and tried not to think of where she would emerge when it was finally done with her.

Days passed with no memory for her other than the word. Her hair grew tangled and she considered shaving it but then reminded herself that she was too chickenshit. She chewed her nails until they bled. A chickenshit way of dealing with stress. She stopped making eye contact with the guests at her tables. chickenshit!

Midway through July, the owner's wife called her into the office and asked her what was wrong. Heather shook her head (no need to say what kind of answer that was). The owner's wife, a pretty red-haired woman two years older than Heather, explained that there had been complaints about, well, a lot of things. She told Heather, in a kind voice, that she was being switched from the dining room to housekeeping, but that anytime she felt up to it she could try a few tables at lunch, for a start.

—Is that okay?

Heather nodded and looked to the door where the head of house-keeping was standing.

—Gladys will show you what to do.

After a week of making beds when the guests were on the lake, vacuuming when the guests were playing shuffleboard, dusting the photos of Muskoka in the golden age of leisure when the guests were doing whatever they did when not out on the lake or playing shuffle-board, chickenshit lost its stranglehold. She didn't wait on any tables at lunch, for a start, and she still chewed her nails, but she stopped muttering to herself and she no longer felt the need to carve things into trees.

In the years after, her life became a careful study in keeping out of everyone's way. Even her parents, who had moved to Port Carling when they retired, had a hard time remembering that she was only a thirty minute drive away. She told herself, in the days before she hit Naomi's magic twenty-five mark, that she was hibernating, saving her energy. For ten years, she hibernated in a cave of alcohol and weed, two-for-one movies at Muskoka Video and the odd screw whenever she had the resolve to stick around after last call at The Albion. Ten years she waited for something she couldn't put a name to and was surprised when it turned out to be Larry. Her Larry, who didn't mind that her ass looked like every other 38 year-old's ass in town, who once said he liked nothing better than a gal in sweat pants, who showered when he got home from work and also before they had sex. Larry, who never told her that he loved her but who, when she brought it up, said the word had been ruined for him and that whenever he sneezed he said to himself, Heather bless you, so that whenever she sees him sneeze she should tell herself that he's thinking about her and wishing the word hadn't been so damaged. Larry. One of the good guys. Her good guy.

—Pardon?

—Huh?

The line of cars had disappeared in front of them. A few stragglers raced up Wellington, their high beams switching to low beams switching to high beams. Heather looked around. They were walking past the skate park built beside the community centre before it had been shut down. The lights were on but a dozen spectators were crowding the mesh fence enclosing the cement ramps and steel rails, making it hard to see what was happening beyond.

—You said chicken shit.

—Did I?

—Yes.

—Well, I guess I've earned the right. Once in a while.

—I'm sorry?

—Nothing.

A burst of applause and a few high pitched whistles erupted from the spectators. Heather craned her neck, peering through the cracks in the bodies. She saw what looked to be a bloody arm, held up like a trophy. With another burst of applause the bodies closed in the crack, obscuring the injured boy from Heather, and Winnie's hand clutched at her wrist, pulling her out of the way of the skateboarder bearing down on them.

The boy gave an extra kick for speed then popped his board into the air and jumped the small stretch of grass separating the sidewalk from the parking lot. He was wearing a white sleeveless undershirt, a pair of combat boots and black cargo pants held up by suspenders. The overhead lights glinted off his bald head (except it wasn't bald, Heather corrected herself, it was shaved). She couldn't see any tattoos, which meant he wasn't a real skinhead, just a kid trying something on.

—Watch it, you little punk.

She said it in an offhand way, like a sister scolding her little brother for jumping out from behind a door and scaring her. The last word was lost under the wheels of a passing car so she couldn't have said it too loud. Surely not loud enough to make the skinhead pivot on his board, popping it into his hand as the experienced skaters do, making it look as easy as walking up a flight of stairs. There wasn't any real anger in her tone, she was sure of that. Just a startled gasp was all it was, nothing to make him stride towards her, holding the board flat against his side, his other arm swinging stiff - a soldier's arm - his feet marching over the grass and up the ten feet of sidewalk that separated them until he was close enough for Heather to smell the grape-flavoured bubble gum on his breath.

Winnie's hand tightened on her arm and Heather struggled not to blink against the splatter of spit on her cheeks while he called her a fucking bitch and dared her to call him a punk again.

—You dumbfuckingbitch. God, you're ugly. Did you know that? You uglyfuckingbitch.

☐☐☐

From An Interview With Jack Welland, WellandGood Kennels
Recorded by Deacon Riis, *Bracebridge Gazette*
July 15th, 20–

Dogs were barking something fierce. This'd be about 9:30. Usually I lock 'em up at 9:00 but it was hot all day and I wanted to let them stay outside as long as I could. I figured it was just a 'coon. Get a lot of them around here with the dump being just across the highway.

Little sons of whores, I swear they like to taunt the dogs. They do. It's a big joke to them. They'll be standing there half a foot from the outside runs hissing, getting them all riled up. Happens a couple times a month and's been happening since we opened the kennel in, uh, '95. 1995. First time I saw one of them crotch-grabbers I didn't have anything on me so I took off my boot. Big old Kodiaks. Steel toe, not like these slippers I got to wear now, my back being what it is. I took it off and a hoofed it at that black bastard. I mean I wailed it. Hit that shit-eater right in the back of the head. That boot'd hit a man, he'd be talking to Jesus, I don't care if he was alive or dead. But that nasty little bastard, he just turned and looked at me like I was throwing flowers at it. Didn't even hiss, that's how much of a threat I was to it. I went in and made my first 'coon stick that very night. This here one's the fifth, maybe the sixth. And, uh, I'd 'preciate it if you didn't mention anything about 'em when you write your piece, if you get me. Have them damn animal people out here and ah, hell... Looks a lot worse than it is. Really just finishing nails in the end. Enough to give them a little sting, they got skin like shoe leather. I ain't out to hurt them. Just want 'em to leave the dogs alone. Anyway, here's the kennel. The runs on the outside there. This is where I found the one. I understand her name was Juliet, like in that book. She was laying there in that little hollow, head was tore open. A real mess. Missing the one eye. She was still breathing though, I could see that. First thought I had was that one of the dogs had got out of the kennel, tore her head up squeezing through the fence, I figured. It happens. I'd like to say it don't but it does. Course I didn't recall us having a Stafford at the time but, well, the wife does her fair share around here so who's to say? I went down on one knee like this, and put my hand on its neck. She lifted her head so her good eye, the one that she still had anyway, could get a look at me. That's when I heard the growl. I turned around, real easy, and saw Romeo standing by the corner of that last run. He was holding a bowl of dog food in his mouth. I get 'em ready at night 'cause I got enough to worry about come morning, what with all the shit and piss and whatnot. I backed away from the bitch which seemed like the sensible thing to do given the way her mate was looking at me. I told him I meant him no harm and he seemed to get that because he stopped growling. He walked over and put the food down beside her head. I don't know how she managed to get to her feet but she did. She finished the bowl off then looked at me like she was asking for another. I guess Romeo knew better because he trotted on past her and disappeared into the woods, just over there. A second later she took off after him. I don't know how long I stood there afterwards. I guess it must've been a while because the wife started yelling from the house, telling me it was after ten. If we don't have the dogs inside by ten it's a fine, our neighbours make damn sure of that, so I went to get them squared away. When I heard about what happened to that boy- No, not Chris, I didn't hear about him until after. The one at High Falls. The teenager. Mark, right. When I heard what happened to him, I called the police. They came out, couldn't have taken them more'n ten minutes to get here, which was a damn sight faster than after someone broke into my trailer last year. Asked me why I didn't call them earlier. I said, it didn't occur to me. Well, a boy's dead because it didn't occur to you, the officer says to me. Maybe he was right, maybe that boy is dead because of me, but he didn't need to say it like that. That was uncalled for. If you ask me, he was just being plain mean.

□□□

Heather stood on the sidewalk in front of her car and watched the door close behind Winnie. The trace of a scream carried over from the midway, and her fingers fumbled with her keys although she knew the Sunfire wasn't locked. They hadn't spoken a word on the way back and Winnie hadn't released her hand from Heather's until they were within sight of her street. When they reached her walkway, Winnie said goodbye then bowed her head and hurried towards her front door.

—What the hell was I thinking?

Her hand shook as she jammed the key into the ignition.

—God Heather, Jesus. Idiot.

The lighter popped out and the distraction was enough to remind her that she was driving. Her eyes caught sight of the sign passing at the intersection. Quebec Street. The exact opposite way from home. Past Monk Field, past the community centre, past the skate park. She took her foot off the gas and turned onto Dill, letting the car coast in neutral, wondering if there'd be enough speed to make it to the end of the block.

On the side closest to the park, the houses were brick and sat on large lots with big driveways and two car garages. On the other side of the street, vinyl siding covered flimsy wood frames betrayed by sagging roofs. The yards there were small and cramped with piles of leaves and brush, Fisher Price toys and rusted out snowmobiles. It was where she was taking Winnie.

She coasted to a stop in front of her parents' old house. It was two stories stacked like cardboard boxes covered with yellow siding. A scarecrow sat in a wicker chair beside the front door, chewing a corncob pipe. A wooden sign in its lap read, All That Wander Are Not Lost.

She opened the door and got out. A van drove by and wind whipped an ash from her cigarette into her eye. She rubbed at the sting then closed the car door and hurried across the road. She stopped at the corner where Dill met Victoria. The streetlights and the sidewalk ended a few houses beyond as the road fell towards the falls. Heather turned left and walked past the four houses spanning the distance between the corner and Victoria Street School, where they kept the retards when Heather was a kid and that's what they still called them.

She'd walked past it every day on her way to and from school until one afternoon in February. She was in grade six or maybe seven and was coming home. There'd been a few warm days followed by a quick freeze and the sidewalk was pockmarked with ice. She'd already fallen a couple of times. Her knee was hurting and she had a lump on the back of her head that was big enough to tighten her toque. As she approached the Victoria Street School she'd seen a student throwing handfuls of salt onto the driveway. He was huge, like Frankenstein's monster if Dr. Frankenstein had pieced him together out of gangly teenagers. He was wearing a blue winter jacket, the puffy kind, the front soaked through with the drool sputtering from his mouth, and his wool gloves were encrusted with chunks of rock salt. There was no one else in sight. Heather tried to walk faster but she kept slipping and her knee ached. She bent her head low, hoping he wouldn't see her. Little girl, he called. Little girl. Heather looked up and he was on her. He grabbed her in a bear hug and she felt his wet mouth on her cheek. The next thing she knew they were on the ground and he was on top of her. A man was yelling something from the school but Heather couldn't see him. She was pinned and couldn't breathe. She tried to scream but when she opened her mouth a great gob of spittle gushed inside. She was drowning. She thought she was going to puke. Then a man was helping her up, wiping her face with his shirt. A woman was trying to talk to The Monster but he wasn't listening. He just kept repeating, The little girl fell. The little girl fell. The woman said something else, and touched The Monster's arm. He let out a shriek, then stuck his hand in his mouth and bit down on it, hard.

Fifteen minutes later, Heather stood in front of the principal's office listening to her mother yell at the woman who had tried to talk to The Monster outside of the school.

—She was attacked! I ought to call the police.

—I know it must look that way but it's all a misunderstanding. If you'll just let me introduce you to him I'm sure you'll see that he never meant to hurt your daughter. He wouldn't hurt anyone.

She called for The Monster. He shuffled out of her office, still wearing his jacket and gloves. His head lowered, he said, I'm sorry, little girl. I'm sorry.

Heather's mom led her out of the school and on the way home she made Heather promise that she would walk the long way from then on. Heather never saw The Monster again and she never told her mother that she got the bump on her head falling a half block before he'd slipped and landed on top of her.

□□□

From An Interview With Constable Kevin Sullivan,
K-9 Unit, Bracebridge O.P.P.
Conducted by Deacon Riis, *Bracebridge Gazette*
July 13, 20-

Me and Zoom have been together for eight years. He's a good officer. A hell of a good officer. Uh, you know it's, it's not like in the movies where they give a dog a sniff of somebody's you know, like a piece of their clothing, and the dog tracks them through the wilderness and finally finds them hiding in a haystack in some abandoned barn fifty miles away. It's not a science, you know. More like an art. The dog is kind of like the paint brush and, I'm not saying he's not important, of course he is, but tracking something has got as much to do with the handler, more so really, so if somebody's to blame for what happened, then I guess you'd have to blame me. Dogs are like people in some ways and other ways they are not. They each have their own peculiarities, you might call it personality, you might call it character or, what's the word I'm looking for? Their own themness, what makes them act one way when another dog would act in a completely different way. That's just like people, you see what I'm saying, and because we have this in common a lot of people, most people maybe, think that it makes them like us in a lot more ways. My experience is that this isn't true. We want it to be, for whatever reason, so we pretend that it is when the reality is a whole other thing. When I was growing up, we used to play this game, you probably did too. Three wishes, right? You get three wishes, anything you want. Most of my friends wanted to be superheroes or have a lot of money, live forever, that kind of thing, but me, and maybe I was just saying this to be different, I always said that I wanted to be a dog. For a day, an hour, whatever. My friends'd ask me, Why would you want to be a dog? I'd tell them it was because if you could be a dog for even a little while, it would all make sense. What would make sense? Everything. Now that might sound a bit vague but I meant everything and, I guess, if I were to think about it, which I haven't in a long time, I'd still mean it today. Here's an example, why do we have eyes? It's an easy one right? To see, that's why. But why do we need to see? Maybe someone out there's smart enough to have answered that but, hell, it sure isn't me, and it's beside the point anyway. Dogs don't ask why they see. They just do it, and I don't mean it's just because they're stupid animals and they can't talk and all that, I mean seeing is a part of them. They don't create little packets of everything like seeing was salt and hearing was pepper and smelling, I don't know, was ketchup or whatever. They just see and hear and taste and smell and – what's the other sense? – and feel and they all kind of mesh together like eggs and flour when you're making bread. And he just accepts that he's bread instead of trying to figure out, hey where'd that egg go, or how many grains of salt are in me, or some other such nonsense. I guess what I am saying is, that dogs are present. He's here, fully situated, you know, in his environment. Someone, an ex-girlfriend, ha ha, but that's a whole 'nother thing that we'll just, you know. Anyway, this woman, she was into all that New Age stuff, tried to explain to me what holistic meant one time. She said it was seeing the whole world as it really was and I said, you mean like a dog. She got real angry when I said it, I don't know why, maybe she thought I was making fun of her but whatever, it's true. Dogs are holistic. That's why you can't lie to them. They pick up on things, make their choices based on a whole set of facts we can't possibly even imagine. We can train them to be focused, to sniff out drugs, or guide blind people, or herd sheep, or whatever, but we can never really train them to forget what they are. So you can't lie to a dog, and even if you try, he's not going to believe you, and that's why old Zoom here didn't find those two pit bulls. After I saw what they did to Christopher Allen, he knew what'd happen if I found them, and he knew I loved dogs too much to want to have anything to do with that. He was protecting me, pure and simple. That's what partners are for.

□□□

Beyond the Y where Victoria Street bled into Quebec, the old high school sat perched on top of a hill, inert like a buzzard after eating a buffalo. A message lingered on the notice board in front of a row of windows on the bottom floor. See You In September, it read. Who the message was from wasn't clear. Probably it was left by the student council, or maybe the principal, but to Heather it seemed that the school itself had written the note as if nobody had told it that the only people who'd be coming back were the men with sledgehammers and pry bars. She looked past the sign at the papered up windows hiding the cafeteria, searching for an empty square so she could look in to see if the table in the front corner, her table for four years, was still there but there weren't any open spaces.

She walked up the stairs leading to McMurray Street and stood, breathing hard, in front of the Presbyterian Church. A woman sitting on the porch of the house beside it called over, asking if her she was all right. Heather waved back at her then let gravity pull her back down the hill towards Wellington Street.

The last time she'd been to her parents' church was to hear her brother Mike speak about his mission work. She'd sat in the back, feeling silly for being there when she hadn't been to church since she was a teenager. The chapel smelled of mould and burning candles and her nose itched the whole time. After the children had left for Sunday School the minister remained on the steps leading to the pulpit. He was new to the church, or anyway, Heather didn't recognize him. He was a thin man, with a flood of hair that washed over his eyes. He laughed when he told the congregation that they were doing something different this week and Heather saw that his teeth were long and straight and yellow, like a horse's. He introduced Mike, and her brother shuffled up to the pulpit. He stood there for a moment, his head lowered as if thinking about what he wanted to say, the same thing Heather'd seen the preachers on TV do for dramatic effect. Then he said something that everyone in the congregation knew and, maybe because they did, it put them at ease.

He said:

—Being a Christian is hard.

Everyone Heather could see in front of her nodded, as if that's exactly what they'd wanted to hear.

Then he'd gone on to say:

—A lot of times we wish that it wasn't so hard, so we go out of way to make it easier for ourselves and those around us. Maybe this is understandable. Maybe it's natural. But, and this is what I am here to tell you today, it is most certainly not Christian.

For the next few minutes he listed off the ways people try to make it easier on themselves, and by the time he was done there wasn't a single person sitting there who was nodding their heads. Then he talked about some of the people he'd met, some of the poorest people on this planet, people who'd never been to a church with more than a thatched roof, people who made their living rooting through garbage, but people who put nearly every Christian he'd ever met to shame because of their generosity, their sacrifice and their humility. The meek that Jesus had talked about were living amongst us, he said, and true to His word they had inherited the earth, a world that we had thrown away, a world that we no longer had any use for, one that they had claimed for their own and had made better than the one from which it came.

On he went until he'd run out of words on the page in front of him, leaving him red-faced with sweat at the crease of his hairline. Taking a sip from a water bottle on the floor beside the pulpit, he opened his Bible and read a passage from the book of Matthew then handed the congregation back to the minister.

Heather snuck out of the church as soon as he was finished and didn't see her brother again until the day he'd left for Africa, a few months later. Mike and his fiancée had collected shoes for six months beforehand and their plan was to travel through Ghana handing them out. Heather had driven to Pearson airport to see him off with her family: her sister Lara, her uncle Bill and Aunt Eugene, her Grandpa Gus, her three cousins, two of them still in booster seats and the third lost inside a handheld video game he played the whole trip. She'd sat in the back of her parents' van wishing she was going too, knowing she didn't really mean it, and thinking about darkness and light and finding the path like happened to people in the Bible but never to people like her. She stood alongside everyone else at the security gate, crowding around Mike and Annika, their backs to customs, and the plane, to Africa and their lives together, all of them waiting to get in a last handshake or a hug. Not wanting to be forgotten, she'd forced her way up beside Grandpa Gus and saw him slip an envelope into Mike's pocket, telling him that he'd seen a fair bit of the world himself.

—This was during the war mind you, and I'd be lying if I told you we were doing the Lord's work like yourself. Still, an extra couple of bucks always came in handy and sometimes meant the difference between... But then well, I don't expect you'll have any of the trouble I had.

Grandpa squeezed him on the shoulder and kissed Annika on the cheek, though everyone knew what he felt about the two of them together, and then Mike was standing in front of Heather, smiling like he hadn't expected to see her standing there even though they'd driven up in their parents' van together.

—Sis.

Hearing him call her Sis made her feel special because he'd never called her that before, and she'd hugged him closer than she would have if he'd only called her Heather. And didn't he notice that there was a tear on her cheek, and he laughed, his brow crinkled like he couldn't make sense of it and laughing was the only thing he could think to do. She wiped at the tear, laughing too, laughing along with her brother, her Bro, and that's when she'd said it.

—Watch out for the cannibals.

She'd meant it as a joke and, seeing the look of tired understanding wipe away his laughter as he set down his bags, she'd instantly regretted it.

—There are no such thing as cannibals. It's a myth. You see, when white man first came to Africa they were alarmed that so many of the coastal people they first encountered warned them about going inland because inland, they were told, was populated by cannibal tribes. Everywhere they went they heard the same stories until finally greed overcame their fear and they voyaged into the jungle. When they encountered the inland tribes they were greeted with as warm a welcome as they'd had on the coast and when they'd lived with them long enough to learn their language they discovered something odd.

Over and over again they were asked how they had got past the coastal tribes without being eaten. You see–

Annika tugged at his shirt and reminded him that it was getting late.

—Of course, of course.

In a flurry, Mike gave mother a final peck on the cheek, shook dad's hand for the tenth time then snatched up his luggage and hurried after his soon-to-be-wife.

On the drive home from the airport Heather sat in the van's back most bench trying to distance herself from the two hour Mike-a-thon her mom was hosting in the front. By the end of the trip, the anger she felt over her little brother talking to her like she was a child in front of the whole family had trickled out of her, replaced by the troubling sensation that Mike was right. That night, she prayed for the first time since she was sixteen and asked God that her life be filled with her brother's spirit, so that he might guide her. Afterwards she lay awake in bed, afraid to fall asleep, worried that the morning would rob her of her new found faith just as it always did her resolve to quit smoking.

Walking back towards Wellington she thought of that night and of how many times since she'd woken up on Sunday Morning, hung over, and promised herself that she'd go to church next week and that she wouldn't drink on Saturday but then Larry'd have a few and she'd give in, and even if she didn't wake up with a headache she'd stay in bed until it was too late to bother with anything but lunch. She counted the seconds between cars flashing by at the end of the block, clicking her tongue against the roof of her mouth the same way she did when she was a child kept awake by a storm. She reached seven before another light surged briefly then fell away, like lightning arousing thoughts of thunder.

At the intersection she turned left and cut across the parking lot separating the sidewalk from the skate park. She lingered in the shadow cast by the Rotary building and scanned the ramps beyond the fence for the skinhead. The spectators had disappeared, leaving only a couple of pre-teen girls leaning against the wire mesh with their backs to the show, alternating between sips of pop from a two litre bottle and handfuls of Reeses Pieces or M&M's. She watched him glide down a ramp, his body crouched and lithe as he approached the ramp on the far side. Halfway up, he jumped off the board sending it catapulting over the top and slamming into the mesh wire. He screamed fuck all the way over to his board then mounted the ramp again and did the same thing, except this time he stayed on the board until they were both in the air, the board flipping under his feet, and even landed one foot on it before it spun out from under him, sending him to the concrete. Over and over he repeated the trick with subtle variations that didn't change how every attempt ended with the board skittering off towards the fence and the skinhead swearing, until finally he swung the board and sent it careening into the parking lot.

Kicking the door to the enclosure open he stormed out, followed by another teenager with a bleached blonde Mohawk, tall like a sail but with enough metal in his face to keep him from drifting away.

—You ain't never going to do it.

—Fuck you. I'll do it.

—Monkeys'll fly on the moon before you do it.

—I told you I'll fucking do it so why don't you fucking shut the fuck up about it.

—All right then, fuck, you'll fucking do it. Have a fucking stroke, why don't you?

The skinhead snatched up his board and turned it over, inspecting it tenderly. It was the punk who saw Heather emerge from the shadow and walk to within a parking space of them. Heather could see that he had a bad case of acne and that he was self-conscious about the way she was staring at him. He shifted on his feet and nudged the skinhead.

—Well, what do we have here?

—I forgive you, for you know not what you have done.

—If it ain't that ugly fucking bitch.

—I forgive you.

—God, you still ugly.

—I forgive you.

—I got that. You forgive me.

—I forgive you.

—Is that fucking right?

The skinhead was right up in her face now, stabbing at her with his nose, trying to make her twitch.

—I forgive you.

—Come on, Trev, she's fucking crazy. Let's just–

—I forgive you.

—Fuck you!

He screamed it so loud that her ears popped. The sound of cars on Wellington became distant, like they were under water, and it wasn't until the punk and the skinhead had rolled out of sight that the street noise leaked back, too quiet even then to drown out the high-pitched whine burrowing into her head and the sound of her own voice muttering to the empty parking lot.

□□□

Interview with W. & B (names withheld at their request)
Recorded by Deacon Riis, *Bracebridge Gazette*
July 17, 20-

W: We was at the dump for reasons I'd rather not say.
B: It was because of the weed.
W: Shut up.
B: It'll be gone by now anyway. The cops ain't that stupid.
W: What the fuck?
B: The cops had all this weed, right—
W: Shut the fuck up.
B: Don't mind him, it's that time of the month.
W: I will fucking—
B: They had this weed—
W: It'll get ugly, brother. It will get ugly.
B: And they didn't know what to do with it so—
W: Ugly.
B: —they buried it at the dump.
W: Don't forget to draw him a fucking map.
B: It's fucking gone alright. Fuck, get over it. Christ!
W: Fuckwad.
B: Can I continue?
W: You don't tell this story for shit.
B: You keep interrupting me.
W: You got to start at the beginning.
B: That's what I'm trying to do.
W: We heard about the weed from (name deleted).
B: But that happened after the cops buried it—
W: You've got to be subjective when you tell it. First time we heard about the weed was when (name deleted) came over to ask if he could borrow dad's bolt cutters. Said he'd lost the key to his bike and—

B: We knew he was lying, right away. That fucking guy is so full of fucking—

W: I knew he was lying. I told him I could pick the lock, right, and if he was smart—

B: He's smart like my shit tastes like chocolate covered roses.

W: If he was smart—

B: Which he ain't.

W: —he'd've told me it was a combination lock but—

B: What a fucking retard. He doesn't even own a bike. Have you ever seen that fucking retard on a fucking bike? If you did, it'd have to have fucking training wheels.

W: But instead he gets all sulky. I just need your dad's bolt cutters. It ain't much to ask after I gave you that PS2 for 10 bucks, fucking boo hoo hoo. I thought he was going to start crying. So I grabbed that motherfucker by the balls—

B: No you didn't.

W: I slammed him up against the wall—

B: That never happened.

W: I leaned real close to his ear and whispered, You're going to tell me what the fuck's going on or I am going to get my dad's bolt cutters and we're going to find out how many Es are in squeal.

B: He did say that.

W: So then (name deleted) gets all fucking excited. Spit spraying out of that fucker's mouth. I thought he was going to fucking jizz in his pants.

B: That's when he tells us about the cops burying these bags of weed at the dump. You see his brother works there.

W: He drives a bulldozer.

B: It was his job to cover up the shit.

W: Said there was maybe a dozen black garbage bags.

B: Full of fucking weed.

W: He had a map and everything.

B: So we went out to the dump.

D: With the bolt cutters?

W: You don't need bolt cutters to get into the dump.

B: You just hop the fence. There's a spot around back.

D: So you've been there before.

B: We go there to shoot the rats, sometimes. Dad's got a .22—

W: And does dad know we use his .22?

B: No.

W: Then why don't you shut the fuck up about it?

B: He ain't going to tell dad. Tell him you ain't going to tell dad.

D: I won't tell your father, I promise. So when did you see the dogs?

W: Like I said, we were around back looking for the place we hop the fence.

B: And that's when we heard the siren.

W: Fuck. Found out later that (name deleted) wasn't the only one his brother told. Some dumb shit—

B: (name deleted).

W: —drove right up to the front gates and cut the lock—

B: Dumbfuck.

W: He had four bags of weed in the trunk and was tying a couch from the recycle shed to the roof of his car when the cops showed up.

D: And that's when you saw the dogs?

W: No.

B: Dogs weren't at the dump.

W: Who told you the dogs were at the dump?

D: I just thought—

W: We saw the dogs at High Falls. It was hot and I felt like going for a swim. High Falls is the best place around.

B: The fucking best.

W: We was just getting undressed when we saw the one, standing there on the rock below the falls.

B: It was messed up, real bad. Looked like a fucking zombie fucking dog, you know all (makes zombie noises).

W: I don't think it even knew we were there.

B: That other one sure did.

W: Yeah.

B: It came out of nothing. Out of darkness.

W: A set of teeth, you know, and a growl.

B: I thought we was done for.

W: He fucking shit himself.

B: That's a fucking lie.

W: God's honest.

D: So what'd you do?

B: Nothing. We was too fucking scared to move.

W: Then all of sudden the one fell over—

B: The zombie dog.

W: —she just fell over, standing there.

B: The other one stopped growling and ran over to her.

W: When he got there he gave her a nudge—

B: I was already halfway back to the truck by then.

W: —but I think she must have been dead.

D: And did you tell the police about seeing the dogs?

B: Fuck no.

W: But we would've. If we'd've known what was gonna happen.

B: Sure we would've. Wouldn't wish that on nobody.

W: No, sir.

☐☐☐

After the victory with the skinhead – and it was a victory as certain as her feet had led her back to the Sunfire – Heather pointed her car towards town. At the end of Quebec Street she coasted left through the yield, meaning to go up to Manitoba Street, take a right, and be well on her way home. Instead, she parked across from the United Church, got out and walked the half block to the alley leading into Chancery Lane.

At the entrance to the alley sat Smellie's Stationary. The store was empty, abandoned, but nobody had gotten around to scraping the lettering off the window. Eventually a drunk teen would throw a rock through it and whoever owned the place now that Mr. Smellie had retired would have to put a board over the hole. Until then, kids would always have an excuse for a fart and a laugh whenever they walked past on their way to Chancery Lane.

Beyond the store the alley jogged right, leading Heather past the row of small, unkept yards behind the Manitoba Street apartments. She'd been in one during the fall after the chickenshit summer. She couldn't remember exactly which; she was drunk and had come and gone through the front. After the guy she'd followed home had finished his business and was smoking a joint on the bed, his free hand playing idly with what was left of his erection, she'd gone to the window. The moon shone on a lake beyond the yard's fence and a loon bleated in the distance. It was as picturesque a Muskoka moment as she'd ever had and it took her longer than it should have to realise that the ripples on the water weren't moving because it was a mural and the loon was a car alarm.

—Get away from the window or put some clothes on. You'll have the cops busting the door down.

Heather let the sheet he was using as a curtain fall back and walked to the bed. She picked her pack of smokes off a stack of three milk crates and bent to collect her lighter from the floor. He asked her if she wanted to fuck again and she said, Sure. The next morning he dropped her off at her parents on his way to work. He hadn't showered and she could smell the stink of sex on him the whole trip. Probably carrying it around so that he could show it off to the other guys, she thought. She imagined him sticking his finger under his workmates' noses and laughing.

—See, even an ugly prick like me gets laid sometimes.

He didn't say he'd call and she didn't ask for his number.

She hadn't seen the mural after that night but then she'd avoided the alleyway, afraid that she'd run into the ugly prick again. It wasn't until she'd met Larry that she'd come back. His favourite bar was The Gryphon, an English-style pub that shared a wall with Chancery Lane. The first time he'd taken her there was a few weeks after she'd moved in. They hadn't been out of the house together for more than a swim at High Falls then, one night after dinner, he'd said that it was about time they stopped hiding.

She was disappointed that he wanted to vary their routine of a joint, a foot rub in front of the TV and a slow grind that made her spend the next seven years trying to figure out how exactly he'd made her feel so good. She covered by coughing into her arm.

—What are you thinking?

—I'm thinking about showing you off, that's what. You got a problem with that?

She told him she didn't.

They left the dishes in the sink and jumped in his truck.

He was renting a clapboard bungalow off the 117 towards Baysville, not more than two kilometres from the house they'd eventually buy together. The drive took ten minutes and there wasn't a second of that time that Heather hadn't wished the engine would blow leaving them stranded, alone, miles from anyone who might recognise her.

They parked in the big lot between the train tracks and the Royal Bank and walked up the stairs to Manitoba Street. It was a Friday and the stores were all open. Would-be shoppers drifted along the sidewalk drinking take-out coffees and eating ice-cream cones. Larry lit a cigarette while he surveyed the scene and waited for Heather to catch up. From behind, she could see his underwear through a hole below the back pocket of his jeans where he kept his wallet and despair almost buckled her legs. Oh god, she thought, we're going to The Concrete Monkey and I'm going to become one of those girls who sit in a chair drinking coolers while he gets drunk and plays pool with his buddies. She stepped up beside him and he grabbed her hand and gave it a gentle squeeze. She offered him a smile in return. The first step was like the first step off a dock in May with nothing to look forward to but a quick freeze. She closed her eyes and was surprised when he didn't pull her left towards the pool hall but between two parked cars and out into the street. Heather let herself be carried along, onto the sidewalk and past the old fashioned sign at the entrance to Chancery Lane.

The cobblestone walkway, wedged between two brick walls, led up a steep slope and Heather was panting by the time they reached the top. A young woman stood smoking in the doorway of a shop at the crest of the hill. The sign in the window read, The Silver Snail. Other signs offered body piercing and tattooing and Heather was unsure if the girl was a living advertisement for the store or just an employee grabbing a butt between customers. She had three rings through her lips, two in her nose, a multitude in her ears and a lattice of chains spanning the distances between. Tattoos poked out from within the long sleeves of her black dress and from beneath the hem what appeared to be barb wire, or thorns, curled around her calves before disappearing into her lime green Converse runners. Heather tried not to stare and the young woman responded by flicking her cigarette into the alley and slinking back into the store.

The sighting, and that's how she thought of it as if she'd just seen Big Foot or the Loch Ness Monster, had stirred in her memories of the forays she took with Naomi into Toronto's east-side. She quickened her pace, anxious to find out what else the alley might have in store for her.

At the end of the cobblestones Larry turned right and stepped up onto the raised platform that served as The Gryphon's patio.

—Ray!

An old man missing two of his front teeth and with a face that looked like a burlap sack stuffed with dirty socks lumbered off his stool and stuck his hand out. Larry shook it and asked the man how he was holding up.

—Like a eunuch in a brothel.

The man's laugh doubled him over and wormy strands of mucus spewed onto his beard.

—Easy there, Milky.

Larry patted him on the back and Heather glanced about. In the hazy light she could just read the sign above the door in the back of the building opposite: Smellie's Loading Only. Customers Use Front Door.

—There used to be a mural there.

Larry followed her finger to the patch of grey smoothing the bricks.

—They must have painted over it.

—Hey, Milky you remember a mural on the wall over there?

The sound of his name snapped his head out of its slow descent towards the counter running along the patio's rail and he once again lurched off his stool.

—Ray!

Larry grabbed Heather's arm and guided her past Milky's out-stretched hand. Inside the pub, music with Celtic fiddles played in the background while a waitress wearing a frilly dress, laced at the belly, served pints of darkish beer to a table of middle-aged men, doc-tors or lawyers who'd forgone suits for jeans and fleece sweaters with the sleeves pulled up to show veins marking their hours in the gym. At the table by the window overlooking Chancery Lane a group of young secretaries, or maybe bank tellers, talked over one another in an excited gibberish that mostly left their squat glasses of whiskey or scotch untouched. The doctors and lawyers took turns flirting with them and the ladies responded with shrill laughs. A red haired man wearing the green jersey of the Irish National Football team sat at the bar and watched a soccer match on a wall-sized TV. He muttered a play by play of grievances to the bartender and the bartender nod-ded in response between stocking glasses and pouring drinks. In the corner, a bearded man read from a hardback book that looked an-cient and was certainly not on any Best Of Beach Reading lists for the summer. Every few seconds he jotted something down on a notepad, glanced about the bar furtively, then went back to reading. While Heather was standing at the door taking it all in, the waitress filled his coffee cup and dropped two creamers beside.

—Larry. Christ is that you? God, you're an old man.

The bartender, his hair shaved to the wood as Heather's dad would have put it, wiped his hands on his apron then placed both hands on the bar as if he was getting ready to arm wrestle.

—Hey Cal, how's the chemo going?

Cal nodded grimly then picked up a pint glass and spat into it.

—You still drinking horse piss?

—Only when it's fresh.

—What about your friend?

—She likes horse piss too.

Wiping the spit from the glass with his apron, he stuck it under a tap marked HP while Larry scanned the remaining tables and chose one in the back, out of sight of the bar.

—He spit in your glass.

—He always does.

—Is he going to spit in mine?

—Couldn't say. Maybe.

Heather wriggled out of her jacket and propped it on the back of her seat.

—Hey Loose.

The waitress set two pints of beer on their table and a couple of napkins beside.

—Larry. Thought you'd gone back up north.

—Damn near. Heather, this is Lucy. If it wasn't for her, Cal's mouth'd look like his head by now. Heather smiled.

—Heather Asche?

—That's right.

—Lucy. Dobson.

—Lucy?

—Yeah, shit. When'd you get back into town?

—Um, a few months ago.

—Nice to see you.

—Thanks. You too.

On her way back to the bar Lucy touched the bearded man's shoulder. He shook his head without looking up and she collected his empty creamers.

—We went to school together.

—That a fact.

Rubbing his hands together, Larry snatched up the mug of beer.

—Here's hoping the tests come back negative.

He tilted it back, took a sip, paused, then took another. When he set it back down, half the beer was gone. Heather leaned over and sniffed hers. It smelled like Canadian and a quick taste told her it was.

—Hey, you want to play a game of darts?

□□□

From the *Bracebridge Gazette*
July 5th, 20–
By Deacon Riis, Staff Reporter

Rampage Ends At High Falls

A pair of Staffordshire Terriers (commonly known as Pit Bulls) are dead following a day long rampage that resulted in the death of two boys. The dogs escaped from a Hiram Street residence when police attempted to execute a warrant during an early morning raid and proceeded to kill a neighbour's child, Christopher Allen, aged 3. Their subsequent disappearance sparked an area wide search that ended with the discovery of their bodies at High Falls Park just before midnight on Saturday.

Police were responding to a 911 call regarding an animal attack. When they arrived they found a teenager with no vital signs, and the two dogs, both deceased. The 16 year-old male from Regina, Saskatchewan, was transported to South Muskoka Memorial Hospital and pronounced dead on arrival.

Police would not comment on the details surrounding the death of the two dogs, stating that it was an ongoing investigation and that information would be released as it became available. However, Sergeant Ball, the O.P.P.'s Community Relations Officer, told this reporter that there were several witnesses to the incident. One of them was a friend of the deceased while the other, a local man in his twenties, was the friend's brother. The latter killed at least one of the dogs with what Ball referred to as 'a rather large hunting knife' and is currently in custody while police investigate a possible parole violation related to the possession of this weapon.

The name of the 16 year-old victim is being withheld pending notification of his next of kin.

□□□

—Get your fucking hands off me.

Cal dragged the woman whose arm he was clenching out the door and planted her in the alley. She was wearing a pair of dirty flip flops, an orange tie-dyed tank top and cut off jean shorts. From where she stood at the far corner of the patio's rail, Heather could smell her B.O. mingled with sex and rotten teeth. Spit sprayed out of her mouth, speckling Cal's back, already walking away.

—You fucking piece of shit. Cockfucker. Asshole.

—Good night, Corrie.

—Fuck you.

Cal waved, the door slamming shut behind him, and Corrie took up a stance in front of the patio, looking like she'd do battle with anyone who made a go for The Gryphon. Heather strode by her and dipped down into Chancery Lane thinking, That's what you get for helping someone.

It'd been four years since Lucy had made a project out of Corrie, giving her free bowls of soup with garlic toast, and bags of clothes, some with the tags still on them, and personal hygiene products so she didn't look and smell like a drugged out bag lady when she was begging for money from the tourists, which she did up and down Manitoba Street, seven days a week from June to September. Heather had overheard Pearl tell Mavis that she'd run a side business buying smokes and booze for minors until the police had warned every store in town that they'd be paying the fine if they caught her doing it again. She'd also said that Corrie made two hundred dollars a day, and sometimes as high as five, depending on the weather and how bad she smelled.

Why Lucy was so determined to help her out had been a mystery to Heather until one afternoon when they were sitting on the Gryphon's patio drinking Margaritas. Larry was up on the roof with Cal fixing a leak that had been souring the ceiling for years. Heather had come with him to get out of the house and because Thursday was one of her days off. Lucy had offered her a drink, gratis, and for an hour and a half she'd sat and listened to Lucy's wry take on small town life (she was born in Bracebridge but had spent ten years in Vancouver). There'd been a lull in the conversation after Lucy went to get refills. To spark it up again Heather had mentioned that she'd seen Corrie down at the falls the other day.

—Was she talking to the squirrels?

—No, she was just sitting there with a coffee. It was like she was taking a break from being a crazy fool.

—Did you know, I was the first person in town to see her?

—Really?

—Well my Nana was the exact first. She has a place out on Wilson Falls Road, down near the hydro station. She was out in her front yard, ever since they banned the pesticides she's got a hate on for them dandelions so she was probably bent over digging them out with a fork, which is how she spends most of her days. Corrie came walking out the woods, wearing nothing but a man's sleeveless undershirt. She was howling like a banshee. Damn near scared the wits out of Nana.

Lucy gave her impression of a banshee and Heather admitted she would have been scared out of her wits too.

—My mom called me from work. Said I ought to get over there. We were living on Charles Street at the time so I was just around the corner. I hopped on my bike and got there in under five. Sure enough, there she was. First thing I noticed was the bush hanging between her legs. Looked like she was giving birth to an octopus. I sent Nana in to get her some underwear then followed her to the door and told her to call the cops.

The police? she said. Do you think we should?

Unless you want a new roommate, I told her.

That got her moving. I don't know if it was because she took me serious or because it suddenly occurred to her that this woman might be dangerous. When I turned back to Corrie, course I didn't know her name yet, she was sitting on the ground with her legs crossed. She was high, no doubt about it. Acid or shrooms, something heavy. She was sitting there watching an ant crawl over her hand. The whole thing was kind of amusing, if you want the god's honest, and I was having a hard time not laughing. Didn't know what to say to her so I started by asking what her name was. She said something like she's the sun, the moon, the stars above. Some really lame hippy bullshit, right. So sun's your first name, and stars above's your last? I asked. She smiled at me like I was a child and went back to staring at the ant.

God, where the hell is Nana? I thought. I figured she was probably stuck on the phone with the police because they'd told her to stay on the line and she's got one of those old cord ones that's always getting tangled so even though it's fifty feet long you have to stand right up next to it.

I'm looking for my mother, Corrie said all of a sudden. What's her name? I asked. Maybe I can help you find her. Madonna, she said. That would make you Christ, I guess, I said. Maybe, she says. My dad's Michael Jackson but he don't want nothing more to do with me since I broke his Ferris wheel. That got me moving towards the house. I found Nana, as I expected, having difficulties with the phone. She'd somehow got her dog all tangled up in the cord and her attempts to get him loose were only making matters worse. I don't know how long it took me to get the dog untangled but between that and getting the underwear, by the time I got back out to the yard a cop was helping Corrie to her feet. And God was he good looking. Couldn't have been older than 15, if you know what I mean, and just ripped, right. And the tan that boy had. I walked over to him and say, Hi, you know, like I was a friggin' teenager, and he looks at the pair of old lady's underwear in my hand then back at me like he's trying to figure out how old I was. They're my Nana's, I told him and handed the briefs to Corrie. She said thanks and right there slipped them on. The cop was staring at the river and I was staring at the cop. I mean he was really good looking. Like one of those Greek statues and I was having a hard time not imagining him in a fig leaf, you know, when Corrie walks over and just wraps her arms around him.

I like cops, she says.

And he's all like, Ma'am I'm going to need you to remove your hands and step away, Ma'am. Ma'am. Ma'am.

But Corrie wouldn't let him go. She just stood there hugging him and talking about how her brother was a cop and that he'd dropped her off at the motel on the highway because he knew the people in this town were friendly and that they'd take good care of her.

I've got to hand it to the cop, he was real patient with her. Just kept saying, Ma'am, I'm going to need you to remove your hands. Ma'am. Ma'am.

Finally, she lets him go and he tells her he needs her to get in the car. She doesn't argue or nothing, just gets in the back of the car like he said. He shuts the door and turns back to me. He asks for my name and phone number in case he has any questions. Well, I told him, you could ask me anything you want, Officer. He must've stared at me for fifteen seconds and I knew what he was thinking was, Is every woman in this town completely fucking nuts? Anyway, I gave him my name and my phone number. He never did call. The very next day I saw Corrie again. She was standing in front of the 7-11 drinking a Big Gulp when I stopped to get some gas. Came right up to me, said, I know you. I said yeah, from yesterday. No, she said, from a past life. What were you then? I asked. She took my hand and

gave it a gentle squeeze then said, Your mother. Sounds ridiculous, I
know, but the way she looked at me, it took my breath away. Made
me feel like I'd be a fool not to believe her. So I help her out once in
a while, figure it doesn't hurt, there but for the grace of God and all
that.

□□□

From the announcement's page, *Bracebridge Gazette*
July 5th, 20-

Family and friends of Christopher Allen will be gathering to celebrate
the three wonderful years he spent with them on July 21st. A private
viewing will start at 11am and will be opened to the public at 1pm.
A brief service at 3pm will be followed by a procession to St. James
Cemetery. The Allen family wishes to ask that, in lieu of flowers,
donations be made to The Make-A-Wish Foundation.

□□□

A few cars idled by on Manitoba Street, too late to be in a hurry, too
early to be going home. The clock in the tower of the old post office
said it was nine. The stores were all closing, the clerks wheeling racks
of sale items off the sidewalk or folding up sandwich boards, but a
red neon Open sign was still visible in the window of Muskoka Bean.
    A blast of cold air met Heather at the door. It prickled at the hair
on her arms and swept along the sweat laminating her shirt to her
chest but it didn't feel fresh. Not like a breeze coming off the lake or
the momentary shudder you get when you open the fridge on a hot
day knowing there's a beer in there. A shiver ran through her and she
looked at herself in the mirror opposite the entrance, a sign below it
reading: Another Happy Customer. Tangled curls of soggy hair hung
limply over her cheeks, dotted with blackheads, and there was a sore
on her jaw where'd she'd picked a pimple to scab.
    God, she thought, I look like I should be hanging from a meat
hook.
    The teen-aged girl behind the till was counting her money. Eight
hours serving coffee had left little mark on her except a slight scowl.
    I'm sorry, we're closed.
    —But the sign says—

—We're closed.

—I just want a cup of coffee.

—I've cashed out.

—I'll give you five bucks for whatever you've got left in the pot. Won't even have to ring it in.

The teenager didn't respond but when she was done counting her float she poured a large take-out cup and set it beside the five dollar bill Heather had fished from her wallet.

The street was empty when she stepped from the coffee shop. The sticky July heat landed on her like it was poured from a bucket and made her feel tired and silly for buying a coffee so late with the thermometer pushing thirty. The stores were dark and the only noise was the faint squeal of tires as a car peeled away from the four-way stop at the other end of town. She sipped at her coffee and walked up the hill towards the library.

A pick-up truck idled at the lights and the driver took a long, slow look. His face was lost in shadow and Heather couldn't tell if he was checking her out or staring at the mannequin in the window behind her. She glared back, straining to see past the cloud of night. Her eyes itched and the coffee was burning her fingers. She shifted it to her other hand. The light changed and the pick-up truck drove on.

Crossing Dominion Street, she heard people drumming in the park. For a moment it took on a jungle beat, the kind savages played in old movies about Africa. Usually they're war drums and when the hero hears them he knows there's going to be trouble. He also knows that the trouble won't start until the drumming stops and that gives him enough time to figure out how he's going to save himself and the lady who's just fallen in love with his strong, silent ways.

The drums trailed off all of a sudden, a few beats lost on the way bumping into each other before falling quiet. Stepping around the corner of the Norwood movie theatre, Heather turned to the park. The bandstand looked to be on fire before her eyes adjusted and she could see that the light was coming from torches arranged in a circle around its perimeter. Beyond the ring of flames the bandstand was dark, although Heather could see several figures walking around inside. She skirted along the edge of the lawn and sat on a bench in the corner. The glow from the street behind it was shaded by a tree so it was possible to imagine that she was invisible to anyone not looking directly at her. She blew at the steam coming out of the hole in the lid of her coffee then set the cup in the space between her lap and rubbed her hand on her pant leg to ward off the heat.

A young man with a beard and wearing a colourful robe and sandals helped an elderly woman with a flaming bob of red hair out of a black VW Golf parked beside the theatre. He then reached into the back seat and pulled out two drums. Heather recognised the old woman but couldn't place her. One of her elementary school teachers, maybe. She looked like she'd just stepped off a boat at some African village and wasn't sure if it was safe. Another bearded man, this one taller and wearing a golf shirt, jeans and a skullcap as colourful as the other man's robe, hurried across the lawn towards them. The old woman didn't see him until he was two or three feet away and she jumped when he called out her name, which sounded to Heather like Martha.

—You made me pee my pants.

Heather heard what she said clearly, the car was parked only ten or so feet from where she sat, and also caught the look of horror on the second bearded man's face.

—It's okay, I have something on. He never lets me leave home without it.

The elderly woman laughed and placed her hand in the crook of the first bearded man's arm. Heather lit a smoke and watched the two men guide the woman past a sign stuck into the ground at the foot of the bandstand's stairs. Memorial Park Drum Circle, it read, All Welcome. Sunset to an Hour Past Sunset, Saturday. A spry old geezer, showing off by taking the four steps in two strides, waved as he passed and the old woman shook her fist at him. Over the next few minutes a dozen or so people mounted the stairs, half of them retirees and the rest scattered in age from there to the classroom. Most wore loose hanging outfits with splashes of colour added by way of the sashes they wore tied around their waists and the bandanas they'd wrapped around their heads. The last person to climb the steps was a middle-aged man wearing a Tilley hat and a pair of sturdy brown boots, beige kakis and a beige fishing vest over a plain white T-shirt. Like the others he was carrying a hand drum.

An old couple, wearing tennis shirts and white shorts, set up lawn chairs at the foot of the bandstand and shortly after the spry old geezer went to each torch and extinguished them with a little brass bell on the end of a stick until there was only one. This he took onto the bandstand and dipped into a colourful ceramic bowl, big enough to hold a full bag of nachos with salsa in the middle. A single strand of smoke poured out of it and the bearded man wearing the colourful hat handed the bowl to the spry old geezer then brought his hands together over the bowl, pulling the smoke into his face. The ritual was repeated with each of the members then the bowl was placed on a stool in the middle of the bandstand next to the chair in which the second bearded man sat with his drum propped against his knees. There was a moment of quiet, then a slow pum pum pum. The other drummers joined in, a few awkward beats tugging at the rhythm then being drawn back in line until all were one.

—Jeremiah!

A young boy ran up to the bandstand. He made it onto the first step before the girl who'd called his name grabbed him by the hand and pulled him off. Both had blond curly hair, the latter in pigtails, and Heather guessed they were brother and sister. The boy, who couldn't have been more than three, protested and slapped the girl in the face and she responded by holding both of his hands.

—You're hurting me!

The girl knelt to face him and said something that Heather couldn't hear. When she let his hands go, he raced right up to the old couple yelling, po'corn, po'corn.

The old lady strained to reach the shoulder bag on the ground at the foot of her chair and shimmied a bag of microwave popcorn and two bowls out. She handed one bowl to the boy and he sat on the grass. She filled it to overflowing then gave the girl the other bowl and did the same. The whole exercise seemed to exhaust the old lady and she slumped back in her chair, her head thrown back so that Heather could tell she had a sense of humour about being old and having grandchildren to worry after.

The drumming had slunk into the background while Heather watched the scene unfold. Now it came rushing back to the foreground with a dramatic stuttering of beats that made it sound like it was recorded and the CD was skipping. The burst died down and blended into the steady pum pum pum again. A few seconds later another drummer broke free and mimicked the first, only the drum sounded different, deeper, and the drummer was a little less sure. Back and forth across the circle it went, each drummer trying to copy the previous drummer's beats. It's like the grapevine game, Heather thought, where one child whispers into another's ear and so on down the line until the last child says what she heard and it's nothing like what the first person said. Or really, it's a conversation. The drums are speaking to each other, each with a separate voice, each with something different to say, until all the voices are heard, and then what?

Heather leaned forward on the bench as a new beat emerged from the middle of the circle. The other drums struggled to make the shift except one, or maybe two, Heather noted, who were still playing pum pum pum. The new beat was quicker, more determined than the first, and the drummers responded with their own variations, continuing the conversation. But while the first conversation might have been about the weather, this one was about something more serious.

Maybe they're talking about Corrie, Heather mused, or Christopher Allen.

Something brushed past her leg and Heather let out a yelp, jerking her feet off the ground. She shot a fearful look down, expecting to see a snake but found only her coffee cup, its spilled contents pooling in the hard packed dirt rubbed clean of grass at the foot of the bench. Picking it up, she wedged the lid into it sideways and squished it down before setting it beside her. Out of the corner of her eye a shadow moved and she glanced over at Winnie stepping from between two trees. She made her way slowly towards the bandstand then paused before she reached the old couple on lawn chairs.

—What's she doing here?

The sound of her own voice drove Heather off the bench. It wasn't so much a question as a challenge. She was just cresting the edge of the shadow cast by the tree when the drums choked to a stop and the bearded man with the hat skipped down the stairs, hurrying over to Winnie. He took her hand, not taking the way she shook her head for an answer, and led her onto the bandstand accompanied by a sharp burst of applause. A short time later, the drumming started again. Heather turned towards the street but she didn't want to leave; she was enjoying the drumming and had other reasons besides that kept her from returning to her car. Stepping out from under the tree, she scanned the bandstand and found Winnie standing beside the one remaining torch. Her eyes were closed and her hips were swaying to the beat. Heather watched her for a moment, trying to think of something to add fuel to the anger that was even now beginning to ebb, then let her eyes drift to the boy, dancing in frenetic circles while his sister stood close-bye, wanting to join him but not quite brave enough to start.

□□□

Chris, you left me
Like a bird I once kept
That opened his cage
And flew out the window
I called out his name
He looked back in regret
Not wanting to leave me
But in the sky nonetheless.

A Poem by Casey Allen
Read at Christopher Allen's Funeral, July 21st, 20-.

□□□

—You were amazing.
—No.
—Just wonderful.
—No.
—John, tell her she was amazing.
—You were amazing.

The three year-old tugged at the old man's arm and yelled that he wanted to go. The old couple sighed in unison and did impressions of limp marionettes. With a wry glance at the bearded man (John Williams?), they let themselves be dragged, the boy clenching their hands, back to the station wagon where the girl stood holding the folded-up lawn chairs.

Heather took a drag off her last cigarette and, dropping it into the grass, stood. It was late, well past ten. Winnie's dancing had distracted her from the drumming and she was never able to get into the groove like she had before. She'd retreated onto the bench, smoking and hoping that it would end before she ran out of cigarettes, but the drumming went on and on. The longer it went on the more impatient Heather became, as if she knew how the night was going to end and also that the longer she held off going home, the worse things were going to get. Still she sat, the foot tapping on the coffee soaked mud beneath the bench barely able to keep her mind on the beat. When it was over, she stood and watched Winnie talking to the elderly couple on the lawn chairs. Sweat grew in dark patches under her armpits and her dress clung to her breasts making it obvious that she wasn't wearing a bra. Heather could tell by her strained expression that she didn't really want to talk to the elderly couple and, also, didn't want to talk to John Williams when he appeared, taking Winnie's elbow in his hand and leaning in close. She shook her head at him and smiled, her lips pulled tight.

John pointed towards his car, the last left in the parking lot. Winnie backed away from him saying, Thank you, and bowing, wanting to turn, Heather could see it as clearly as she saw that once she turned she'd break into a run. John took a step towards her, holding out his hat, filled with the change he'd collected as the drummers had filed past him at the bottom of the bandstand's steps. Winnie shook her head again, saying she had no pockets, and John pressed the hat into her hand. She took it and John turned back the torches and the extra drums lined up beside the stairs. He pressed the remote in his hand and at the ba-weep of his car unlocking Winnie took off like it was a starter's pistol. Heather let her get to the edge of the park then ran after her. Her legs protested the strain of jogging across the street, and there was a sharp pain every time her left heel made contact with the sidewalk. Winnie paused at the end of the block to let a car roll through the intersection and by the time that Heather'd reached it herself she didn't have the energy to run anymore. Stooped over, breathing hard, she saw Winnie disappearing down the path leading behind Bracebridge Public School, where she'd gone from kindergarten to grade eight.

The schoolyard was brighter than Heather had remembered it. Two large overhead banks of lights bracketed the playground making the darkness they didn't reach all that more black. Standing with her shoe tips pressed against the railway ties framing the sandbox, she couldn't see anything outside the field and the school and the charcoal grey sky. She bent down and picked up a handful of sand. She let it sift between the cracks then brushed the grains clinging to her fingers and heard a moan. She took a step forward, forgetting about the railway ties, and fell face first into the sand.

—What was that?

—What?

—I heard something.

—It is nothing. Please.

A moment: Heather lying with her face in the sand, afraid to move more than it took for a breath. Winnie moaned again, and it seemed to open her up, making her whisper, please, please, please, yes, please, oh yes, please, yes. Heather pushed herself up, trying to get to her feet without making a sound, not wanting to disrupt those pleases and yes's and those gasps in between moans. On her feet, she heard the crackling of gravel and turned. The lights above the playground exploded in her stomach, or at least that's how it felt. She fell to her knees, gasping for breath, then rolled onto her side, clutching at her belly, looking up, wondering why the sky was so bright above her, and why she couldn't breathe, and why it hurt to even try. Then a hand was lifting her by the hair, off the stones pitting her cheek, and she smelled grape bubble gum soured by whiskey.

—Do you forgive me now?

She let loose a scream but it came out sounding like one of Winnie's moans. Her head fell back against the asphalt, a sharp stone cutting into the ridge over left her eye, leaving a gash that she'd see the next time she looked in her bathroom mirror, her alarm tempered by the passage of time and the words she hadn't, as of yet, spoken to Larry who, when she arrived home, would be passed out drunk on the bench he'd built into the deck outside their kitchen door.

—Hey!

and

—Did he steal anything?

and

—Heather, is that you?

brought her back to the present too fast to remember what she'd seen, just then, a glimpse, she'd been certain, of things to come. A hand was on her arm, helping her sit up, and she looked past Winnie to the boy bent down behind her, his hand resting on the curve of her back. Blonde hair washed over his eyes, their blue sharpened by specks of grey. He scrunched his brow, staring back at him, trying to match the face, and it struck her that she knew him, he was a cook at The Riverside. Him being here with Winnie meant something but she couldn't think of what it was before she caught her first real gulp of air since she'd been hit and the word came pouring out of her like Michael was there in her stead.

—Yes!

mathew&mark

They'd been standing there, beneath the overpass leading to a town called Huntsville, for the better part of four hours. The sun had gone down but it was still bright enough that if Mathew squinted he could read the big green sign a few hundred metres down the highway: Bracebridge 37 km.

—Goddamnit, these bugs are killing me.

Beside him, Mark scratched at the back of his arm, already red with bites and dried blood.

—You ever seen so many goddamn bugs?

Electricity crackled above them. The light bolted to the wall behind a cage of steel mesh flickered then settled into a dull yellow glow. A moth appeared a moment later, battering against the bars, and Mathew watched it thinking, Only pervs pick-up kids after dark.

Miguel had said it to him not two weeks ago. He was going to university in the fall and late in June Manuel had asked Mathew if, starting in September, he could come in on weekends to do his prep work. He added, loud enough for Miguel to hear in the cold room, that he didn't know why Miguel couldn't still do it, as he was going to the U of R.

—Such is the life of a father. He works sun up to sun down so his son can have a better life then the first chance he gets, his son turns his back on him. I will be lucky if he sends a card at Christmas.

Miguel came out of the cold room carrying the box of old vegetables that he'd use to make stock, the secret ingredient, he'd confided to Mathew, that made El Norte the best Mexican food restaurant in Saskatchewan.

—Ah, the prodigal one returns.

—Only long enough to stab his father in the heart.

Setting the box of wilted carrots and bruised peppers on the counter, Miguel drew the butcher knife he always kept in a scabbard on his belt and made to attack his father. Manuel tore open his shirt offering a clean shot.

—How long I have waited for this day? Make it quick so your poor father doesn't have to suffer no more.

The kitchen door flew open and Maria strode in, shooing her son back to the counter with a menu.

—What did I tell you about attacking your father? As if I don't have enough to do without spending all night sewing buttons on his shirt.

Snatching up a plate of enchiladas from the heat rack she threw Manuel a scowl then hurried back into the dining room.

Working at El Norte was like living in the margins of a book, outside of the action but still able to watch everything unfold, and the day Mathew came in to apply for the job was like a first page he kept flipping back to remind himself how far he'd come. It was a Saturday afternoon and he'd been riding the city bus for a couple hours, to get out of the house, and had seen the sign through the window. He got off at the next stop and ran back. Dishwasher Wanted, it read in a swirl of colors, hand painted on a piece of cardboard with plastic flowers glued around the edges. He pushed open the door and stepped inside. The dining room was empty. Dirty dishes from the lunch crowd littered the tables and angry voices rose from the kitchen.

The door slammed open and Maria stormed out, waving her arms about her and yelling in a language that Mathew barely recognised as Spanish. She wore a billowing red skirt and a low cut blouse and when she saw him she scrunched her face and fixed him with a fiery look.

—What do you want?

—I'm here about the job.

Maria turned back to the kitchen and called, Manuel!, then slumped in one of the booths and plucked a paperback novel off the tabletop.

Manuel came out a moment later shaking water from his hands. His apron looked like a desert landscape, splattered with eggs and beans and chilli sauce, and patches of greying scruff clung to his cheeks and jaw. He said something long and scrambled in Spanish then stopped mid-sentence and tapped his finger on his forehead.

—Ah, hah. You are not a Mexican.

—No, I'm an Indian.

—Ah, hah. Have you ever washed dishes?

—Sure, at home.

—But never in a restaurant?

—No.

—It is easy. Come, I will show.

For two years, Mathew manned the dishwasher and scrubbed pots five nights a week while Manuel and Miguel battered about the kitchen like two bulls tied by the tail, and there was no place he felt more at home. When Manuel gave him the chance to spend a few more hours there on the weekends he leapt at it. Halfway through his shift, Mathew remembered that the busses didn't start running until seven o'clock on Saturdays and eight o'clock on Sundays, so he'd have no chance of making it by six, when Manuel told him he'd need to start. Walking to work would take almost an hour at a brisk pace and, in a place where -40 was a certainty during the winter months, the thought was enough to drain him of enthusiasm for the promotion.

—What's a matter, Chico?

Mathew picked up his sprayer and rinsed down a tray load of dishes then fed it into the washer and jammed the door down, starting the cycle.

—Nothing.

—Come on, Chico. You can't fool a fool.

Miguel leaned against the dishwasher, his usual position for playing what Maria called The Older Brother Routine.

—If you don't want the promotion, I'll have a word with Papa. No worries.

—I want it. I do.

Mathew told him about the bus and about how long it would take for him to walk.

—You got a bike?

—I did.

—Stolen?

—The first one was. Then someone tried to steal the one I bought to replace it. They couldn't cut through the lock so they slashed the tires and snipped the cables.

—Hmmm.

—Yeah.

—If Papa had a car, I'm sure he would drive you. You could hitch-hike. You know–

Miguel stuck his thumb out as if Mathew had never heard of hitchhiking before.

—I used to do it all the time. I didn't have much choice. I was the only kid in my class whose father thought cars were the devil's work.

Miguel said the last bit loud enough to cause Manuel to stick his head in through the back door, a cigarette and a book fighting over the fingers on his left hand.

—El Diablo, si.

He said something else in Spanish that Mathew couldn't understand then ducked back outside to escape Maria, popping her head in to harangue him for smoking in the kitchen.

—There's always someone willing to stop and pick up a kid, especially if it's cold.

—I'm not a kid.

—But you got that baby face. Don't worry. Give it a shot. If it doesn't work, Papa will fire you for being late and you'll be free. It's a no-lose situation.

Mathew promised him he would think about it and Miguel went back to slicing vegetables for the stock, only pausing a few moments later to advise him against hitchhiking after dark.

Now, with the sky a deepening shade of blue, the thought had Mathew straining to see the drivers inside passing cars, their faces obscured behind the hazy shield thrown by their headlights.

—We'll give it another ten minutes.

—Then what?

—I don't know. We'll get off the road.

—Why?

—Only pervs pick up kids after dark.

—We ain't kids.

—I know.

Mark chewed that one over in between swatting at the flies and picking at his bites. A transport rumbling past at a hundred clicks an hour kicked up a cloud of dust. Mathew shielded his face with the back of his arm and beside him, Mark did the same. Overhead, moths assaulted the streetlight. Beyond the tunnel, the sky was too dark for even stars.

□□□

I died the moment I told Matt I would go with him. It wasn't fate or nothing. Destiny don't play the role people think it does. You're born and fated to die, besides that it ain't got nothing to do with nobody. He asked me to come and I said yes. I didn't know what would happen then, but I knew it would be bad. Otherwise he would have told me where we were going and all he said was, I need you to come with me. Okay, I answered and that was that. It was my choice and if someone had told me that I was going to die because of it I wouldn't have believed them, and even if I did I still would have gone, so it was my fault I died, except really it was Matt that killed me, same as if he stuck me with the bone handled hunting knife he sewed into the lining of his bag. I don't hold it against him. You can live an eternity inside sixteen years. Any more, I think, it'd drive you crazy. Seventy or eighty years, you'd go bat shit for all eternity, especially if you ended up in a hospital bed, staring at the ceiling, wondering if it was over yet or if you was still living in between breaths. So you'd wander back trying to find something to make sense of it, all the while thinking that the only thing you got to look forward to is counting the tiles in the ceiling. Maybe a fly would land on one of them. Whoop - dee - fuck. I could live a thousand years inside my death and then a thousand more. I've just had a taste so far. A little lick. I need to get lost for a while so it's a surprise again. Here I go.

□□□

—Can I have a smoke?
—You just asked me ten minutes ago.
—I did?
—Yeah.
—Well, d'you give me one?
—No.
—Then can I have a smoke?
—Nobody's going to pick us up if they see you smoking.
—Shit, nobody's going to pick us up anyway.

They'd been back in the same spot, under the overpass, for two hours after spending the night in the most comfortable bed Mathew had ever slept in. It was in a trailer in an RV lot just off the main road leading into Huntsville. Mathew had led Mark up the slope beside the onramp hoping that there was some cover close by they could crawl into for the night. When they got up onto the road, he spotted the lake of trailers gleaming white, stadium lights standing guard over them. It had looked like an oasis and he rubbed his eyes to make sure it was real.

They climbed the fence surrounding the lot and walked through the rows, checking the doors to see if one of them was unlocked. Each had a different name written on the back and a painting on the side to match. There was one called The Horizon, with a picture of a setting sun sending orangey-red rays streaking across the doors and windows, and one called The Explorer with a man wearing a coonskin cap and carrying a rifle standing on top of a hill. On others, animals prowled or flew or growled or just stood there looking proud. Mark added sound effects to everyone they passed until Mathew told him to quit making so much noise and he lowered his squawks and bleats and roars to a whisper.

—Hey, there's a picture of you on this one.

Mark pointed to The Mohawk, where an Indian sat astride a horse wearing a rainbow coloured headdress and staring solemnly through the window of the trailer across from him.

—I'm not a Mohawk.

—But you're an Indian, that's what I meant.

Mark cupped his hand and slapped it against his mouth for his Indian call while Mathew checked the door. It was locked and he moved to the next. The door of The Eagle, a few trailers down, was open and it was in there that they found the most comfortable bed he'd ever slept in. The toilet wasn't so bad either and come morning Mathew took his time in the bathroom, pleased that he wasn't crouching in the bushes, the grass and sticks poking his ass making him worry about what might be crawling into his pants.

—Can I have a smoke?

Mathew reached over and pinched Mark hard on the soft flesh under his armpit and Mark let out a yelp.

—What was that for?

—You were gapping again.

—I was not.

—You asked me the same question three times in the last ten minutes. You were fucking gapping.

Mark shook his head, refusing to believe it, like him gapping out was something Mathew had made up just to mess with him. He turned back to the road and cocked his thumb to the traffic, unmoving like a statue made of denim and melting wax. Mathew sat down heavily on his duffel bag. You shouldn't be so hard on him, he thought. If it wasn't for his curly blond hair and his slack-jawed innocence, we'd never have got as many rides as we did. It was only when he'd got in the car that they started looking at him like he'd beamed down from outer space and had lost half his brain on the trip.

He counted off the seconds and wondered if Mark was gapping out again. At 96, he moved to scratch a bite behind his ear and Mathew ran through a few clever replies to the inevitable plea for a cigarette.

—How long would it take?

—What?

—If we walked. How long would it take?

—We're not walking. We'll get a ride.

—But how long would it take if we did walk. A couple of hours?

—Longer. Ten, maybe.

—Bullshit. You could walk to Saskatoon in less than ten hours and that's twice as far.

—I don't know about Saskatoon, but it'd take us ten hours.

—I like to walk.

Mark lowered his arm and went back to chewing on what was left of his thumbnail.

—We ain't never going to get a ride. We should start walking.

—We'll get a ride.

—You think the cops will pick us up?

—No.

Mark peeled off a section of nail and Mathew cringed as if he'd heard a fork being dragged across a piece of slate. Holding his thumb up, Mark squeezed a drop of blood out of the nub and Mathew got back to his feet.

The highway was still for a moment and he looked down towards the hump of a bridge where the road disappeared. A black blur shimmered momentarily at the crest and Mathew squinted trying to see what make of car it was. It took only a moment for him to recognize the box shape of a Jeep, probably a Cherokee. When it was almost upon them, he saw a dream catcher hanging from the rear-view mirror and got his hand into the air the moment before it raced past.

□□□

I have spent five hundred years in the biggest surprise of my life besides the last one. I was twelve. I was in bed. Can you guess what it was? It was only seven O'clock but I was curled under the covers. It was the only place that was mine. The room wasn't even mine. It was also Matt's. We'd been together for three years by then, thrown together by Ted, who some people might have called Fate or maybe Mr. Destiny but who was really our social worker. We were closer than brothers, or at least I was closer to him than to any of my real brothers, but Matt always went out after school until curfew, and sometimes later. I didn't mind except when he tried to tell me he was at work and not out having fun like I knew he was. Most of the time I understood. He needed his own space just like I needed mine. His own space was the whole world outside of the home we shared with seven other kids, all boys between the ages of ten and sixteen; my space was my bed. When I was lying there, wrapped under the covers, I wondered what would happen to me if I went out of the house by myself. Would I have been set upon by roving gangs? Beaten to an inch of my life? Called fucking retard and stupid? Would I have had shit smeared in my face and hair? Would I have been forced to eat shit? Would I have had my pants stolen? Would someone have kicked me in the nuts? Would someone have pushed a pop bottle up my ass and broke it off inside? Would a girl have looked at me and smiled? I imagined all these things happening but can never know for sure, even now. The dead only know one thing. Can you guess what it is? Just wait and see. Back to the bed. Five hundred years under the covers. Five hundred years thinking, it'll never happen. Never. Never. Never. Then oh my god, oh shit. Five hundred years of wiping my hand on the sheet. Five hundred years of wonderful surprise.

□□□

—Sure nice of you to stop.

The bearded, middle-aged driver of the Cherokee unwrapped a stick of gum and popped it into his mouth.

—No problem.

Shifting into gear, he did a quick shoulder check before gaining speed and rejoining the flow heading south. A song about patio lanterns ended on the radio and the news announcer came on.

—Police have issued a warning to people in the Bracebridge area to be on the lookout for two pit bulls responsible for an early morning attack on a three year-old boy who was playing in his backyard. One is brown with white spots and the other is white with a brown eye patch. Police strongly urge-

The driver pushed a tape into the deck. Bob Marley replaced the urgency of the announcer's voice with a laid back beat that perfectly matched how Mathew was feeling, now that the end of their journey was in sight.

—How long you been waiting?

—Couple hours.

—Tough to get a ride out of Huntsville.

—Hey mister, how long you think it'd take to walk from here to, uh-

—Bracebridge.

—How long do you think?

Mark leaned forward as far as his belt would allow, a single curl of hair all that made it past the seats.

—Let's see. It's about thirty-seven clicks. Average walking speed is about four kilometres per hour. That'd be-

—Ten hours like I told you.

—About ten hours.

—Like I told you.

—I like to walk.

—You part Indian, or something?

—No.

—Thought you might be 'cause of the dream catcher.

It was made of brown suede strips tightly wound around a ring then crossed in the middle. A large black feather with brown stripes hung suspended below it.

—Oh, you mean the medicine wheel. When I was out east a Mic Maq woman gave it to me. She said my car looked sick.

—I'm a hundred percent, pure blood Cree. When I turn eighteen I get fifty thousand dollars. It's my cut from the casino.

—Sweet.

Matt crossed his arms over his chest like The Mohawk he'd seen on the trailer and imagined himself looking just as proud.

—Cree? They mostly live up north.

—We're from Regina.

—Really? I spent a semester there at the university. This'd be in 1990. Before your time, I guess. It was the year of the Oka crisis. You hear about that?

—Sure. My dad told me about it.

—I'd flown in on Sunday of the Labour Day weekend. Nobody was showing apartments until Tuesday so I wandered around downtown for most of the day. Everything was closed. The place was dead. Never seen a city so empty, it was weird, almost post-apocalyptic. I stowed my gear in a locker at the bus station. Figured I'd just spend the night in the park. There was a fountain on one side and a big field on the other. It was right downtown.

—You mean Victoria?

—Right. By the river.

—The Wascana.

—Yeah. I sat on a bench and read the book I'd brought. *The Sunlight Dialogues* by John Gardner, don't suppose you'd know it. It's one of my favourites. Anyway, there was something happening on the other side of the park. I couldn't tell what it was because of a row of trees that were in the way. Figured it was a family reunion or company picnic or something. When it got dark I found this bench that was kind of hidden in this stand of cedars.

—I sit there all the time.

—It's still there?

—Sure.

—I lay down on it and tied my bags around my arm, in case someone tried to grab them, and closed my eyes. Don't know how long I lay there. I couldn't fall asleep, I was too nervous or excited or whatever. I heard a crackling sound, like footsteps, and when I opened my eyes I was surrounded by four of the biggest Natives I'd ever seen.

—Whoa.

—Black leather jackets, hair down to their asses. I thought I was going to be scalped.

—No shit.

—I mean that was the first thought that crossed through my mind, you know. I was pissing myself, right, and then one of them says that it was supposed to rain that night. They told me they were having a vigil for Oka on the other side of the park, said I could come and sleep in one of their tents. The tents were these two huge tepees, must have fit thirty people although they were mostly empty from what I recall. They fed me, gave me some pillows and a blanket. I stayed with them for a couple of days.

—Cool.

—I went back a few times after school started, but things were getting pretty heavy. They were blockading the train tracks and the RCMP had the park staked out 24/7, off duty of course. Don't know how it all turned out. Did your dad say?

—The cops raided the park. Threw everyone in jail except for a few guys they took on a moonlight tour. That's what they call it when they take an Indian out into the middle of nowhere and drop him off.

—Hard to believe they have a name for such a thing.

—They didn't get my dad, but he had to leave the province for awhile.

—He was there?

—Yeah. He was probably one of the guys who took you in. My dad was always doing stuff like that.

—I never did thank them.

—No need to. It's the Indian way. It'd be like thanking a bird for flying.

□□□

I killed a man once. He was my history teacher. I called him Mr. Shitface, I can't remember his real name. He didn't bathe or change his clothes or shave or do all the things teachers are supposed to do before they come to school. He made me sit at a desk in the front after he caught me talking the first day I was in his class. The only empty desk was right in the middle of the front row so I had to sit there for an hour every day. Sometimes he'd sit on his desk and take off his shoes and socks. He'd scratch his toes with his ruler. He was too fat to scratch them with his hands. His toes were all red and flakey and when he scratched them with the ruler bits of skin would fall off. I would stare at the bits of skin on the floor afterwards and if he caught me he'd smack the ruler down on my desk and tell me to pay attention. Sometimes I'd find bits of skin on my desk and I'd be afraid to touch it for the rest of the class. One time I found bits of skin in my notebook so I burned it. The next class he asked me where my notebook was and I told him what I'd done. He didn't say anything to me after that. Next class I returned to my desk in the back and he acted like he didn't notice. When I was in the back I used to think about how many ways I could kill Mr. Shitface. I bet I thought of a hundred different ways. If I'd had my notebook I could have written them down so I would know for sure how many ways I came up with but I didn't so I'll just have to guess. My best guess would not be a hundred because a hundred's not a number you reach by accident. It'd probably be 97 or a 103. I like 103. That would be my best guess. Of the 103 ways I thought of killing Mr. Shitface, my top five favourites were: 1) run him over with a steamroller 2) crush him with a garbage compactor 3) lock him in a room and force him to eat himself 4) feed him to a crocodile and 5) glue his eyes shut and drop him into the middle of a demolition derby (which maybe wouldn't kill him but it'd sure be fun to watch). I'd sit and think about these and the other 98 ways all class long, imagining what they would look and feel like. One hour a day, from 855 to 955 staring at Mr. Shitface and thinking up different ways I could kill him until one morning when I got to class Mr. Shitface's desk was empty. The Principal arrived a few moments later and told everyone that Mr. Shitface didn't come to school that day. That's all he said. Not that he was sick or on vacation or had a doctor's appointment, just that he didn't come to school that day. For the next couple of weeks we had a pretty, young substitute teacher (she even went and got me a new notebook from the supply room when I told her I had burned mine) and between 855 and 955 I thought about what she would look like naked instead of how to kill Mr. Shitface. Then, one Friday, I came to school and this is what it said on the sign in front: We Will Miss You Mr. Shitface. Except it didn't say Shitface, it said his real name, so it took me a while to figure out who they meant. There was an assembly before class and The Principal got up and said what everybody except me already knew: Mr. Shitface was dead. Then he went on to say a few things about Mr. Shitface that almost nobody knew. Like that he had graduated at the top of his class from a big university and that he had also been a champion rower at the school. Then he lowered his voice and talked about Mr. Shitface's wife and child who had been killed in a drunk driving accident ten years ago and how Mr. Shitface had never been the same since. Everybody clapped afterwards and the girls who always cried and hugged each other when someone died cried and hugged each other in the hallways. What The Principal didn't tell anybody was how Mr. Shitface died. It took me until lunch to find that out. And how did it happen? He slipped in his shower and broke his leg. He crawled to the bathroom door but couldn't reach the knob because of his broken leg and the fact that he was so fat. The police say he was probably alive for two weeks before he starved to death. No mention was made about how much of himself he'd eaten.

☐☐☐

The Cherokee dropped them off at a 7-11 on the main street of Brace-bridge. There was a big map bolted to the wall beside the front door. Water had seeped beneath the plastic cover, fogging it over, but when Mark leaned close he could still read the street names.

—Can I have a smoke?

Mathew set his bag on the sidewalk that led from the store to the bathrooms. He dug past his sweater and extra pairs of underwear until he found the Ziploc bag of reserve smokes. He passed one of the rollies to Mark.

—Can I have two? In case we get separated.

—We're not going to get separated.

—I know, but just in case.

Mathew handed him another cigarette and cinched the bag. Mark stuck it behind his ear and lit the one in his mouth with the Zippo that Mathew had given him last year for his birthday. It had a skull and crossbones engraved in the steel grey finish. He'd chosen it because when they were ten he used to dress up like a pirate and hide Mark's toys around the house. Mark'd spend hours looking for them and Mathew couldn't recall him ever being happier. Rosie had confiscated the lighter after Mark had set the bathroom drapes on fire playing with her hair spray and the last thing Mathew had done before he left with Mark was to nick it from the top drawer of her desk.

—Man, I've got to get me some of that.

Following Mark's gaze, Mathew caught sight of the some-of-that strolling into the parking lot: three teenage girls wearing bikini tops, gym shorts and flip flops. All of them had belly button rings and jos-tled each other whenever their giggles trailed off, as if their summer joy needed a nudge every few seconds to keep it from stalling.

Mathew looked back at the map. He put his index finger on the red *You Are Here* arrow and traced outwards in a circle until he found Hiram Street. It was only a couple of blocks away.

—God, it's like they're just asking for it.

Mathew walked past him and Mark followed a few steps behind, craning his head so that he could steal an extra second's worth of the girls trying on sunglasses at the rack beside the till before jogging to catch up with Mathew.

—You think that guy who picked us up was a perv?

—No.

—He sure talked a lot.

At the edge of the parking lot they turned left and cut onto the road to avoid an old lady pushing a walker. A plastic grocery bag hung from one of its handles loaded with a big bag of Doritos, a half dozen chocolate bars and a two litre bottle of Tahiti Treat.

—It true what you said about getting all that money?

—Yeah.

—How come I never heard anything about it?

—I must've told you a million times.

—Really?

—Yeah.

—So what you going to do with it?

—Don't know. I haven't got it yet.

The street dead-ended at a dirt parking lot beside an arena. It was half filled with minivans and there were two school busses on the far side. Teenage hockey players wearing sports coats and ties milled around the front of the building while groups of parents, sweating in team jackets, smoked out of sight around the corner. A few discreet nudges prodded those with their backs to the street to turn around and a half-dozen set of eyes appraised Mathew as he approached. He was almost six foot tall and was wearing the plain, black sleeveless shirt that he'd taken to ever since he managed to fight through five hundred push-ups a day. While he walked, his shoulder length hair swayed like a skyscraper during an earthquake and his size 13 converse high tops padded the ground with all the grace of a jack hammer in ballet shoes. He imagined himself cutting an impressive figure, fierce even, and the reflection he caught of himself in the sliding door of a dust-caked Caravan agreed. With the duffel bag slung over his shoulder he could have been a hockey player come to do battle with their children and he was pleased to detect a tremor of fear in the way a squat woman with black, steel wool hair glanced over at the group of boys blocking the front entrance. One of them, deeply tanned with the squared blond hair of a comic book colonel, shuffled

a few feet to his right, clearing a space for Mathew and Mark to walk
through the doors. Mathew smiled his thanks then strode on by.

—I got to take a piss.

—You can go at my brother's place.

—Your brother's place?

—We're almost there.

—Since when do you have a brother?

—Since always.

Mark's brow creased and he looked down at the ground, the way
he always did when he was trying to figure out if Mathew was bullshit-
ting him or if the gaps he didn't believe in had once again swallowed
something he already knew. They reached the end of the block and
turned onto a street called Anne before he looked back up.

—If you got a brother, then what's his name?

—René.

—How come he ain't never come and visited you?

—Because.

—Because why?

—Because he was in jail.

—Your whole life?

—Pret' near.

—What'd he do, kill someone?

—Yeah.

—Really?

—Yeah.

—Are we going to stay with him?

—That's the plan.

They walked in silence for as long as it took to pass a dentist's
office and a three story building that looked like a house but that
had windows filled with signs advertising the names of insurance
companies and financial planners.

—I really got to go. Bad.

—It's just around the corner.

Mathew stopped at the intersection and, scanning the numbers to
see which way they went up, turned left onto Hiram Street. Past a
blue house with boarded-up windows there was a large brick building,
a sign in front calling it The Hawthorne Medical Group. A woman
wearing a blue nurse's uniform struggled to pull a wheelchair from
the trunk of a white Outback in its parking lot while a middle-aged
man wearing a bathrobe sat in the front passenger seat, one foot

bent at an odd angle on the pavement while the other resisted his attempts to get it out of the car. Next door, an old man the shape of a balloon filled with Jello sprayed his driveway with a pressure washer and a woman, wearing a full body bug suit, yanked weeds out of her flowerbed.

It had been six days since they had followed the train tracks out of Regina and caught their first ride in a souped-up VW Rabbit that took them halfway to Winnipeg. On day two, riding in a Winnebago with two German couples who couldn't speak a word of English, the familiar blocks of earth and sky had become speckled with trees and the first creeping toes of The Canadian Shield poking through the ground. After that there hadn't been much to see except the ditch, an unbroken line of trees, and the violence of a road that carved itself through layers of stone too old to know that its guts were cleaved open, exposing deep red fissures.

Other than the Rabbit and the Winnebago the rides were, for the most part, little hop-skips crammed into the front of a pick-up truck with a dog or a wife; good to the next dirt road that led only to the horizon or, later after crossing through most of Manitoba, were eaten by a tangle of trees and rusty cow fences. Then it was back to waiting for the next which might be two hours in coming but would more than likely be four. By Mathew's calculations it took twenty-three rides and a hundred and forty-five hours to get within a few houses of the address on the envelope his brother's last letter had come in. Tracking the cracks in the sidewalk leading towards 240 Hiram Street, his hands felt for the photo pressed flat into the back pocket of his pants. He didn't need to pull it out to see his brother standing shirtless in front of a waterfall. René's hair was longer than his by six months and there were crudely etched prison tats covering his chest and his arms but otherwise Mathew could have been holding a picture of himself from ten years in the future. They had the same gangly limbs that ate up muscle as fast as weights could put it on, and the same smile which Rosie said was his best feature because he could turn it on in a wink but it took him three days to turn it off again.

When the Cherokee had pulled off the highway, passing a Home Depot, a Wal-Mart and a Tim Horton's before the town started good and proper, he had kept a keen eye out for his brother. The worry that he might not recognise him quickly disappeared, buried under an endless stream of pasty faces.

A group of them were standing around looking up at a tree in the yard Mathew guessed was right across from 240. Branches lay scattered over the lawn, one was poking a few feet onto the road, but no one was making a move to round them up. Instead they gaped upwards, laughing and rubbing the sawdust out of their eyes. Mathew followed the grind of a chainsaw to the man straddled in the crux of the trunk, thirty feet up. He was wearing a white sleeveless shirt that exposed skin the colour of apples too long on the ground, shorts and work boots. His hair was black and cropped short. His back was to Mathew but he detected something familiar about the way he flicked the chainsaw out at the frayed ends of a snapped branch, chopping at the sinews keeping it attached until it fell without a sound. The onlookers offered sparse applause then shuffled off to the garage patting each other on the back and jostling for position at the beer fridge.

The man in the tree wedged the saw at his feet and unclipped a water bottle from his belt. He drank from it then splashed some on his face, wiping drips from his dense beard over his forehead before tossing the empty bottle to the ground and picking up his saw again. Mathew turned to the house he was passing on his side of the street. The number was written in frilly lettering on a board hanging from a post beside the door. Two Hundred and Thirty-Eight. Its porch stretched almost to the sidewalk, obscuring the house beyond. Mathew stuttered his stride out of a nervous impulse to do something to mark the moment when the address on the letter from his brother became a house. When it came into view, the first thing he saw was the white sheets hung in the windows in place of curtains. The second was the yellow police tape barricading the stairs leading to the front door.

—This the place?

—Yeah.

—Well ain't you gonna knock?

☐☐☐

There is a book written about me. I saw it once. It is a big book with a plain white cover. My name is written in one corner. Mark Jensen. A book all about me. Ted showed it to me when I asked him about my mother. He flipped to a page near the front and looked at me like he wasn't sure whether he should tell me what it said. Finally he took a sheet from the book and set it in front of me. I am not a good reader. My English teacher said really I am just lazy but it amounts to the same thing, so I asked him what it said. He picked it back up and looked up and down the page. He told me it was written by the police after they took me from my mom. He read what it said then put it back in my book and closed the cover. Do you still want to meet her? he asked. Yes, I told him. He looked at me like the people at McDonalds look at you when you don't know what you want and it's your turn. I glanced over his head and pretended I was choosing something from the menu board. I tapped my finger on my lips and made clucking sounds. I thought about ordering a chocolate shake and large fries with spicy cheese sauce but I didn't get a chance before Ted told me that he would see what he could do. He never talked about my mom again and neither did I. I didn't really want to meet her anyway.

□□□

While Mark relieved himself, hidden in the house's backyard, Mathew kept guard by the steps leading to the side door, marked with police tape just like the one around front. He watched the man climb down from the tree across the street and wondered how he could have thought that it was René. His hair, that looked short from a distance, was actually tight curls, like an afro except that it clung to the man's head, plastered with sweat and sawdust. And only the skin on his arms and neck was tanned. White folds of flesh carved rings under both his short sleeves and around his neck. Dark spirals of hair, almost as thick as those on his head, scratched at the back of his shirt.

Two kids sucking on jumbo freezies stopped in front of the house to look at what the man had done to the tree and Mathew walked over to them.

—Hey.

The older of the two boys looked back. He was six or seven and missing his two front teeth. Scabs carved out a riddle on his knees. The other one was half his size and was busy squeezing a piece of blue ice up the plastic tube.

—You get those at the 7-11?

—Huh?

—The freezies.

—No, at The Shoppers. They got a big freezer full of them.

—Where's that?

—In the front of the store.

—No, I mean The Shoppers.

—Oh. It's across from the KFC.

—And where's that?

—Down there.

The boy pointed back the way they'd come.

—You live on this street?

—Uh huh.

—You see the cops bring a big Indian out of that house. Looks like me except with tattoos up and down both arms.

—F'rest?

The younger boy tugged at the older's shirt but he pretended not to notice.

—Nah, they just brought out some white guy and a lady. She was white too.

—F'rest?

—What?

—Too cold.

—Well hold it with your other hand.

The younger boy switched the freezie to his other hand and, beaming, stuck the end in his mouth and began to suck the juice out.

—Thanks.

Mathew turned back to 240 Hiram Street. He couldn't see Mark through the gap between the house and the garage and when he looked back at the sidewalk the kids were gone.

—Mark?

He stepped to the edge of the garage. A few dots of sunlight speckled the uncut lawn making the shadows that covered the rest all that darker. A deck took up almost half of the yard. Three nails with a chunk of wood that looked like Styrofoam protruded at odd angles from the nearest post, missing its rail, and the deck's floor was pockmarked with holes that could have been footprints if the person who'd made them was too drunk to find the door. A fence at the edge of the property was held up by strands of clothesline wire tied to the jack pines that concealed this yard from the next, and it was from behind this rickety construct that Mark's head appeared.

—Watch out for the dog shit.

Mathew scanned the lawn. It was covered with little spirals and fat logs, giant splats and fresh ones seething with worms. He threaded his way to the fence where Mark was cleaning a mashed turd off his shoe with a stick. His other shoe sat upside down on a table fashioned out of a piece of old plywood and two saw horses.

—Have you ever seen so much dog shit?

—Can't say as I have.

—I need a hose. Did you see a hose?

—No.

—God. It's fucking disgusting.

Mathew picked a stick off the ground and used it to scrape the brown/green blob off the other shoe then dropped it on the ground at Mark's feet.

—I ain't wearing it like that. It's still got shit on it.

—Then go in your socks.

Mathew started down the path leading between the trees in the far corner of the yard. The ground was springy at his feet and squeaked though Mathew couldn't see beneath the layer of pine needles and leaves to tell what was down there. Probably an old mattress someone had buried. The question as to why someone would want to bury a mattress occupied him until he was standing in the parking lot on the far end of the path. A middle-aged woman with purple streaks in her hair and wearing institutional whites leaned against a red brick building under a sign that said, Patient Parking Only. She smoked a cigarette in between bites from a banana and stared at Mathew in the same way he imagined she'd have stared at Sasquatch if he'd just appeared at the edge of the parking lot.

—Hey, lady. You know where I can find a hose?

Mark stood beside Mathew holding up his shoes. The lady looked away, took another drag of her smoke then stubbed it out on the side of the building. She pocketed the butt and took another bite of the banana before pitching the peel into the yard of the house neighbouring the doctor's office.

Mathew waited until she disappeared into the porch stuck to the side of the red brick building then headed for the street. The aroma of KFC, familiar and tantalising, blocked out the stench of dog shit. He followed the smell of fried chicken to the next corner and turned towards the giant spinning bucket on a pole that stood at the intersection a block down.

—I'd kill for a bucket of chicken right now. We could split it.

—It's too expensive.

—We could at least get a couple of snack packs. They're cheap.

—Maybe.

They cut into the parking lot and approached the door. There was a closed sign on the front window over another one telling them that it opened at eleven.

—It sure smells open.

—Yeah.

—There's a McDonald's at the bottom of the hill. They're definitely open.

Mathew shook his head.

—There's a Mr. Sub across the street.

—I like Subway.

—They're too expensive.

—I'd fucking kill for a bucket of chicken right now. What time is it?

—Don't know.

—It's got to be close to eleven.

—We could wait.

—Yeah.

—You want to get a freezie?

—A freezie? You mean while we wait?

—Yeah.

—Now that's what I'm talking about.

□□□

I go back to the beginning. To a place I don't know, to a time I don't remember. It's not like I thought it'd be, being a baby. It's weird. It's like I'm looking at the world while spinning out of control on a merry-go-round. Colours and sounds and smells and light and dark and my fingers in my mouth and a pressure on the back of my head that could be the floor or a mattress, I can't tell. Something green scares me. I don't know what it is but I start crying. Then the something green is gone, so gone I don't even have a memory of it but still I cry. I cry and cry and cry and cry. Then I hear her, or rather feel her. She is a presence, a force, and I shake with her being near. Now I'm floating. My cries grow louder. I want to look her in the eyes so she'll know about the something green but there's a pressure on my feet. Her hands are holding me by the ankles. The colours and the sounds and the smells and the light and the dark all blur. I hold my breath. I am too afraid to cry. I am flying.

□□□

They ate their snack packs at a picnic table behind the KFC amidst a scattering of flies on vacation from the dumpster a few feet away. They'd barely sat down when a boy wearing red and white stripes opened the restaurant's back door carrying a bag of garbage. The bag was clear and Mathew could see that amongst the wadded up paper towels there was at least four buckets worth of chicken, wings, thighs and drumsticks smeared against the plastic. Mathew watched him until it became clear that he was just going to keep on standing there then picked up his chicken leg and peeled the crispy skin off with his teeth, burning his lip on the layer of grease inside. Mark had his back to the door and didn't notice anything out of the ordinary until the door slammed shut making him startle and drop his half-eaten thigh. It tumbled off the table and into his lap. He let out a shriek and snatched it back up, tossing it into his box.

—Shit, that's hot.

He rubbed his leg vigorously then took his unopened can of Sprite and rolled it over the burnt area, cooling it.

—I ought'a sue.

Mathew dipped a fry into his coleslaw and watched the door. Halfway through his last fry it opened again. A red-faced man ventured out carrying a gut big enough to make Mathew wonder how many buckets of chicken he'd see if his shirt was clear like the garbage bag.

—This table's for staff only.

Mathew finished off his fry and thought about asking why they didn't serve Grecian bread in their snack boxes like they did in Regina.

—The sign says so right there.

The man pointed to a sign bolted to the wall. It was pockmarked with cigarette burns and reminded Mathew of the max speed signs on the side of the highway that farm boys in Saskatchewan used for target practice.

—The ones inside were full.

—You the boys who made that mess in the bathroom?

Mark laughed through a mouthful of chicken, spraying bits onto the table and Mathew kicked him.

—We'll be done in a moment.

The man may have shaken his head or pulled at the wiry strands of his moustache or made some other gesture to show his frustration, but whatever he did while he stood there waiting Mathew didn't bother to notice. He thought about the picture he had of René and tried to come up with a plan as to how he was going to track him down now that 240 Hiram Street was a dead-end.

—There a waterfall around here, Mister?

Mathew hazarded a glance at the red-faced man and was met with the unwavering stare of a man certain that he was being wronged more with every passing tick. Mathew chucked a chicken bone back into the box and closed the lid. He considered opening his can of pop just to see how long the man would stand there before he did something. The aroma of chicken venting through the grates above them didn't seem so inviting now that his stomach was full, and he settled for farting loudly as he stood. The door banged shut before they'd made the corner of the building.

—Sucks you don't get greasy bread with the snack pack like you do in Regina. I love that greasy bread.

Mathew nodded then scanned the street looking, he supposed, for some sort of sign like Indians did in the old days, or maybe just in the movies. Best he could find was a poster stapled to a light post by the curb with a picture of Santa on it.

—Christmas in July. What do you think that is?

Mathew shrugged and read the fine print that promised sleigh rides, candy apples, reindeer, a midway and more.

—We should check it out.

Two pre-teens sitting on the curb eating handfuls of popcorn chicken pointed them down the hill towards the McDonald's and said they couldn't miss it. A couple of minutes later they stood at the edge of a parking lot full of old midway rides, games like ring toss and balloon darts, and cars trying to get from the grocery store to the Canadian Tire without ploughing through the swarms of children already crying that they'd dropped their candy floss or that they wanted another chance to win a stuffed crocodile or to see Santa but he was off smoking behind the grocery store. In the far corner, by the gas pumps, there was a penned in area with lots of straw but no reindeer.

—I guess Santa's a no show.

—You want to go on a ride?

Mathew paid for three tickets then stood along the metal fence with a group of moms and dads taking pictures as their kids whizzed by on The Twirler. Mark sat alone in a bucket holding his hands over his head and he slid back and forth across the seat every time the mechanical arm jerked him in the opposite direction. He waved at Mathew when he flew past.

—What a rip off. It wasn't even scary.

—At least it was festive.

—Huh?

—Nothing.

—Fuck me.

Mathew followed Mark's slack jaw to the girl walking past. She was wearing a mini-skirt and a tight tank top and was trying not to smudge her bright orange lipstick while eating a candy apple.

—She's like, twelve.

—Girl's didn't look like that when I was twelve.

—You want a candy apple?

—Shit yeah.

They joined the queue, five deep, at the window of a chip wagon. A large inflatable sleigh sagged in the breeze on top of it and a hand written sign taped over its menu offered Jolly Fries, Elf Burgers, Candy Cane Shakes and Rudolph's Red Nose Reindeer Apples. Two teenage boys leaned against the back of the converted van flicking wadded-up balls of cotton candy at each other between bites. One had a six inch high Mohawk, blonde, the dark roots showing, and was wearing a black leather jacket spackled with bits of white-out that might have started as a skull or a demon. The other boy was wearing a white sleeveless undershirt, a pair of combat boots and black cargo pants held up by suspenders. Pink flecks dotted his shaved head and each burst of laughter that he forced between chews was a challenge to those around who didn't know how easy it was to have a good time.

—Let's just forget about it.

—What?

—The candy apples.

—Why?

—They're too expensive.

—They're only four bucks.

—It's too expensive.

Mark furrowed his brow and dropped his jaw and Mathew fished a five dollar bill from his wallet.

—Just make it quick.

He waited for Mark beside the ring toss. He watched the punk and the skinhead finish their floss then share the smoke that was perched behind the skinhead's ear. They snatched it back and forth from each other, taking deep drags and holding in the smoke for as long as they could. The line was moving at the pace of an Elf Burger and Jolly Fries every two or three minutes and it was ten minutes before Mark came walking over to him, showing off his nuclear red ball on a stick like it was a humanitarian award.

—I got the last one.

Running to catch up with Mathew, now crossing the grassy divide between the parking lot and the street, he bit into it but all he managed to do was break a piece of the coating off. It fell to the ground, shattering on the asphalt. On the road a solid stream of traffic ploughed by and Mathew looked to the lights at the intersection a half a block away, waiting for the red to create a gap.

—What the fuck? You see this shit. It's all brown inside.

He held up the apple. The skin was all wrinkly and the small hole Mark had made in it revealed the flesh to be the colour of fresh motor oil.

—Christmas in July. What a joke.

Halfway up the hill leading back to the KFC there was a blue sign with a big white question mark above an arrow pointing right. Mark trudged along behind Mathew, the stick from his apple hanging crooked from the side of his mouth. A shard from the candy coating clung to the lace on his left shoe and bits of it hung from his shirt. His lips were tinged red giving him the appearance of a vampire after an all-night feeding frenzy.

—God, have you ever seen so many hotties?

A sporty black convertible crammed with them turned into the parking lot just ahead accompanied by a loud, throbbing beat. They were older, university students maybe, and wore movie star sunglasses and serious expressions. They didn't look at Mathew and Mark as they passed and none of them seem to notice that Mathew had to grab Mark by the arm to stop the car from clipping him.

The convertible pulled into a handicapped space in front of the Great Canadian Bagel and the car emptied save for the driver who sat with the engine running, drumming her nails in time to the song. Her hair was pulled back into a pony tail to show off the freckles swarming both shoulders. Mark stared at her the whole way past and Mathew counted four other men doing the same in the time it took to make it across the lot.

—Now that's a fucking woman. What do you think it would take to get a woman like that?

—Money.

—That's all?

—Yep.

The parking lot dumped them back onto the main street. After the heat radiating from the asphalt, walking on the pale sidewalk was like stepping from hot sand into cool water and for a moment Mathew felt a surge of energy. He shifted his duffel from one shoulder to the next and allowed himself a deep breath before converting the energy into his stride. Mark scurried to keep up beside him. Another arrow beneath a question mark pointed straight ahead. Cars lined the curb and idled by on the street and Mathew couldn't remember a Saturday morning when he'd seen so many in Regina. Strange how the city can seem so empty while a small town looks about ready to burst.

—Do you really think we're going to find your brother?

—Sure.

—How do you know?

—Because that's just the way it is.

☐☐☐

Something is wrong. I am lying on the floor. I am crying. I am flying through the air. Then...Nothing. More nothing than I can imagine. More nothing than I think can possibly exist, even though I know that nothing makes up almost everything. That's what my science teacher told us, anyway. She said the universe is made up of mostly empty space. There is more empty space in a chair than wood, that's what she said. I think the whole class touched their chairs, not really believing. But I believe, now I do, because there is more empty space in me than me. How do I describe it, this nothing, this empty space that makes up more of me than me. I can't. I am gone and yet I am still here but am I still here only because I have come back or was I here to begin with? I don't know. I live in this nothing for one hundred years to see if there is something there with me. There is not. I go and stand at the edge of the nothing, although I am nothing so I don't have legs and can't really stand. I am here, anyway, at the edge of where nothing ends. At first I just hear a faint sound. Thumppathumppathumppathump. The beginning of me all over again. Then there is light, there is dark, there is colour, there is smell, there is everything that there was before but something has changed. The nothing has come with me. I am the nothing and the nothing is me.

□□□

The lady behind the desk at the information centre had the look of a kindly librarian and the smile of a person who had grown used to people dropping in just to use the bathroom. She scanned Mathew in the offhand way clerks always did then returned to fumbling with something under the counter.

—There any waterfalls around here?

The question caught her off guard and, startled, she dropped whatever it was she was fumbling with. She bent to retrieve it and was out of sight long enough to make Mathew think she'd snuck off and was waiting in a back room for him to leave. When she did appear the friendly librarian smile had reset and she addressed Mathew as if he'd just walked in and she hadn't just been hiding under the counter.

—Good morning.

—Waterfalls.

—Yes?

—Are there any waterfalls around here?

—There are five waterfalls in the immediate area.

Tearing a placemat-sized map from the stack on the counter, she made circles on it as she listed them off.

—There's Bracebridge Falls, Upper and Lower Muskoka falls, Wilson Falls and High Falls. Do you have a car?

Mathew shook his head.

—The first four are within walking distance. High Falls is a little further.

—Which one's the closest?

Mathew stepped out of the information centre doors and listened for Bracebridge Falls which the lady had said was just across the street. All he could hear was the thump of traffic on the bridge. Mark sat on one of the decorative granite boulders that framed the cobblestone square at the bottom of the stone steps leading down from the street. The cigarette in his left hand had burnt itself out at his fingers and he wore the glazed over expression of a stuffed deer perpetually caught in the headlights. Mathew walked over and leaned down inches from his face. He blew at the wisps of hair curled over his forehead and, when that didn't rouse him, he wet his finger with a juicy gob and stuck it in his ear. He squished it around and Mark snapped back.

—Huh?

—You were gapping.

—Bullshit. I was just thinking, that's all.

—Oh yeah, thinking about what?

—I-I-I don't know, just thinking. Jesus, my ear's all wet. What the fuck?

Stone stairs at the side of the building led them down to a concrete walkway overlooking the river. Some kids were hanging from the trestles below a railway bridge and daring each other to jump past a sign that said, No Swimming. They followed the slow flowing current to a footbridge spanning the width of the river. From the footbridge Mathew could see that this wasn't the falls René was standing in front of when the picture was taken. Most of the water was diverted to a hydro station on the right bank so that only a trickle made it over the actual falls. A father helped a toddler climb over the dry bulges of rock, glittering with quartz and broken glass, while in a viewing area on the far side his wife yelled for him to be careful. Skipping down the cement steps that led to the base of the falls, Mathew saw that part of the viewing platform had been fenced off with the same chain link that guarded the stairs on either side and a metal plate had been tied to the mesh. Danger! Fast Moving Current. Stand Back. Mathew guessed the sign was meant for the spring runoff when the falls were likely to be more active. He took the photo from his pocket and held it up, just to be sure. Water poured over René's head in a thick stream. Behind him, written on the rock face in white spray paint, there was a squiggly doodle. He scanned the rock here but none of the graffiti matched the one on the picture.

At the bottom of the falls the cement steps gave way to a wooden bridge. A few dead fish, small brown trouts or bass maybe, floated in the stagnant pools on either side of it and the breeze was hot with the stench of rot.

—I remember what I was thinking about.

—Yeah.

—I was thinking about getting laid.

—Really.

They'd crossed the bridge and were walking along the crushed gravel path that curved along the bay until it met up with a boardwalk where a dozen or so teenagers were engaged in summer rutting activities. Two brawny teens grappled with each other on a stack of three picnic tables piled against the rail, trying to knock each other into the water, and five others were gathered in a circle around a surfer-looking dude while he demonstrated how to fight multiple opponents. None of the five were willing to get too close though and most of the time he was just kicking and hitting into the air. At the edge of the path, six girls, all wearing bikinis, bunched together like zebras doing their best to ignore the show.

—How old were you when you first got laid?

—Depends on what you mean.

—Huh?

—It's complicated.

—No it ain't. You stick it in, right. What's so complicated about that?

—You don't understand.

—What?

—Never mind.

—No, tell me.

—I was thirteen, okay.

—Shit. I'm already sixteen.

—Yeah.

—I ain't even kissed a girl.

The surfer-looking dude and two of his attackers suddenly broke ranks. Running to the picnic tables, they heaved up the side of the top one sending the two brawny teens into the water.

One of the girls left the herd and strode to the surfer-looking dude, busy dishing out high fives all around. Mathew was too far away to hear what she was yelling and he looked to the bigger of the brawny teens stomping up the ramp leading from the dock.

—Stay here.

—Can I have a smoke?

—I ain't going to ditch you. Just stay here. I'll be back in a second.

Mathew cut across the lawn to where three shirtless longhairs sat on a bench picking at the pubes poking over the waist of their jeans.

—You know this place?

All three longhairs took a moment to check the picture then looked away. Mathew turned back towards the river. The brawny teen had the surfer-looking dude held suspended over his head and was carrying him towards the rail while the latter's girlfriend was screaming for him to put him down.

—Could be the potholes, I guess.

Mathew traced down the row, searching for which longhair had spoken. The one on the end was picking lint from his belly button but looked up to let know Mathew know that it was him.

—Where's that?

Mathew held the map in front of the longhair. He took a moment to orient himself then pointed to one of the circles.

—It's here.

—I just follow the river?

—Easier to take the train tracks. After about a half click there's a path that'd take you right down. It's just before the bridge.

—Thanks.

The scene on the boardwalk had broken up. The brawny teen was flexing his muscles and bellowing wrestling taunts at the surfer-looking dude doing a back stroke towards the pier on the far side of the river. His girlfriend was yelling at him again and her friends were lighting smokes or heading up to the playground to go for a slide or use the swings.

Mark stood at the fork in the path where it split between the river and the playground, watching the girls walk past. There was a small brick building between him and Mathew. Both its windows were covered with plywood and secured with black metal bars and its door was bolted shut with a new padlock. Mathew ducked behind it and pressed himself against the wall. The sun leaked through the leaves in the maple trees mounting the hill towards the road and Mathew closed his eyes. Sparkles flared in the darkness, stars caught under a curtain. He raised his face to the light and a blanket of red blotted out the galaxy of sparks. He counted to ten then turned away from the sun and opened his eyes. The world appeared in negative. The people at the playground were suddenly purple and the trees were orange and the sky was red and they were all surrounded by a silver aura that made it seem like they were part of the same thing before his eyes adjusted and he could see they were not.

□□□

I spend less than a second in the hospital. A second is enough to know that nothing interesting happens in there. People live, people die. People do their jobs, people eat their lunches, people leave. That is all. On TV lots of other stuff happens in hospitals. Things that make people laugh and cry and wish that they could get sick just so they could laugh and cry all over again. For the less than a second that I am there nobody laughs and nobody cries. They are all too busy living and dying, doing their jobs, eating their lunches and leaving. So I join the flow. I live. I eat my lunch. I leave. Now wasn't that interesting?

□□□

When Mathew first came to live with Rosie she would take her boys for walks along the Wascana, which all the maps and signs called a creek although it was big enough to be a river and that's how Mathew liked to think of it. Every few hundred feet along the path there was a bench and near the bench there was usually a stake stuck in the ground with a plaque attached to it. Rosie always stopped at the plaques and read aloud what each said. Most of them were about what someone or some group of someones had done to the creek, like one about how the CPR had damned it up in 1921 to make Wascana Lake, which Mathew liked to think of as just another part of the river, and one about how the Wascana Centre, which is what they called the jumble of parklands and buildings scattered along the shore, was designed by the Seattle architect Minoru Yamasaki whose most famous building, the plaque also said, was the World Trade Center in New York city. Only one plaque was about the river itself. It said that the Wascana originated 45 kilometres east of Regina in a farmer's field, no one knew exactly where.

Rosie always sat down at the bench in front of this plaque to smoke the one cigarette she allowed herself every day since she'd quit and most often she commented that it was fitting that the Wascana started in a farmer's field because, one way or another, everything in Regina started in a farmer's field.

Rosie herself had come from, if not a field, then at least a farm close to one. She had moved to Regina to go to school and had never left, falling into her current occupation after her husband disappeared three years into a twenty-five year mortgage, leaving her with two kids and a whole lot of empty rooms. When Mathew was old enough to ask such things, he asked Rosie why she had never returned to the farm if she liked it so much and she answered that she didn't have to because the farm was all around her.

—Regina was a city built by farmers and if the people around here just remembered that once in a while then maybe they wouldn't be having so many of the problems they do.

Mathew enjoyed these walks along the gentle, even sloping banks of the Wascana and he kept on enjoying them after Rosie had her hip surgery and could no longer make the trek. Even then he always sat on Rosie's smoking bench and, closing his eyes, recited from memory what the plaque said. Sometimes he imagined a search party of pasty faces wearing lab coats and carrying the latest in technological gadgetry stomping through one field after the next while a bunch of pasty farmers leaned on cow fences chewing stalks of grass and taking bets as to who'd be the first to find the fabled source of the mighty Wascana. It seemed impossible that such a simple thing as where a little bit of water came from could elude these great scientific minds and he tried to think of what it might mean. One morning while he sat on the bench with Mark, the answer came to him.

—Some mysteries are best left unsolved.

—Huh?

—Like with the Wascana. Where it comes from.

—What?

—The river.

—I thought it was a creek.

—You're missing my point.

—And what's that?

—That it's a mystery.

—What is?

—It's a mystery where the water comes from. You know, like the plaque says.

—What plaque?

—The one stuck in the ground right there. The one Rosie's read to you two hundred times and I must've recited, from memory, at least a dozen times on top.

—Right. Yeah. It's a mystery. About the water and you know, like the plaque says.

Mark reached behind his ear for the cigarette he'd already smoked while they were sitting there and, not finding it, gnawed on the skin of his thumb.

—Water comes from rain, don't it?

Mathew didn't have an answer for him but later, when he lay in bed, he thought about it again and told himself that Mark was wrong. The rain didn't give birth to the river, the ground did, and the rain just fed it. But the certainty he'd felt on the bench that morning eluded him and he kicked the covers off then wound them tight again and buried his head under his pillow. He imagined that he was floating underneath the Wascana, drowning, and in the next moment that he was the Wascana. He fell asleep and dreamt that he was flowing backwards, the water trickling out of him until all that was left were drops glistening on buried field stones and the dirt around him was like a womb.

After the first of three letters from his brother René arrived, he lay in bed unable to sleep and once again culled the image of himself as a river, this time full with the thaw and raging. After a time he imagined the summer sun on high and the rapids dwindled until there was only a single eddy left in the otherwise calm waters. Enough to spin a leaf, maybe, and not much else.

June 4, 20-

mathew,

you probably saw the address on the envelope and your wondering why someones writing you from an ontario correctional facility. well mathew matt? im your brother. my name is René descartes and it might not sound like it but its about as funny a name as an indian could have judging from the laughs i get whenever i tell it to a white person. i looked up the real René descartes or the other one anyway and as far i could tell he didnt do a hell of lot except making up things to confuse people more than they already are. i don't know if he made any money doing this but i guess he mustve since people are still laughing over his name five hundred years later. im not going to write any more about him now because if you ask me hes got too much press as it is. im just telling you about him because youll probably google my name like i did when i wanted to know something about the real me and youll wonder why im in there 2380000 times. most of those 2380000 times its about this other guy but im in there too kind of hidden which isnt such a bad thing if you ask me. if you look long enough youll find out why im in jail which im sure is what youre wondering right now. itss okay. its the first thing everybodys always asking you in here and they dont even halfways trust you until you look them in the eye and tell them why your a worthless piece of shit just like them. id like to tell you i was different. that im not a worthless piece of shit. but im in here for the same reason that most of the other worthless pieces of shit are in here for and thats because i hurt a woman. i wont tell you i didnt do it. i pled guilty so i guess i must be. and i also wont bore you by telling you what its like inside. youve seen enough movies to get the general idea. of course what the movies dont say, or at least the ones i seen dont say, is that most of the time its like being in school but instead of teachers you got guards and instead of desks you got cells. they even let us go out in the playground and make sure they give us enough room so that when we get back to class we aint pissing all over the place like a bunch of dogs marking their spot.

im not sure what else i have to say but my teacher tells me that no one is allowed to leave until we write a page. his name is roger and hes big and fat and if you were to tell me he showered twice a month id have to call you a liar and maybe wed get into it afterwards because boy does that guy stink. i can tell you this because when he told us that we had to write a page he also told us that he didnt care what we wrote and that he wouldnt even read it hed just check to make sure it was made up of full sentences and not like that guy in the shining wrote before he tried to hack up his family with an axe. all work and no play makes jack a dull boy was what he wrote i think and i couldnt agree more.

ive been sitting here for i dont know how long but boy does it feel like forever. i dont know exactly what time it is because roger took down the clock before he told us to fill up a page. he said its a writers worst enemy but if this is what he means by writing id say my worst enemy is the pain im feeling in my ass because these fucking chairs were made by someone who obviously didnt think anyone would ever have to sit in them.

anyway thats as close to a page as im gona get.
your brother,
René.

Mathew kept the letter in his bag and read it over whenever he had a few moments, more because it made him chuckle than because of any questions it might have awakened in him about where he came from. A week later, a second letter arrived. He didn't open it until he was sitting on Rosie's smoking bench by the Wascana and he was good and sure that nobody was around. Why he wanted to be alone this time, when the first letter hadn't raised more than an eddy in the calm and happy waters of the river Mathew Descartes, he couldn't say. All he knew was that the second letter felt different and he didn't want to take the chance that he'd start bawling and have to endure a month's worth of stupidity from the other kids and maybe even give out a few bloody lips because of it.

June 11, 20–

matt,

me again. im sitting on my pillow this time so my ass should hold up better than the last time. it came to me last week after i finished that letter that i didnt say why i was writing to you. i ment to but i guess i ended up filling the page anyway so it doesnt really matter. roger my teacher who is so big and fat that ive seen chairs faint when he walks in the room told us we could write anything we wanted as long as it wasnt gibberish but that hed prefer we wrote something that was useful like a story or instructions on how to build something or maybe a letter to someone we hadnt talked to in a long time. well im not any good at telling stories and even though i am pretty good at building stuff writing a page about building stuff sounds about as fun as watching your fingernails grow but there was one person id been meaning to talk to sometime and just never got around to it. thats you in case you didnt guess. we are brothers as i said in my first letter. we have never met but i did see you for a little while if you can call a big belly you. that was before our mother left me with our grandparents and took off for i dont know where. the reason i know about you is that after you were born our grandparents got a visit from a woman named mrs romp. i remember her name even though it was a long time ago when i was eight or nine because she looked just like it sounded. she was even bigger and fatter than roger my teacher and her face was like something you'd puke up in a toilet. there was a red blotch that covered most of it and there were chunks of skin hanging off her cheeks and one big notch of skin dangling from her eyelid. every time i was being sick after i saw her i always thought of her because her face looked like something youd puke up in a toilet and her name sounded like the noise you made when you was doing it. one time i had a urine tract infection and i was so sick i was romping for three days straight. i spent most of my time in the bathroom with my head on the toilet bowl and i dont remember much about it except that the toilet was cool and it felt better than laying on my pillow and romping into a bowl. grandma said that the whole time i was in the bathroom i was laughing. she thought that the fever had made me delirious but really i was thinking about mrs romp and laughing because her name sounded just like it did when i threw up.

mrs romp sat at our grandma and grandpas kitchen table and told them about you being born in saskatchewan. i was hiding in the pantry which was a little closet at the top of the stairs to the basement where my room was. i always hid in the pantry when grandma and grandpa had guests over because i could listen to what they were saying and they wouldn't know i was there. i dont know why it was so important that they didnt know i was there. if i wanted to listen to what they were saying i could have sat right at the table and had tea and homemade oatmeal cookies with them which is what grandma always gave people when they came to visit. it wasnt like i was a monster or something that they were hiding in the basement and who they only let out when no one was around but for some reason i dont know why id rather hide in the pantry. i could stay in there for hours if i needed to but when mrs romp stopped by i was only in there for a few minutes. as i already said she told grandma and grandpa about you being born and grandpa told her that they were too old to take on a baby. mrs romp said she understood and the floor creaked so bad when she walked to the side door that it sounded like she was going to fall through it. it was when she was putting her shoes on that i saw what she looked like. there is a hole in the pantry door where the nob used to be and i looked through it and there she was huffing and puffing like putting shoes on for her was like climbing a mountain for anyone else. i think she must have heard me because she looked my way. she was a mighty strange sight for a boy of eight or nine and if i live to be a hundred i dont think that i will ever forget her name. after her visit i thought about you once in a while and wondered if wed ever meet. i guess so far we havent but i hope that maybe one day we will.

your brother,
René.

Mathew didn't start bawling but he did feel something other than an eddy rising from his belly. It took him most of the way home before he realised it was anger; a gut clenching, teeth gnashing, kick the shit out of the cat rage and it was coming from a place he'd never even known was there. Maybe that place was his source or maybe it was the rain that fed the source or maybe it was the moon that made the tides that blew the wind that brought the rain that fed the source. Mathew didn't know and he didn't care but he knew that if he went home feeling like that he'd end up going after the first kid who said more than boo to him and then Rosie would call Ted and the three of them would have a sit down to discuss what was making him so angry. Thinking about that made him angrier still and he kept walking until, finding himself downtown, he cut over to Scarth Street and bought a dime bag from a guy he knew was always carrying. Everyone called the guy Midget because he was really a giant and whenever they did his laugh left little doubt that one day the wrong person'd call him that and afterwards the people that came to Scarth Street because he was always holding would have to go somewhere else. Mathew didn't call him anything, just showed him a ten and kept his hand at his side, tense like a gunslinger trapped in a town where the dust and the sun were his only friends. Midget threw in a couple of papers, free of charge, and a cigarette to roll it with since the stuff, he said, was still pretty wet.

Mathew rolled the whole gram into a torpedo shaped joint on the bench hidden in the stand of cedars on the far side of Victoria Park. He rarely smoked dope. Rosie made it known weekly that anyone caught stoned in her house had better like sleeping outside, and after a couple of tokes he knew it was a mistake. He stubbed it out on the ground then dug a hole with his finger and buried it, just to be sure.

Right away he started feeling paranoid, like the guy walking his dog was staring at him, even though he couldn't really see him hidden in behind the cedars, or the lady in high heels and a pant suit wasn't just talking on her cell phone she was calling the cops. He got up and fought his way through the cedars then cut across the street and lingered a moment at the foot of the stairs leading into the Hotel Saskatchewan. There was a bathroom just inside the front doors and a sign on the wall beside it that said, For Hotel Guests Only. Waiting until he could see the person at the front desk had his back turned, he slipped through the front doors and ducked inside. He washed his hands and face at the sink, took a leak, then washed his hands and face again. On his way out he grabbed a chocolate mint from the bowl on the stand beside the door.

Back on the sidewalk, the mint rattling against his teeth, he stuck his hands in the pockets of his jeans, trying to act casual, and felt paper crumple beneath his fingers. Confused, he pulled the letter out. It took him a couple of seconds to remember what it was and when it came to him he asked himself why it had made him so angry. A voice that he immediately recognized as Ted's answered him in the remote way that Ted always answered his questions.

—It's because you're not a river, you're a person and people need to know where they come from.

Mathew mulled over the answer for the twenty-five minutes that it took him to walk to Rosie's Place. Jeremy, an autistic eleven year-old, sat on the porch steps. His feet were bare which meant Rosie had hidden his sneakers to keep him from wandering away, as he did every couple of days. He looked at Mathew with the saddest pair of eyes this side of the dog pound.

—Shoes.

—You said it, brother.

Mathew slumped down on the step beside the bone-faced boy. The thought that he was not a river wound through his mind as Jeremy took up his hand, kneading it like it was a Rubik's cube, but all he could think to do about it was to wait for the next letter.

Thirteen months later, after working his shift at El Norte, Mathew came home to find it sticking out from his compartment of the shoe shelf. Unlike the others it was printed by hand in a messy sort of scrawl using only capital letters, the words mostly legible except in the places where the cheap ink was smudged by a carelessly placed knuckle. He took it to the kitchen and, after staring at the photo that came with it long enough to make his eyes ache, he read it by the light over the stove, the only one Rosie ever left on for him.

MATT,

FIRST OFF I WANT TO SAY IM SORRY FOR NOT WRITING TO YOU AFTER THOSE 2 LETTERS I SENT. THAT TEACHER OF MINE ROGER TURNS OUT HES NOT JUST BIG AND FAT HES A LIAR TOO. HE RED BOTH OF THOSE LETTERS AFTER I DELETED THEM FROM THE COMPUTER WHICH I DIDNT KNOW WAS POSSIBLE BUT IT TURNS

OUT IT IS. I GUESS HE DIDNT LIKE SOME OF THE THINGS I SAID ABOUT HIM SO I GOT WORD THAT I WASNT IN HIS CLASS ANYMORE. THAT WAS OKAY BECAUSE I ENDED UP DOING OUTSIDE WORK WICH I LIKED BETTER ANYWAY. COURSE I COULD HAVE STILL WRITEN YOU LIKE IM DOING NOW USING MY OWN HANDS AND A PEN BUT TO TELL YOU THE TRUTH I NEVER THOT ABOUT IT UNTIL I WAS OUT. NOW IM LIVING WITH A GUY I KNOW NAMED DARREN EVEN THO HES SERVED TIME TO AND A CONDITION OF MY PAROLE IS THAT I DONT HANG OUT WITH GUYS THATS BEEN IN PRISON. HES BEARLY HERE ANYWAY ON A COUNT HE HAS A RICH GIRLFRIEND AND SPENDS MOST OF HIS FREE TIME WATER SKING ON HER PRIVATE LAKE AND PLAYING TENIS ON HER PRIVATE COURT. THATS WAT HE SAYS ANYWAY AND MAYBE ITS EVEN TRUE. WENEVER HES NOT PLAYING TENIS AND WATERSKING OR DOING WATNOT WITH HIS RICH GIRLFRIEND HE DOES LANDSCAPING AND GOT ME A JOB DOING THE SAME. THE MONEYS NOT GREAT BUT BOY SOME OF THE PLACES IVE SEEN. THERE WAS THIS ONE THAT WAS OWNED BY A HOCKEY PLAYER I CANT REMEMBER HIS NAME BUT HE WAS A MAPLE LEAF WICH MEANS HE COULDNT HAVE BEEN ALL THAT GOOD AND I HAVE NEVER SEEN THE LIKES OF THIS COTTAGE. IT WAS AS BIG AS A CASTLE AND MADE ME FEEL LIKE JACK WHEN HE CLIMBED THE BEANSTOCK. THE HOCKEY PLAYER WASNT A GIANT THO HE WAS SHORTER THAN ME. I KNOW BECAUSE I SAW HIM STANDING BY THE BACK DOOR WAITING FOR HIS DOG TO TAKE A CRAP AND AFTER HE WENT BACK INSIDE I WENT AND STOOD IN THE SAME DOOR AND I BET I GOT TWO INCHES ON HIM MAYBE MORE. WEN I WAS STANDING THERE DARREN CAME AND ASKED ME A FUNNY QUESTION. HE ASKED ME HOW MUCH I THOT THAT DOOR WAS WORTH. I SAID I DIDNT KNOW MUCH ABOUT DOORS BUT HE PRESSED ME TO TAKE A GUESS SO I DID. DARREN LAUGHED THEN TOLD ME WHAT IT WAS REALY WORTH. I STILL DONT NO IF I BELIEVE HIM BUT I DO NO THAT THE NUMBER HE SAID WAS MORE MONEY THAN I EVER MADE IN A SINGLE YEAR WICH SEEMS LIKE A HOLE LOT OF MONEY TO SPEND ON A DOOR WHEN YOUR PLAYING ON A TEAM THAT HASNT MADE THE PLAYOFFS SINCE I CANT REMEMBER WEN.

ANYWAY I GOT TO GO NOW. DARREN WILL BE HERE TO PICK ME UP FOR WORK ANY MINUT. IF YOU HAVE SOME TIME MAYBE YOU COULD WRITE ME A LETTER AND IF YOU DO PLEASE IN-

CLUDE YOUR PHONE NUMBER SO THAT I CAN CALL. I DONT HAVE
A PHONE RIGHT NOW BUT DARREN TOLD ME I COULD USE HIS IF
I GET A PREPAID CALLING CARD SO IT DONT COST HIM NOTHING.

YOUR BROTHER
RENÉ

OH AND HERES A PITURE OF ME DARREN TOOK ON MY FIRST DAY
OUT. MAYBE YOU CAN SEND ME ONE OF YOU SO I KNOW WHO IM
WRITING TO.

    After he read it, Mathew went to his room and stuffed his duffel
bag with whatever clothes would fit then woke up Mark. He told him
they were leaving and that he needed to get ready. While Mark got
dressed Mathew fetched Rosie's spare office key from a nail under the
bathroom sink, and got his bank card from the top drawer of her desk
along with a Ziploc bag of Rosie's rez smokes and the skull Zippo he'd
given Mark for his birthday. Locking the door again, he returned the
key to its hiding place under the sink and went to collect Mark and
his bag.
    He did this all in such a carefully calculated way that an observer
might have assumed he'd been planning it all along but the truth was
that he was working on autopilot, like a secret codeword in the letter
had activated a program lodged in his brain and he was powerless to
do anything but what it told him. It was only after he'd helped Mark
over the fence protecting the trains from deer and cattle and was
walking south along the tracks that he'd snapped out of his trance.
By then the cool breeze blowing in his face and the moon glint on
the lines of steel, set by the same people who'd made a river out of a
creek and a lake out of both, seemed as good a direction to follow as
any.

▢▢▢

A man's got to know his limitations. This is a very famous line from a
very famous movie that I never saw. I know the line because Mathew
said it to me whenever he caught me staring at some girl. After about
the fiftieth time he said it, I told him to cut it out. He asked me
what I would do if he didn't. I told him I'd slug him. He said, Go
ahead, make my day. That's another very famous line from another

famous movie that I never saw. Or maybe it's from the same movie. There's no way for me to know for sure because knowing only what I knew is my new limitation. When Mathew told me that a man's got to know his limitations it was really just another way of reminding me what my old limitation was. Being a little bit retarded used to be my limitation and I am glad to say that I got over that one. Of course, not being a little bit retarded isn't much help since all I know now is what someone who was a little bit retarded knew. That's my new limitation, as I said, and I wish I could get over it too because I would sure like to know what it was like to stare at a girl and have her stare back without making a face like she was about to puke. Mathew did it all the time. Girls that he stared at most often smiled then turned away so that Mathew couldn't see how happy him staring made them. Sometimes they blushed or talked quietly with their friends if there were any around. Once a girl even sent another girl over to him and she whispered something in his ear. He went off with the girl, the one he smiled at, and when he came back he told me to sniff his fingers. I did and they smelled sour, kind of like vinegar. I told him so and he said, That my friend, is the sweet smell of success. I nodded but didn't understand what he meant (and still don't). It was probably just another line from a movie I never saw, although it was the only time Mathew ever said it to me so the movie couldn't have been all that famous.

□□□

The thought that he wasn't a river didn't cross Mathew's mind again until he was hop-scotching the boulders imbedded in the south branch of the Muskoka. It had ceased to hold any meaning for him and he dismissed it as another dumb-ass thing Ted had said to make him sound like he knew what he was talking about when it was plain that he sure as hell didn't. Balancing on the tip of a slanted rock, the rest of it submerged in two feet of water, he listened but couldn't hear anything above the sharp buzz of mosquitoes. If there were any falls close by, they were likely to be as dead as the one in town.

He spat into the water and pondered the river ahead. Aside from neither having as much water as a river should, there wasn't much in common between the south branch of the Muskoka and the Wascana. Where the Wascana had the look and feel of something man made, with its gentle sloping sandy/gravel banks and the way it wound so

purposefully towards Wascana Lake, the Muskoka zigzagged errati-
cally between a tangled mess of rocks and fallen trees with pockets
of pine needles, dingy foam, plastic bottles and take-out containers
collected in between. On the far bank, a green tube stole most of its
water for the hydro station planted where the south flowed into the
main branch, leaving only a trickle that was barely a creek much less
a full-fledged river.

—Fuck, I'm thirsty.

Mark stood behind him on a great square of stone. With his foot
forward and his hand shading his eyes he looked exactly like the
explorer on the RV they'd seen in the lot outside of the town whose
name he could no longer remember.

—Have a drink then.

—What do you mean?

—It's a river isn't it?

—Ain't much of one, if you ask me.

—Still, it's got water in it.

—Probably bear shit too.

—There ain't no bear shit in it.

—How do you know?

—I just do.

—Well I ain't drinking it.

—Suit yourself.

Mathew bent down and dipped his lips into the water.

—Taste's fine.

—You barely took a sip.

—That's because I'm not thirsty.

Mathew stood back up, wiping his mouth with the back of his
hand.

—Well?

Mark lay down with his head hanging over the edge of the rock
and extended his hand towards the water.

—It ain't going to bite you.

Cupping his palm he dipped it then drew it to his mouth and
slurped whatever water hadn't slipped through his fingers.

—This is going to give me the runs, I know it. God, I hate the
runs.

Drop by drop Mark quenched his thirst and Mathew sized up the
stretch of rocks pebbling the river ahead, wondering how far he could
make it without getting wet or having to jump onto the thick tree roots

jumbled on the shore. The first leap looked to be the hardest as there was a good five feet between his rock and the next one. Setting his left leg behind him, like a sprinter in the block, he pushed off with his right and leapt, swinging his hind leg forward to give him added thrust. He landed square on the rock but it wobbled, throwing him off balance and he quick stepped onto the next. It was round and wet, the size of a watermelon, and he could feel his foot slipping the moment it touched. Momentum carried him to the next stone, wide enough to do a two step, and he got enough push to skip over five smaller rocks, his sneakers barely touching any of them. Beyond, there was open water for as far as he could see around a bend but there was a steep sheath of exposed shield forming the left bank. Mathew aimed high and managed four strides on it before he felt himself slipping under the force of gravity then pushed off hard from the wall and by sheer dint of luck stuck a crouched landing on a car sized boulder planted in the middle of the river. Pausing for a half-breath, he lunged at a toppled tree, spanning the distance between the two banks at a sharp angle. The tree gave under his weight then sprang back giving him an awkward boost that catapulted him onto a sloping ripple of shield set between two stagnant pools of murky green water.

Feeling every bit as fierce as a cougar stalking a lamb, Mathew balanced on top of the ripple and caught his first sight of the falls. It wasn't more than a thin stream of water pissing through a crack between canyon walls that rose fifty feet on either side. Beneath it, the water pooled in a deep basin twenty feet wide and maybe twice as long. Mathew didn't need to check the photo to know it hadn't been taken here. He tightrope walked to where the ripple squeezed under the rock face and climbed up onto a smooth platform overlooking the pool, careful to avoid the shards of glass that filled every crack big enough for a hand to find a hold. He unhitched his duffle, slung off his shirt and shoes then stepped to the edge of the pool and peered into the black water ten feet below, trying not to think of how many horror films had started with a teenager hiking through the woods to a secluded swimming hole. When he couldn't, he slumped onto his duffle and sat flicking fragments of glass into the water until he heard a splash close by.

—Shit!

Mark sploshed through the shallow river. His clothes were soaked and his hair hung in damp curls that bobbed against his cheeks.

—Watch out for the glass.

The sound of Mark cursing and of his shoes scuffing against the rock wall lasted until Mathew had cleared all the glass from within arm's reach. He pried up a flake of the pink rock and sent it spinning over the edge as Mark's head popped into view.

—I thought you'd ditched me.

—You'd know if I'd ditched you.

—How?

—Cause you'd be lying in a pool of your own blood, watching me walk away.

Grunting, Mark heaved himself up onto the platform.

—That's fucking cold, man. Fuck. Cold.

Tossing his knapsack beside Mathew's, Mark crept to the edge of the platform on all fours and looked down into the water.

—Go ahead. Jump.

—No fucking way.

—I did. Water's great.

—How come you ain't wet?

—You took so long I'm already dry.

—Bullshit.

—Just jump.

—What if there's something down there?

—There's nothing down there.

—How do you know?

—I told you, I already jumped.

Mark leaned a little further over the edge then glanced nervously at Mathew, on his feet and stretching.

—Don't you fucking push me.

—I ain't going to push you.

—Stay back. Get the fuck away from me.

—Just jump.

—You go first.

—Jesus.

Something flesh coloured dropped past and water splashed high enough to speckle the ground at Mark's feet. He startled away from the edge of the platform and Mathew stepped around him to see a girl swimming towards where the rock sloped out of the water. At first she looked naked but as she reached the shore Mathew saw that her tan bikini was the same colour as her skin. Turning onto her back, she kicked her legs out to keep her against the stone slab and cast a discrete glance up at Mathew. Her red hair was splayed out around her and even wet Mathew could see it was frazzled like a show horse's mane after its braids had come out. A faint shadow hung over her top lip but Mathew couldn't tell if it was a moustache or just a trick of the light and the nub of her nose was pitted with a dent big enough for a gnat to swim laps in. In a crowded room, Mathew wouldn't have passed her a second look but out here, in the middle of nowhere, with her kernel hard nipples pressing against her bathing suit, he had a hard time not staring. For her part, she acknowledged Mathew by drawing herself out of the water and adjusting her g-string, giving him a hint of the trimmed outline of her bush.

A pink knapsack clomped onto the platform and Mathew turned to the girl climbing down a thick tree root. Grey gym shorts concealed the shape of her rear but not its breadth and folds of doughy flesh squeezed out from under the armpits of the one piece bathing suit that served as her top.

—God Sam, take all day why don't you.

Sam dropped the last few feet to the platform and pulled at her shorts, dislodging them, as the other girl skipped over the ledges filled with broken glass. Between the time it took her friend to snatch the bag from her and scrounge through it for a silver cigarette case, Sam noticed they weren't alone. She bent to her friend and whispered something that Mathew strained to hear but couldn't.

—You're such a pussy, Sam.

Sam recoiled and crossed her hands in front of her chest as her friend touched flame to the end of the joint in her mouth. She took two long tokes then passed it to Sam who snatched it without looking, took a quick toke and passed it back. Her friend drew heavy on it then held the joint up to Mathew. It was poorly rolled and there wasn't a finger width left of it beyond the filter. Half way through his second inhale he felt the sharp prickle of burning cardboard in his throat and he rolled the roach between his thumb and forefinger and flicked it into the water.

—Hey.

Mark scowled at Mathew.

—You ain't got it to lose.

—What's that supposed to mean?

—You gonna jump or not?

Mark glanced towards the edge and Mathew gave him a little nudge.

—So do it why don't you?

—Don't fucking push me.

—You don't want to jump from there.

The nameless girl was sitting with her arms propped on her knees. Sam was laying beside her, eyes closed, and laughing quietly.

—There's a metal bar sticking up from the bottom. Friend of mine tore her leg up pretty bad. Needed, like, thirty stitches.

—Fuck.

—If you want to jump from down here, go to the far side. It's deep there.

—How deep?

—Twenty feet, maybe more.

—That's deep.

The nameless girl smiled like she was thinking of something else then turned to look square at Mathew.

—You're an Indian, right?

—Well, I ain't no Mexican.

—I'm sorry, I didn't-

—It's okay.

—A lot of people mistake you for a Mexican?

—You'd be surprised.

Nameless crinkled her brow as if she was trying to figure out if there was anything hidden behind what he'd said.

—You want to jump? I'll show you the best spot.

—Sure.

He followed Nameless as she climbed up the tree root that Sam had come down. The folds in her bathing suit seemed to wink at him and Mathew, not more than two feet below her, had to fight the urge to inhale deeply so he could catch a whiff of the scent that lay buried beneath.

The best spot to jump from turned out to be a cedar tree bent over the edge of the cliff that someone had nailed six slats of wood to. Nameless clambered up the makeshift ladder and edged out onto a branch suspended over nothing, the end broken off and frayed. She looked back at him and smiled then, holding her nose, stepped off the branch and dropped out of sight. A distant splash told Mathew how far she'd fallen before he could see for himself. While Nameless wasn't exactly an ant swimming in the thin slice of water below him, when he looked down from the jumping branch he had a hard time coming up with anything bigger that captured the scale.

—God, am I ever high.

It was about all that he could think of to delay the moment so he let go of the trunk and stepped forward. As he dropped he could hear Sam shouting and the piercing shriek of alarm in her voice provided the perfect background to what Mathew would later call the worst three-two-one of his life, the blast off coming as an explosion of pain like getting smacked in the nuts with a sack of frozen oranges. Between hitting the water and registering the need to kick, his ears popped so that when he finally reached the surface Sam's frantic yells had all the urgency of a foam rubber cattle prod.

—Get the fuck off me. Help! Get him off me!

Mathew reached the shore at the same time Nameless made it onto the platform.

—Get the fuck off her. Jesus. Fuck.

The rock that sloped into the water was slippery and it took a couple of swipes before Mathew managed to get a hand hold.

—What the fuck! You little shit. Get the fuck–

Pulling himself to his feet Mathew watched as Nameless grabbed two handfuls of Mark's hair and dragged him off Sam's thrashing body. She swung him hard enough to lift him off his feet then let go, sending him skidding off the platform. His feet landed flat on the ledge below it but, his arms pinwheeling, he couldn't fight the force toppling him over. He sat down hard, wedged between two ripples of stone. Above him, the girls clawed their way up the tree root. Neither looked back and the nameless girl's bathing suit didn't appear to be winking at Mathew anymore. He turned to Mark, holding his arm up, a gash smiling a wry grin just below his elbow. The cut wheezed open like fish gills out of water before it darkened, filling with blood.

Mathew leapt onto the platform and grabbed his shirt. He froze a moment, thinking of how much he loved it, then tore it down the seam anyway. Confusion curled Mark's lips into question marks and blood oozed out of the gash, soaking the lower half of his shirt and his shorts. Mathew knelt beside him and wound a four inch strip of his shirt around the wound and tied it off tight then helped Mark to his feet.

—You okay?

—Yeah.

The chunk of beer bottle that sliced Mark's arm open lay between the two folds of rock. It was green and the shape of a tear, curved as if it was rolling over someone's cheek. Mathew heaved it into the deep part of the pool then scanned the area for any other pieces that might be lurking in the cracks. Mark wavered and Mathew grabbed him by the arm, steadying him. Blood was already seeping through his dressing, bringing the black fabric to life before the red streamed down his arm in a thin line.

—Matt.

—Yeah.

Mathew saw it in Mark's eyes before he puked and managed to get him bent over so that he threw up in the water. The red mush of the candy apple and the green KFC coleslaw swirled in the river looking, Mathew thought, quite festive before the current carried them away. Mark dry retched two more times then lay down with his head resting on his hand.

—I told you I shouldn't have drank that water.

□□□

My memory was never any good. I was always forgetting things like my lunch, the combination to my locker at school, and, Rosie said, pretty much anything she ever told me that was for my own good. Sometimes I even forgot that I had to go to the bathroom, which is what Rosie called it when I pissed my pants. Now my memory is all I've got and I can't forget anything, even stuff I wish I could, like how many times I forgot I had to use the bathroom. I went back and counted. It was 283 times. I wonder, now, if it's some sort of a record like the one's in that big Guinness book of Rosie's I liked to look at. It had lots of pictures so I didn't have to read and most of the time it was real easy to tell what the person was in there for. Like if it was a picture of a fat guy, he was probably the fattest guy, or if it was a picture of an old lady she was probably the oldest lady or if it was a picture of guy with twenty-seven hot dogs stuffed in his mouth he was probably the guy who stuffed the most hotdogs in his mouth at one time. Most of the people in it didn't do anything special; they just did one thing over and over again until anyone normal would say, that's enough, I'm done. But not this guy or that lady. They said, Hey I can do that two more or ten more or seven hundred and forty-five more times. Just watch me. And don't forget your camera because this one's for the record books. It always made me think that maybe one day I would do something one more than anyone else and I'd get in there too. Now I know that nobody will ever take a picture of me and put it in that book, even if 283 is the record for pissing your pants, which I think it must be because when I went back in my memory to check the book I didn't find anything about pissing your pants and that's exactly the kind of record I would have looked up. So I would have been the first and they would have had to put me in. And there'd be a photo of me standing there with the 283rd wet patch on my crotch, except this time I'd be smiling proudly like the fattest guy or the oldest women, which would have been a whole lot better than the way I looked when I pissed myself for real. Mostly I looked confused or angry or I started crying. I wish, now, I could tell myself that it was okay, that it meant I was just one soaked pair of pants closer to the record books, but I can't. Memory doesn't work that way. Even one that never worked so good, like mine.

□□□

On day four of their trip, a day and a half after they'd crossed into Ontario, Mathew and Mark stood next to a sign pointing to Pass Lake. They'd been there for three hours when a Toyota station wagon stopped and a man with skin the colour of wet charcoal stopped and urged them, quickly quickly, to get in. He said he was going to Montreal which meant he could drive them the rest of the way but that he needed money for gas.

—We don't really have much money. That's why we're hitchhiking.

—How much?

—I don't know. A few dollars.

—Give it to me.

Mathew fished a five and whatever loose change he had in his pocket after using a ten to buy root beers and a big bag of chips from a truck stop a few hundred clicks back and handed it to the man.

—It is very little.

—I told you.

The man discarded it in the drink holder on the dash and asked if they liked the Beatles.

—Sure, who doesn't like the Beatles?

He pushed a tape into the deck and John, Paul, George, and Ringo too were the only voices to disturb the silence that the man imposed on the car until they'd stopped for gas at a diner outside of Marathon, a town on the northern edge of Lake Superior. Mathew and Mark got out to stretch their legs while the man filled the station wagon at the pumps. The sky overhead was a darker shade of grey every time

Mathew looked up and the wind carried in it the smell of rain on hot asphalt. A solitary siren wailed in the distance growing louder and quieter in spurts.

On the highway, a police car with its lights flashing led a line of cars, SUV's and transport trucks loaded with lumber or pulling eighteen wheeled boxes to the entrance of the diner then drove halfway across the road and parked straddling the yellow line. The officer got out and the vehicles streamed past him into the parking lot, stopping only when the officer put his hand up and waved in the oncoming traffic. The line behind him took ten minutes to clear and by the time it did there wasn't a space left on the gravel beside the diner and cars were parking on the grass or on the shoulder.

The man paid for the gas inside then told Mathew and Mark to stay by the car while he went to find out what was going on. He took two steps towards the mass of people gathered on the side of the road then turned back and locked all four of the car's doors before hurrying away. At the wall of bodies barricading the entrance to the parking lot he tugged on the sleeve of a large bearded man. The bearded man shook his head and the charcoal-skinned man pushed his way through the crowd.

A few minutes later, the man scurried back to the station wagon and unlocked the driver's side door. He slipped in and started the engine before reaching over to unlock the passenger door. Mathew opened it and got in, reaching backwards to get the rear door for Mark.

—There is a fire. Very Bad. Road closed. We go to town.

In town, the man told them, there was a community centre with cots and food.

—All free.

It took ten minutes to drive the pothole strewn road to Marathon, a bundle of dark houses cramped around railroad tracks with a general store in the middle, so brightly lit and crammed with people that it reminded Mathew of an airport terminal. A line-up stretched out the front doors and wound through the cars wedged in at the pumps. A large hand written sign hung on the front window and read: No More Bottled Water. Sorry. MGMT.

The community center was on the other side of the tracks, the dull white beacon of an exposed bulb hanging over its front door visible the moment the station wagon passed the fluorescent glow cast by the general store. Five longhairs in leather and denim sat smoking on the stone steps. When the station wagon passed into the parking lot Mathew could see that all of them were Indians. At the back of the building cars cramped the half-acre of dirt and grass and the man drove purposefully along the rows, scanning for a space. He found one, the last it seemed, between a pick-up truck, its tail gate replaced by a rusty chain, and a Dodge Dart missing its plates.

—You can leave your stuff. It is safe. We eat.

Mathew thanked the man but grabbed his duffel anyway and motioned for Mark to do the same. The man circled the car and locked the doors then circled again, double checking. Together the three of them walked around front. The Indians were still there but four women had joined them, dressed the same as the men and smoking cigarettes with the same hunched over determination. One of the men now held a baby suspended by its arms over the path of concrete tiles that dead-ended halfway to the road and was trying to induce it to take a step. The baby resembled a puppet made out of nylons stuffed with cotton and its head swivelled loose, bobbing this way and that. It was the first to look up at the three as they made their way to the front doors and it stared at them, momentarily awestruck by the movement and, possibly, because it had never seen a charcoal-skinned man before. The others took their time in looking but all had at least a glance by the time they'd reached the door. Mathew was last up the steps. He shifted his bag on his shoulder and stuck his hands in his pockets. A man in his late twenties, with a samurai braid and wearing a black AC/DC muscle shirt, leaned against one of the double doors at the top of the stairs. He flipped his head up at Mathew as he shuffled in behind Mark. Mathew offered a weak smile in return and dug his hands into his pockets a little deeper.

The community centre was nothing more than a big room between two basketball nets. Cots with neatly folded blankets and a pillow resting at their heads took up most of the space on the hardwood floor, except for where a fold-up table had been set up along the far wall. Behind it, three old ladies, their faces caked with make-up and wearing pink frilly aprons to protect their white frilly blouses, dished steaming ladles of stew out of a big pot while another cut thick slices of white bread from a loaf too uneven to be from any store. A few dozen people, most of them Indians, stood propped against the walls or milled around the aisles, all carrying bowls.

A man, old enough to be the father of time and wearing a rotary jacket covered cuff to collar with buttons, forced himself off a chair by the front door. He wasn't fast enough to intercept the man on his way to the food table and turned to Mathew and Mark. He unfurled three tickets from a large green roll and tore them off in one strip.

—These'll get you a bed. They evacuated the reserve this afternoon, so most of the cots have been taken, but they're setting up some mats on the stage. They're showing a film downstairs for the young'uns if you'd like to watch. Lights out at ten. Don't lose your tickets.

He held the tickets out to Mark but it was Mathew who reached over to snatch them up.

—What's the movie?

—Huh?

The old man offered his good ear and Mark leaned in closer.

—The movie?

—It's downstairs.

—But what is it?

—Right through that door.

—But what's it called?

The old man shook his head, grumbling to himself, then sat in his chair, his eyes back on the front door.

—We should check it out. You think they'd let us take our food down?

—We're leaving.

—What?

Mark's voice pierced the low din of voices and the scuffle of feet, not loud enough to quiet the room but loud enough to give it momentary pause so that most of the people were watching as Mathew wheeled around and kicked the door open.

—What about the food? I'm hungry. Matt. Matt!

Mathew ignored Mark's pleas as he struggled to catch up to him on the road. The community centre, the general store and the darkened houses were behind them by a half hour when the urgency that had propelled him out of Marathon weakened and his stride returned to the ambling gait his legs knew best. A steady stream of oncoming cars kept them on the side of the road amongst the broken bits of asphalt and corroded mufflers that hadn't survived the constant onslaught of potholes. Mark stumbled along behind him, cursing every time he tripped over a chunk of debris.

—Where are we gonna sleep? You think about that? We should go back. You still got those tickets right? God, I'm hungry.

A drop of rain splattered Matthew's cheek and a second caught the tip of his nose. He looked up but the sky was too dark to see the clouds. A van with its wipers going full bore rattled by and the spray that trailed behind it brought a chill to his exposed arms.

Headlights sparkled in the mist, coming off the roofs and tires of passing cars, and finally touched on the sign Mathew was looking for. He'd seen it on the drive in when it hadn't seemed so far outside of town. Superior Campground, Fully Serviced Sites, Pool with a bright orange FOR SALE painted over it. They made the gate at the moment a sudden front of wind brought the rain, soaking them before they were up and over. As soon as it hit Mark groaned and said that his head was hurting and Mathew dragged him, cursing, to a covered picnic area. They spent the night lying on the tables, a dry change of clothes unable to ease their shivering. Mathew had forgotten to swipe Mark's pills from Rosie's office and his migraine kept both of them up most of the night, his fits of moaning broken only by the screams that usually wore themselves out in a few minutes but once took almost an hour. When morning came, Mathew didn't have the energy to think about what had driven him from the community centre and Mark had no memory that it had happened at all.

Four days later, Mathew stood on a dock staring up at the shades of grey turning the sea of clouds above the Upper Muskoka Falls black and thought that if he had an offer to spend the night in a pit full of snakes he'd take it, as long as it was dry.

—You think it's going to rain?

—Haven't been here long enough to say one way or the other.

—What do you mean? If it's going to rain it's going to rain. Don't matter how long we've been here, does it?

—I guess not.

—It looks like rain.

—Yeah.

Mathew watched a group of kids taking turns on a swing rope on the far side of the river then turned back to the falls. A small brick building stood on one side and a fence guarded the other. There was no way to get underneath except by swimming over to it and even if you did there was nowhere to stand.

—How's your arm?

—Hurts like a motherfucker.

—You want to go to the hospital?

—I ain't going to no hospital.

—All right then.

Mathew stripped off his T-shirt and shoes then removed his pants.

—Stay with the bags.

Diving into the water, he swam hard and let his breath out in short spurts, trying to stay under as long as he could. When sharp stabs in his chest forced him back to the surface, he wasn't even a quarter of the way to the other side.

—Where you going?

Mathew flipped onto his back and ignored Mark calling from the dock, his hands on his hips making him look enough like Rosie to be her sister. He kicked his feet leisurely against the pull of current drawing him towards the string of buoys guarding the hydro station's intake channel. Overhead, a patch of blue escaped the clouds then disappeared again, rolled under by an ocean of grey.

□□□

Here's a surprise. My dreams. I found them by accident. I was trying to stay with myself for one full day, from beginning to end, just to see what it's like to live again. I don't think it's possible. I have tried many times. I have tried days that begin with me waking up feeling happy; I have tried days that begin with me waking up sad; I have tried days that begin with me feeling mad or sick. It doesn't matter, it's always the same. I wake up. I lay in bed until the pressure in my stomach forces me to the bathroom. This is the easy part. Mathew pounds on the door and tells me to stop playing with myself then suddenly, like in a movie, I am downstairs eating cereal. Or the alarm goes off and Rosie tells me to roll out, which is what she always says when I'm late. Roll out! Roll out! I roll out and trip over my bag. It is heavy, full of books that I never read. Then I am sitting at my desk staring down at a piece of paper with questions on it. Hours have passed so I go back. I trip over the bag but make it to the bathroom. I am careful to stay focused. I pull out my dick and aim it at the toilet. My foreskin sticks together and the end bulges a moment before erupting. Pee rattles off the shower curtain and I clamp my hand over the end of my dick, trying to control the flow. Urine drips between my fingers, splattering my pyjama pants. Rosie knocks on the door and tells me it's my day to choose dinner. She asks me what she should take out then I am eating fajitas. I have lost a whole day, but it doesn't matter. I go on eating. I am thinking of Kelly Schneider tying her shoe. She is kneeling at her locker, right across the hall from mine. A piece of her hair slips out from behind her ear and dips into the crack between her breasts, ballooning against her tight sports bra. I can feel myself getting hard. I slam my locker door shut and run to the bathroom. I seal myself in a stall and whip my dick out. It comes off in my hand. I look at my severed penis, unsure of what to do with it and I am sitting at my desk. Kelly Schneider looks over at me and giggles. My dick is still in my hand. I wake up. It is dark and my crotch is cold and damp. I roll over to get away from the wet spot and go back to sleep. I am dreaming. It is all a dream.

□□□

—I ain't never gonna get laid.

—Sure you will.

—Bullshit.

—Even The Elephant Man got laid.

—Who's he?

—A hideous freak. He lived a long time ago. I saw a movie about him.

—But she was ugly, right? The woman he fucked.

—Not in the movie.

They were sitting in front of the train station and eating fresh cut fries. The building at their backs was small and square with a roof like a mushroom cap and their bench was bolted to the side facing the tracks. Taped to the ticket window, a schedule said the last train left three hours ago but there was only a Tim Horton's cup on the counter to prove that it'd happened.

—You really want to get laid?

—Damn straight.

Stuffing his last fry in his mouth, Mathew licked his fingers then bent to his bag secured at his feet. He opened the side pouch and took out his wallet. A quick count told him he had thirteen twenties, a ten and a five with some change besides.

—Where'd you get all that money?

—I got a job, you know.

—Since when?

—You think that's enough?

He slapped Mark on the shoulder with the two hundred and seventy-five dollars worth of bills.

—For what?

—To get you laid.

—Huh?

Mathew led Mark across the street and around back of a four story brick building with The Al ion otel stencilled over the front doors. A temporary fence surrounded it with warnings every few feet to STAY OUT but did nothing to hide the faded picture of a naked woman pinned in the glass display case between two boarded up windows, both promising Live Nude Girls. Behind The Al ion otel there was a building as low and flat as a bus terminal. On the metal doors beyond a cement loading bay it read Feed Store Pick-Up but on the window beside the front door there was a finely rendered silhouette of a ballerina below pink lettering that spelled, Princess Dance Academy. Mathew sat on a parking block and Mark hovered, anxious, beside him.

—What are we doing?

—Waiting.

—Waiting? For what?

Mathew pointed at the front door of the Princess Dance Academy.

—We saw them go in at six.

—So?

—It's almost seven.

—Huh?

—Never mind.

—How's this going to get me laid?

—Just wait.

—Can I have a smoke?

Mathew fetched him a smoke from his bag and held it up in front of Mark's face.

—Save it for after.

—Why?

—Just don't smoke it yet, okay?

—Sure, yeah. No problem.

Mark stuck the cigarette behind his ear and Mathew chose a random number between two and three hundred then started counting. The first girl came out of the Princess Dance Academy at 193, 69 short of the number he'd chosen, which maybe didn't bode well for the plan but then might have been a good sign after all. She was in her late teens, wearing black leotards and a pink hoodie with a purple paw print on it, a bear or a wolf. Her sandy blonde hair was pulled back into a ponytail but a few wisps had come free and dangled across both cheeks, red from the workout. She waved to a car with its motor running then skipped over to it. An older woman, opened the passenger side door for her and Mathew, standing, turned back to the dance studio. A group of four girls came out next. One of them, a cute brunette, tugged at the arm of a red-haired girl, her thick hips out of place with the rest of her body, and the red-haired girl looked apologetically at the other two before letting the brunette drag her towards the street. The door bumped against the back of one of the two abandoned girls and she scowled at the helmet-clad girl pushing her bike out. The helmet-clad girl said sorry but even from where Mathew stood he could see she didn't mean it. Kicking off, she flung her leg over the seat and rode directly past Mathew and Mark and didn't give either a glance. Three more girls straggled out over the next few minutes. All walked off alone after giving the two abandoned girls a cursory smile. Mathew thought about following the first one, lanky, her face dotted with blackheads, but couldn't make up his mind until she was already out of sight. The second one was far too prissy looking and the third was a little on the chunky side.

The lights went out in the academy and a middle-aged woman, dressed the same as the girls, backed out, locking the door as she did. She had a few words with the two abandoned girls then activated the remote in her hand, unlocking the minivan parked in front of the loading bay. The chunky girl circled around behind the building, making for a set of stairs that rose to the main street. Mathew tapped Mark on the shoulder and hurried after her. They'd just crested the building's corner when the chunky girl reached the first step.

—Excuse me?

Startled, the chunky girl jerked around.

—Didn't mean to scare you.

The chunky girl gave a quick glance up the stairs. Her top lip quivered and she clamped her teeth on it to keep it still.

—My name's Mathew. And this here's my brother Mark.

Mark gave his standard head-flip greeting and the girl grimaced.

—What do you want?

—You ever hear of The Make-A-Wish Foundation.

—Sure.

—Well Mark here, he applied and he got accepted too-

—Are you looking for a donation?

—No.

—Because I don't have any money.

—We're not looking for a donation.

—And besides, I already have a charity. I raised over seven hundred dollars last year for the Terry Fox Run and the year before that I raised almost three hundred even though I had the flu.

—Wow, that's great. Amazing. And it's kind of a coincidence too because my friend here, Mark, the reason he applied to The Make-A-Wish-Foundation was because he has cancer, just like Terry did.

—Terry had it in his leg then it spread to his lungs. That's what killed him.

—I know, tragic, it really was.

—Where's your friend have it?

—In his brain.

The chunky girl passed a tentative glance at Mark and nodded sympathetically then looked back to Mathew.

—And when you think about it, the brain's really the worst place to get it.

—Unless you're a runner, then it's the leg.

—I guess you're right.

—Listen, I really have to go now. My dad gets worried.

—Aren't you going to ask what his wish was?

—Huh?

—His wish. You know, his make-a-wish.

—What was his wish?

—To make love with a beautiful girl just once before he died.

—What?

—That's exactly what the people at the foundation said. So, like yourself, I did a little fundraising.

Whipping the money out from his pocket, he held the fan of bills in front of his face.

—Two hundred and seventy-five dollars to fuck my friend here.

—I really got to go.

The chunky girl spun and, grabbing hold of the rail, hastened up the stairs.

—How about a hundred for a hand job? Fifty to let him see your tits?

The chunky girl reached the top of the stairs and hurried out of sight. Looking to Mark, Mathew couldn't keep from sputtering at the dumbfounded slack to his jaw and the glazed sheen in his eye.

—You can smoke your cigarette now.

Mark shook his head, his lips tightening to a scowl.
—Why are you always fucking with me?

□□□

Lost in a dream, in the dreaming, and still I can never forget, not for a speck, which is how time is measured in a dream, like a speck of sand on a beach - each speck a joy, a horror, a release, a wish come true, a moment unmuddied by TV or homework or a car alarm from the street. For how many specks I have been lost, I do not know. Best guess is 10'321'619, although it feels like more. Oh that I could stay here for eternity but I know that I can't. The dead only know one thing. Everything else just fades away, and it is fading fast. Have you guessed what it is? It is now so close, this everything - this what will happen, what has happened, what is happening — and it pulls at me, drags me through the blips of nothing until they are like shadows outside a bus window. The bits of brightness from the streetlights are a blur, and I can't make out who the people are standing underneath them but hope one of them is Mathew. I want to see him one last time, to tell him that it's not his fault even though it is, was and will always be his fault, and something else, but it's too late. The blips are gone along with the specks and the bits and I am scared. Too scared to close my eyes, even though I am nothing and have no eyes, so I can't help but see it. Water falling from high. Words that make sense but don't make sense. And then the words are gone, along with everything else, and it comes, came, will always be coming. Out of darkness. A set of teeth and a growl. My everything. My all. And I am gone.

□□□

When the drums started, Mathew mistook them for distant rumbles of thunder. He opened his eyes and counted towards the flash, worried that the overhang protecting the bench where he sat leaning against his duffel and Mark lay sleeping, his feet kicking out every so often like an old dog dreaming of fields and rabbits, was good enough to keep a drizzle off them but not much else, especially if the wind picked up. Mathew stopped counting at twenty and, slumping back on the bench, too hot and tired to sleep, wondered if it were to start raining whether he'd be able to unlock the train station's door with his bank card like they did in movies or if he'd need to pry it open using the knife he'd brought as a gift for René.

(He'd found it at a pawn shop on Scarth Street. He'd gone in looking to buy some used PSP games as a Christmas present for Mark and saw it under the glass cabinet by the cash register. Its handle was yellowed with age and sweat but its blade was polished and the edge was smooth and sharp and it came with a crude leather sheath, the inside lined with short, hard bristles that made Mathew think of elk's fur. The man behind the counter pulled it out without being asked and set it in front of Mathew.

—That there's a genuine Indian scalping knife. A real cultural artefact, is what it is. Old Indian sold it to me two weeks ago. Said he didn't need it where he was going.

—And where was that?

—Never asked. To the liquor store, I'd imagine.

—How do you know it's genuine?

—Fella from the university authenticated it.

—How much?

—Fella said it was round about one hundred and fifty years old and as far as I'm concerned that's as fair a price as any.

—A hundred and fifty bucks? That's pretty steep.

—History don't come cheap.

—I only got one-forty.

—Sold.

The man said it so quick that Mathew knew he hadn't given the old Indian, if there even was an old Indian, more than the price of a pint, but still he handed the man the one hundred dollars Rosie had given him for presents along with the forty she let him spend from his pay check every two weeks. All the way home he'd tried to think of a good hiding place for it and when he reached the front steps decided it'd be best if he sewed it into the lining of his knapsack. He hadn't looked at the knife until after he'd got the third letter from René and when he'd ripped open the seam of his back pack and pulled it out, he knew that it had always been meant for his brother.)

The drumming started again after Mathew had given up waiting for the next rumble but before he'd resigned himself to sleep. At first he couldn't place what it was, although he knew that it was too organised for thunder. It was familiar and he closed his eyes, trying to isolate the sound from the flapping of tires as cars drove over the tracks beyond the parking lot and the drunken hoots and hollers from the main street, calling to each other like coyotes. There was a definite pattern, he thought, but it didn't sound like it was made by a machine. It was... Drums. Yeah drums. A drum circle, that's what it was. Like the university students, the hippy ones, have at Victoria Park on Saturdays before it gets too cold to do anything but get drunk and pass out on the bus on the way home from some party. Every Saturday afternoon sitting around, getting stoned, and drumming like it meant something. Big, dumb, pasty heads swaying back and forth wearing big, dumb, pasty grins. Not a speck of colour in the bunch unless one of the Chinese exchange students showed up to see what his classmates did when he wasn't beating them at math. Most of the students used African drums that they propped between their knees but a few used the Indian kind. They were simpler, they looked like pie plates only deeper, and they didn't have much in the way of decoration except maybe a picture of an eagle with a feather dangling down from the side. While the people with the African drums used both hands, and the sound they made depended on where and with what part of the hand they hit the skin, the people with the Indian drums used a stick to beat out a single monotonous pum pum pum.

Listening to the faint but steady pulse doing battle with the street noise and the cricket song, Mathew thought about his history teacher, the one who died, the one who Mark always called Mr. Shitface but who was really named Mr. Blake and who gave Mathew better marks than he probably deserved and once gave him a ninety on a test that he was too sick to write. He'd told the class that Indians, though he'd called them Cree, Dene, Saulteaux, Assiniboine and Dakota, had lived in Saskatchewan for over thirteen thousand years, and that was a proven fact. They'd originally come over on a land bridge that was no longer there but which for thousands of years had connected Alaska and Russia so that anyone who wanted to get out of Russia could just walk over and didn't need a passport or a visa and didn't get called a commie when they got to the other side neither. He'd said it like it was a joke, but no one laughed, and then he told the class to turn to a chapter in their textbook that proved what he'd been saying. Afterwards, when Mathew sat watching the stoned university students beat away on their drums, like children with pots and spoons, he thought about what Mr. Blake had said, and how it was no wonder that Indians ended up where they did if the only drum they figured how to make in thirteen thousand years was one that just went pum pum pum.

—What the fuck?

Mathew had drifted into a sleep that didn't feel more than three breaths from being awake. When he opened his eyes, the drumming had stopped and the street was quiet, leaving only the crickets to protest against the still night air. He blinked and looked up at the woman bent over him, swaying like she had ball bearings instead of ankle bones. She wore a dirty orange tie-dyed tank top, a pair of cut-off jeans and yellow flip-flops. Her lips were pursed in the shape of an arsehole squeezing a turd and the smell coming off her was like the sewer.

—Get the fuck off my bench.

Mathew leapt off the bench and she lurched to Mark. Mathew watched, still groggy from sleep, as she jabbed him with a nicotine stained fingernail and thought, God is she ugly. She just may be the ugliest woman I ever saw. I mean, how does a person become that ugly? You can't be born that ugly. That kind of ugliness has got to be earned.

She jabbed Mark again, this time harder, and he groaned, his eyes blinking, trying to focus on the face two inches from his.

—This is my bench.

Jab jab

—What the fuck? Ow. Stop poking me, lady.

Jab

—This is my bench.

Jab

—Jesus.

Jab

—Get the fuck off my bench.

A final jab sent Mark scuttling for cover. Her eyes followed him the whole way to Mathew standing on the tracks as if there was a rope between them and it was the only thing keeping her on her feet. Mark stumbled over the rail and Mathew reached out to stop him from falling.

—What the fuck you looking at? Fucking Indians.

—Lady, you're crazy.

—Mark.

—Don't you fucking say that.

—Crazy old hag.

—Just let her be.

—Don't you fucking-

—Crazy old hag. Crazy old hag. Where's your bag, you crazy old hag?

With a terrible shriek, she lunged at Mark. Mathew grabbed his arm, pulling him away. She caught a fistful of his hair as she tripped and went down, hitting her head on the rail before her body came to a rest, bent at an odd angle between the tracks, a clump of Mark's hair squirreled in her hand.

Mark screamed and felt at the bald patch on the side of his head.

—She ripped out my hair!

Bending, Mathew checked to see if she was still breathing. He couldn't feel any breath on the back of his hand but her chest rose slightly then fell, rose then fell and rose again. He grabbed her under the arm pits and dragged her off the tracks.

—What are you doing?

—We can't just leave her here.

—Is she dead?

—Nah, she's still breathing.

Pulling her down the embankment, Mathew set her in a patch of scratchy weeds then pried her fingers open so he could get at the hair wound around her fingers. He unravelled it, making sure he got every last strand then held the clump up to Mark sliding down the embankment. Clusters of jagged stones tumbled before him.

—You want your hair back?

—No, I don't want my fucking hair back.

Mathew stuffed it in his pocket and stared down at the woman. In the dark, her face concealed under the leaves of a low lying bush, she didn't look quite so hideous.

—Well?

—Well what?

Mathew gave Mark a nudge with his elbow and cocked his head towards the woman.

—She ain't going to say no.

Mark took a step towards the woman then stopped and turned back to Mathew.

—Are you fucking with me?

Light from a car passing on the road beyond the ditch glistened off the red beads forming where Mark's hair had been yanked out by the roots. Mathew ducked low and buried his face in his arm, covering his three day smile, the same one he shared with his brother.

larry&rené

Here's something Carl said that stuck:

—Most people's days don't start when they wake up. Most start last week or last month or last year or on and on until you get to those days that start the day you were born. And you got to be wary of those days because the farther back they start, the worse off you tend to be at the end of it.

If what he said was true, and Larry had no reason to believe it wasn't, then most of Larry's days started when he was sixteen. Tired of waiting to see how long it'd be before he took a swing at his mom's latest live-in screw, he'd bought a pick-up truck from the money he'd saved mowing lawns at the Spruce Needles Golf and Country Club. He drove it off the lot, the bed empty of all but a couple of bags of clothes, a tent, a portable stereo and a box of cassette tapes, and turned south on Highway 144. He made it four hundred and fifty-five kilometres, a little more than half the way to Toronto, when the truck refused to start after filling up at a gas station outside of Parry Sound. Getting it fixed, the mechanic on duty told him, was a two day job and it would damn near eat up what he'd saved for first and last month's rent, which is what they asked for in the city even if it wasn't legal. Larry spent a few moments under the mechanic's unwavering glare before he muttered fuck to himself and told him to do whatever it

134

took.

Next to the garage, the gas station had a diner attached. The waitress on duty was older than his mother but didn't look it from behind and Larry caught himself sneaking peaks at her on her way to and from the kitchen while he sat in a corner booth emptying the sugar dish into his bottomless cup of coffee. She brought him a grilled cheese sandwich for dinner when all he'd ordered was a plate of fries and called him sugar when she shook him awake after she'd come upon him sleeping with his head on the table. She was gentle about kicking him out, telling him that she'd had complaints about his snoring, and laughed in a way that if Larry hadn't been sixteen would have told him that she had kids of her own and thought it was okay to spoil them, as long as they understood that there were lines that had to be drawn too. She said it'd be fine if he slept in his truck and even offered him a pillow and a blanket. Larry turned her down, telling her that he had a sleeping bag of his own. When he woke up the next morning, cramped and aching in the cab, he found a note stuck to the window that said, Good For One Breakfast Special, Your FGM.

While he was eating through a plate heaped with three eggs, four strips of bacon and a mound of hash browns the mechanic dropped by to tell him that his truck'd be ready by noon. Larry thanked him, though the more he thought about it the more he was sure he was being ripped off and that the waitress had known it too, which was why she had been so nice. He finished his Breakfast Special, taking a small measure of revenge by using six creamers in every one of his four cups of coffee and an extra jam on each of his pieces of toast. The rest of the morning he spent reading discarded newspapers and waiting for a pretty young waitress to disappear into the kitchen so she wouldn't notice how often he was going to the bathroom on account of the four cups of coffee he'd drank with breakfast and the three he'd had since. It wasn't much of a gambit because every time he returned his cup would be full again, but it did give him something to do other than re-read the sports section. And if he hadn't been so intent on avoiding her, it was a good bet that he'd never have met Carl.

It happened like this:

In the narrow hall outside the bathroom there was a cork board that took up almost one whole wall. Pinned to it was an overlapping mess of posters for rock concerts and church benefits and ads for lawn care experts, handymen, yard sales, fresh eggs and just about anything else someone on his way to the pisser could possibly need. Larry took to using it as a prop in his increasingly frequent trips. He stood in front of it pretending to scan the notices until he was sure the pretty young waitress had returned to the kitchen and he could slip back to his table unseen. The last time he'd come out of the bathroom, the waitress was camped out at a two-seater by the door chatting with a man dressed as a paramedic. He was doing all the talking and she was answering him with a series of nods and yeahs and noises that sounded like she was cleaning her nasal cavity with a piece of sandpaper. Her back was to Larry and he couldn't tell what her mood was, but she was still standing there while the paramedic babbled on so it couldn't have been too hot. Probably, Larry thought, she was just doing it for his benefit and he tried to summon the courage to slip by her. Every time he made a step, she shifted her weight or tussled her hair or laughed and placed her hand on the man's shoulder and Larry thought she was about to leave except then she didn't. How long he stood there he couldn't have guessed but it was long enough that Larry felt the familiar twinge of pressure. He'd already turned back to the bathroom when the front door opened and a voice with a thick German accent asked the waitress if he could hang something up on the board. Larry didn't hear what she'd said in reply, he was already standing at the urinal unzipping by then. When he came back into the hallway three bright yellow sheets of paper hung at intervals on the corkboard, and everyone of them said: ROOFER WANTED. NO EXPERIENCE NEEDED. MUST BE HARD WORKER. A series of pull tabs cut into the bottom of the notice gave a number to call.

He grabbed the closest sheet and hurried past the waitress and into the parking lot. The man was just getting into his pick-up truck, a weathered Ford that had ten years on Larry. It had a custom built cap on the back with drawers and hooks for rope and ladders, and not a speck of rust. Larry ran over to the truck, blocking its exit, and held up the piece of paper. The man rolled down the window and Larry shuffled over and stood still as the man scrutinized him, all the while rubbing his hand over the scruff dirtying his chin.

—You look strong enough. When can you start?

—As soon as my truck's ready.

—When's that?

—Shouldv'e been a half hour ago.

—Hmm. When your truck is ready, meet me here.

He wrote an address on a piece of paper from the pad stuck to the dash and handed it to Larry.

—I will see you there?

—Yes, sir.

—Good.

The man, whom Larry wouldn't find out was named Carl until he'd finished the day's work, rolled up the window and the pick-up drove out of the parking lot looking, Larry thought, very much like a comically overburdened mule in one of those Italian westerns his mom's latest boyfriend liked to watch. After paying for his truck, he showed the mechanic the address and the mechanic wrested a grease stained map from underneath the sockets in the top drawer of his tool cabinet, giving it to him free of charge.

Larry followed the map along a series of dirt roads to a narrow gap between trees, the mailbox out front the only thing to say there was someone living there. He navigated the patchwork of potholes and exposed rocks that resembled half buried skulls until the trees gave way to a clearing, in the middle of which sat two stories of plywood roughly assembled into the shape of a house. Squares had been drawn in bright orange spray paint in place of windows and a flap of clear plastic covered the hole left for the front door. Carl waved at him from the roof then climbed down the ladder as Larry pulled up behind the pack mule.

—You found it.

—Yes.

—Good.

Carl pointed to the skid of shingles and told him that they needed to go up.

—Like this.

He wasn't a big man, Larry had five inches on him and maybe twenty pounds, and there was nothing about his stooped over frame, bent like a wire coat hanger that had seen too many closets, that gave any clue as to how easy it was for him to heft one of the packs onto his shoulder.

—You see?

—Yes.

Carl waited until Larry had hoisted one onto his own shoulder then strode to the ladder with Larry behind, struggling quietly under the weight.

The first thing Carl said that stuck, he'd said after Larry'd brought up his tenth bundle and Carl told him to take a rest. He stood up from hammering shingles and arched his back, trying to get the stiffness out, and grumbled that there was one good thing about being a roofer.

—It is very hard on back. Nobody wants to do it. You learn to be good roofer, you always have job.

Larry spent the summer living in his tent behind the one room cabin Carl had built outside of a little spit called Orville because, Carl insisted, the neighbours might get the wrong idea if he suddenly started sleeping in the same room as a teenage boy. When the first frost brought a sore throat and a slight fever, Carl spoke to the manager of a trailer park down the road and Larry moved in the same day. They still ate dinner together most nights before Carl drove Larry home (Carl kept track of the groceries and deducted them from Larry's pay). Larry grew used to eating with only the quiet to pass the time so it came as a surprise when Carl blurted out that bit about most people's days not starting when they woke up. Larry nodded and wiped the grease from his plate with a thick slice of buttered white bread. It wasn't until they were following a snowplough back to Larry's place, the blue light on top the only thing they could see besides the swirling snow, that Larry asked Carl when most of his days started. It was more a hiccough then a question; a sudden involuntary contraction that spat out the words in a fully formed sentence, almost by chance.

—The moment I open my eyes. It is the way it should be.

A few minutes later Carl dropped him at the entrance to the trailer park. Larry climbed over the ridge of snow left by the plough and went to get the shovel propped against the Shady Acres Community sign so he could clear it away. When he turned back, the truck was still idling on the road and Larry got the feeling that maybe there was something else Carl wanted to say. Halfway to the ridge, the shovel scraping at the snow dusting the driveway, the taillights flared and the truck lurched ahead, its tires spinning briefly before catching on the snow packed asphalt. Larry gripped the shovel low and, hunkered down, took a run at the ridge. Ice water from the snow packing his untied boots trickled to his toes and he thought about how nice it would be to stretch out in a hot bath instead of making do with a shower.

This day, Larry mused as he lay in bed 13 minutes before 5:30, the time he'd set his alarm, most definitely started three Thursdays ago when Roy threw his back out carrying two bundles of shingles up a ladder. It was the stupidest damn thing because Larry had been telling Roy ever since he'd hired him the summer before last that he should only carry one. Roy assured him that he'd been carrying two bundles since before Larry was born and he wasn't going to stop now. Just after break Larry'd looked down from the garage of the Quemby's cottage and saw him laying flat on his back in the driveway. He climbed down and, lighting a cigarette to keep him from telling Roy he'd told him so, kicked at the skid holding what should have been a day and half's worth of shingles and now held nearly twice that much.

—Give me fifteen minutes and I'll be as right as rain. I've been carrying two bundles since before you were born and I ain't going to stop on account of a little twitch.

A half hour later he was barely able to make it up the ladder and, moaning and cursing, set the shingles for Larry to nail. By lunch it was clear that he wasn't going to be able to do that anymore either.

—Goddammit Larry, I let you down.

—It's okay.

—You took me on in good faith.

—It's okay, Roy.

—And with that big job coming up, too. Jesus Christ, you turn fifty and the whole damn world falls out from under you.

Larry nodded in between bites of his cheese and mustard sandwich and tried to think of someone who'd be able to take Roy's place, already knowing that there wasn't a roofer within three hundred clicks who wasn't booked through to the first snow.

For the rest of the afternoon Larry laid shingles while Roy puttered around on the ground, picking up nails and scraps of shingles that had missed the dumpster when they were tearing off the old roof and, more and more as the afternoon wore on, lying on a flat patch of lawn and sleeping with his ball cap pulled over his face. Mr. Quemby came back just before four, driving his black Cadillac Navigator straight into the garage without so much as a wave. No doubt he'd seen Roy and no doubt, come six o'clock, Larry'd get a call from Jay Moore, the owner of the property management company that took care of the Quemby's summer residence plus a few dozen more besides. It wasn't a call that worried him, Jay had told him that he was the best damn roofer in Muskoka so often it no longer made him blush, but then all it'd take was a few of those calls and the work Jay was only too happy to send his way would start drying up, leaving him scrambling from one job to the next like he'd done for the first ten years he'd been in Bracebridge.

He called the day at 4:30, an hour and half earlier than he wanted to given the slow progress, and drove Roy to the property beside Port Sydney Auto Wreckers that he rented for his mobile home. After dinner he made eight phone calls then printed up the same poster that he'd used to hire Roy: EXPERIENCED ROOFER NEEDED PLEASE CALL with his cell phone number on thin strips of pull-away tabs below. He'd get Heather to pin it to the notice board at Muskoka Lumber on her way to work and then it was just a matter of time before someone, a teenager trying to make car payments most likely, would call and tell him that he didn't have experience as a roofer but he was a hard worker and Larry would hire him because, he'd tell himself, everyone deserved a chance.

Friday he worked until seven and Saturday until he was done the roof which was around four. That left only the eavestrough, a job he couldn't do by himself. He phoned Jay from the site and left him a message saying he'd get to it on Monday, wondering if he was lying or not, then called Morgan Reilly, got his machine and dialled his cell. Morgan answered after seven rings and before Larry'd said as much as hello, he said he'd be home in twenty minutes. The drive from Skeleton Lake, where the Quemby's had 280 feet of waterfront, took him less than fifteen so he stopped by Muskoka Lumber to check if anyone had taken a tab (they hadn't). When he pulled into the double driveway in front of 240 Hiram Street, he told himself it wasn't going to do him any good, but got out anyway. Morgan answered the door on the third knock and Larry handed him four twenties, enough for a quarter ounce of hydro. He smoked a joint on Morgan's back porch then got in his truck and smoked a cigarette down to the nub before turning the key. Heather called as he was backing out of the driveway and reminded him to pick-up a couple of new releases and a two-four of Canadian on his way home. Larry wasn't in the mood to argue and said he would, even though the thought of fighting through the traffic and tourists in town made him itch all over.

It was Heather's weekend off and, as far as he could tell when he walked into the kitchen with the beer and the movies, she'd spent all day cooking. The sink was crammed with dirty dishes and the smell coming from the oven was heaven. She told him to get washed up and when he returned, she handed him a plate piled with stuffed pork, roast potatoes, onions and carrots, all of it dripping with gravy, and promised him apple pie for dessert. After two servings of each, he loaded the dishwasher while she scrubbed the pots. He thought about asking if she wanted to smoke something then thought better of it and resigned himself to beer for the rest of evening. He pulled two from the fridge and held one up to Heather. She shook her head and wiped the soap suds from her hands on the dish towel hanging from the stove.

—God it's hot. You feel like going for a swim?

High Falls was a two minute drive and by the time Heather was pulling off the highway Larry'd finished the first beer and was cracking the second. She parked the pick-up truck in one of the picnic spots carved into the trees lining the roundabout on top of the falls and lit a cigarette while Larry drained his beer in great, hungry gulps.

—You find someone yet?

—Got a few leads. Nothing definite.

—You were always bitching about Roy anyway.

—I know.

—It's probably for the best.

—I guess.

—Don't worry, it'll happen.

—Yeah.

Larry popped open the passenger side door and lobbed the two empties into the woods.

There was a minivan parked at the end of the roundabout but otherwise the parking lot was empty. A family of Japanese or Chinese tourists took pictures of each other on the foot bridge that, one afternoon a few years back, Larry'd watched the army corps of engineers build to connect two sides of the Trans-Canada trail. He caught up with Heather dipping down the path to the swimming hole and skidded past her, the sharp slope quickened by dirt trickling from underneath ragged patches of moss. Emerging from the forest onto the open expanse of shield he stripped off his shirt, squinting against the sudden brightness.

The falls on his right weren't spectacular, the drop was only about fifty feet, but there was always water going over them so the river below it stayed cool all summer long. And there were a half a dozen places of varying heights to jump from, a natural whirlpool at the base of the falls you could soak in, and a sandbar in the middle of the river that was as good a place to smoke a joint as Larry had found.

Across from the falls, the sandy beach owned by the resort was roped off with buoys and a few families were out, their kids bouncing on the trampoline anchored twenty feet from shore or laughing as they splashed off the slide, but there was no one on this side. Larry ditched his shoes and took a running jump off a hump of granite that nosedived into the water ten feet below. The cold water came as a surprise even though he knew it was coming, and he surfaced feeling sober.

—You bring the smokes?

Heather, inching her way down a ridge towards the water, held up her plastic case.

—Should have brought another beer.

Larry dragged himself up onto the ledge and propped himself on his arms. Heather sat beside him and dipped her feet in the water. She lit a smoke and handed it to him. He took it by the filter, careful not to get the paper wet.

—Shit.

—What's up?

—Huh? Nothing.

—Thinking about Roy?

—No. Thinking about, uh, that guy who used to own the resort. The nudist.

—Mitch.

—Yeah. He really naked when he interviewed for that job?

—I told you he was.

—Hard to believe.

—Not hard at all, if I recall.

Larry smiled at the oft heard joke and tapped his smoke. When he brought it back to his lips, it was only the butt end he was holding. The rest was floating away trailing bits of tobacco behind it.

—Bugger.

—Your hand's wet.

—I know. Give me your shirt.

—Get your towel.

—Too late.

Heather lit another and passed it to him and they watched the families on the beach across the river. A shirtless man with a gut the size of a hot air balloon was grilling burgers on a hibachi and the breeze carried the smell of barbecue. Larry heard a splash and looked over at the cliff between the falls and the hydro station that the serious jumpers used. He'd been to the top of it only once and the climb back down had told him that he didn't need to go up again. He waited for whoever had jumped to surface, tracking the ripples in the water lapping against the rock face until a head popped up. Its owner was deeply tanned and had the kind of hair that Larry'd longed for when he was fourteen and drumming in a death metal band. It was thick and dark and trailed behind him like a fishing net. Larry brushed what was left of his hair back over the bald spot that looked more and more like a crater every time he checked, and it came to him that the man wasn't tanned, he was an Indian, and also that he'd seen him somewhere before.

—I know him.

—Who?

—The jumper. He lives on top of Morgan.

—Morgan? Since when did you see Morgan?

—He asked me to come by. His landlord wanted an estimate on redoing the deck.

—When was this?

—I don't know. Couple of weeks ago.

—You tell him you're too busy?

—Didn't need to. He never called back.

The Indian fought against the current sweeping down from the falls, trying to get as close to the rock as he could. He hung there suspended, thrashing madly, not gaining an inch for as long as it took Larry to finish his smoke, then broke off and made for the shore. He pulled himself up onto a ledge three feet above the water, his taut muscles jumping with the strain, and Larry tried to recall if Morgan had said something about him being in the trades. He stared at him, hoping to get his attention but the man, whom Larry could now see had crude tattoos darkening both arms, was doing his best to pretend he was alone. Larry pitched his stub into the water and, pushing himself to his feet, tightrope walked along the ridge to where the Indian was digging in a green army rucksack wedged in a crevice between two folds of shield.

—Hey.

The Indian glanced back at him, nodded then zipped his bag and knelt at the waterfall to wash off an apple.

—You live over Morgan Reilly?

—Used to.
—Andre, right?
—René.
—Right.
Sitting on the ledge with his feet grazing the water he bit into the apple. Larry waited until he'd swallowed before extending his hand.
—Larry.
René took Larry's hand without looking at him and gave it a firm squeeze.
—You working right now?
—Was, until last Tuesday.
—You ever roofed?
—Sure. You looking for someone?
—I guess I am.
René smiled like he'd been sitting there just waiting for someone to show up and give him a job, and Larry asked what he thought about coming back to his place for a beer.
—Best offer I've had all week.
Pitching the half eaten apple into the river, René stood then hefted the army bag onto his shoulder. There was a sleeping bag tied beneath it with binder twine. Larry turned back to Heather, still soaking her feet, and the worry making mountains out of her forehead told him that she'd seen it too.

The alarm went off while Larry was in the bathroom. He heard it bleating the moment he opened the door and hurried into the bedroom to turn it off. The time was 5:36, meaning Heather had been lying there for six minutes, steaming. Larry whispered sorry and slunk out of the room. By the time he was backing out of the driveway, René rolling down the passenger window in the seat beside him, Larry had got to thinking that maybe it was one of those days that started on the night Heather drove him home from The Albion, seven years ago.
—God, I hope not.
—Sorry?
—Just thinking about how hot it's going to get.
—At least we're on the water.
—Yeah.
Larry turned left onto Highway 117 and accelerated to sixty before he had to make another left onto the off ramp leading to Highway 11.

Spots of light hung in the mist creeping up from the ditches, frozen for a second like glow bugs before the vehicles appeared. It was crazy how much traffic there was so early on a Saturday morning and Larry had to slam on the brakes at the end of the merge lane, unable to find a gap big enough to break into. Most of the cars were heading north pulling pop-up tents and trailers, their roof racks packed with luggage or sporting kayaks, and had kids sleeping in the backseats, faces pressed against the glass, and not one of them changed lanes to let him out.

—Goddammit.

Larry gunned the engine and the pick-up clawed onto the gravel shoulder. He got to fifty before he had enough room to swerve onto the highway. The truck jolted on the smooth asphalt and quickly found one hundred and twenty. Just over the bridge spanning the north branch of the Muskoka River the mist thinned but there was no such reprieve from the hazy specks crowding his rear view mirror.

—Can't they see I got my signal on?

The big, green sign pointing down High Falls Road came and went and Larry switched off his signal.

—Fuck it. We'll cut through Utterson. Maybe pick-up a coffee at RJ's.

—Sounds good.

René reached into the 5 lb bag of apples at his feet. He snagged one and rubbed it on his shirt then took a bite deep enough to get a chunk of the core. In between chews he plucked the hard bits from between his teeth. By the end of the day the 5 lbs'd be gone and they'd have to stop at the fruit stand in the parking lot of the Raymond General Store to get another. When Larry'd asked him about the apples on the third day he'd been living in the basement, he'd said it was a habit that he'd picked up in jail.

—They don't let you smoke anymore, so they give you fruit, all you can eat. Oranges make my tongue swell up, and I've always hated the taste of bananas, so I was stuck with apples. Without them, I'd be smoking in a second and you don't want to know me as a smoker.

—Why's that?

—I'm a mean smoker.

—Cigarettes?

—Uh huh. They make me mean.

Flipping on the radio, Larry cringed at the bubble gum rock that came blaring out. He turned it down low and tried to settle his mind enough to focus on what they had to do when they got to the site. It was a hell of a place they were going to, that was for sure. The owner, a Mr. Pace, first initial S., had bought five lots on the southern shore of Lake Rosseau, torn down the cottages and built a summer residence big enough to play a game of football in the living room, with regulation-sized end zones. It was all aged wood and marble inlays with twenty foot ceilings and a fireplace in every room. Two years ago, when Jay had first brought him out to shingle the boathouse's roof, Larry had asked him how much it had cost to build and Jay told him that Mr. Pace probably didn't know himself.

—A hell of a lot for sure, but then he can afford it. He bought a cable TV station back in the eighties, I think he was in real estate before that, and he turned it into one of those speciality channels. He sold it in the nineties for 800 million.

—Whoa. What was the specialty?

—Who the fuck cares?

Over the past winter the boathouse had burnt to the ground and Jay had given him a call, except he didn't say who it was, instead pretending he was a cop investigating the fire. He'd said his name so quickly, and had spoken so authoritatively, that it'd caught Larry off guard and it wasn't until after he'd hung up that he'd realised he'd been had. It had been Heather who clued him in.

—Who was that?

Larry stood frozen with the phone shaking in his hand, trying to make sense of what the officer had just said.

—So?

—It was a cop.

—What'd he want?

—Said the Pace's boathouse burnt to the ground, under suspicious circumstances.

—Which one's that?

—The double on Lake Rosseau. I did the roof.

—What's that got to do with you?

—I don't know.

—Then why'd he call?

—I don't know?

—Does he think you did it?

—Shit, I don't know?

—What was his name?

—Who?

146

—The cop.

—Roddencrutch.

—What?

—I think that's what he said.

—Rottencrotch?

—Oh, Christ.

Larry called Jay back and hung on the line until he'd stopped laughing. After a minute and fifteen seconds, by Larry's Timex, Jay came back on and told him that Mr. Pace had been impressed with what he'd done with the old boathouse and wanted him for the new one.

—Cedar shingles top to bottom and he's willing to pay a premium if you can start the last week in June.

Larry got the specs from Jay a couple weeks later. The boathouse was going to be three times the square feet of Larry's house and when he crunched the numbers he almost fell off his chair. It wasn't 800 million, of course, but it was damn near what he'd made all of last summer and that was for three weeks worth of work, four tops, depending on whether Roy's elbow started acting up. He called Heather over to the kitchen table. Holding up the piece of paper he'd made the calculations on, he pointed to the number at the bottom circled twelve times until it was held to the page by nothing more than graphite and spit.

—What's that?

—My new truck.

—Huh?

—And maybe a set of all seasons for the Sunfire if you play your cards right.

—Geez, thanks.

Shaking her head, Heather went back to watching TV, leaving Larry to stare at the number and to think about how he could squeeze a few more digits out of Mr. S. Pace. After Roy threw out his back the number began to dwindle until it was just a bunch of zeroes knocking around inside his head. With each bump against his skull he felt that much closer to driving his truck off a bridge, just so he'd stop hearing what he figured was the sound of himself going crazy.

—Larry.

—Huh?

—You missed the turn.

Larry looked up from staring at the yellow line just in time to see RJ's roadhouse passing on the far side of the off ramp. He took his foot off the gas but by then there was already ten feet of ditch between him and the exit.

—Ah hell.

Midway through the morning, a moving truck drove up the Pace's driveway to where Larry's truck sat with its back-end blocking the way and honked. Larry waved from the roof of the boathouse and climbed down. He disconnected the compressor in the truck's bed and tried to think of where he was going to move his pick-up to. Mrs. Pace, first initial unknown, sat on the board of some environmental protection group and thought it in bad taste if the construction of her summer residence resulted in the unnecessary removal of any trees. The only places left to park were the double garage attached to the cottage and the designated lot just inside the main fence where, Mrs. Pace had conceded, a few trees would have to be sacrificed. Guests were ferried from the parking lot to the main building by way of golf carts, four of which were kept in a shed at the edge of the lot along with a riding lawnmower, a small tractor and a hardware store's worth of tools.

The moving truck pulled right up to Larry's bumper, leaving him with no choice but to back all the way up to where the driveway split, looping in a circle past the garage and the front doors. It was a tricky bit of driving given the serpentine nature of the driveway and made more so by the dire warning Jay had given him during his first trip to the newly built residence.

Larry had ridden up in Jay's Nissan half-ton. After unlocking the front gate and parking just inside he beckoned Larry over to the black walnut tree that sat in the middle of the driveway, a lane cut on either side. He patted its trunk like it was an old dog too tired to get up from the fire.

—We originally had Ballard in here, you know, doing the excavation work before Mr. Pace hired that outfit from the city. Seems when they were towing in the front-end loader, the trailer caught on old Blackie here. Tore a chunk out of the bark, didn't do any real damage, but you sure didn't have to be looking too hard to notice. Pace fired Ballard on the spot then brought in some thousand dollar a day arboriculturist from the States to save it, on Ballard's bill of course. All he did was put a big band-aid on it and sprinkle some fertiliser, as far as I could tell. Nothing left now but a small scar, and Ballard hasn't had a contract to dig more than an outhouse since. Mr. Pace sure as shit didn't get rich by accident.

Tucked into the lower fork of the loop, Larry waited for the moving truck to pass into the upper then shifted into drive and immediately jammed on the brakes. A shiny, black Jaguar convertible drove around the corner just beyond the boathouse. It crept along the surface of cedar chips lining the driveway with a caution Larry thought was reserved for the elderly or the blind then stopped just shy of the ramp spanning the gap between the shore and the deck that circled the boathouse a few feet above the waterline. Mr. Pace got out of the car and strode to its rear then bent low and disappeared from sight. A moment later he popped back up and threw something into the bushes, a rock or a chunk of wood, Larry couldn't tell. He appeared to be yelling at someone, although the only other person in sight was the woman sitting in the passenger seat of the Jaguar.

Larry had only seen him on two other occasions, both when he was doing the first boathouse, and he did then exactly what he found himself doing now: staring at him like it was Bigfoot driving up in a Jaguar convertible and not a man. What struck him most about Mr. Pace was that he bore an uncanny resemblance to Barry Nichols, the guy who mixed paint at Macnaughtan's Hardware, who himself was a dead ringer for Lanny Mcdonald, the ex-Maple Leaf. They all had the same shock of red curly hair, thinning at the edges, and the same moustache, the only exception being that in Mr. Pace's case, it was probably hiding a full set of teeth.

After a few seconds Mr. Pace swatted at his ear, like he was warding off a fly, and Larry realised he was wearing one of those hands-free headsets that made people look like they'd just been infected by the Borg. Sliding back into his car, he slammed the door hard enough for Larry to hear it above Kim Mitchell's voice on the radio and the car shot forward, no longer looking elderly or blind. It grated to a stop behind the moving truck and Mrs. Pace stepped out the passenger side. She was younger by two, maybe three, decades than her husband and was wearing black pants tight enough to keep Larry from noticing anything else about her. She was gone in a moment, slipping through the heavy oak door opening by itself, and a sudden movement turned Larry to Mr. Pace, now standing beside his car and glaring at him. Larry waved, feeling foolish the second he did, then took his foot off the brake and let his truck drift down to the boathouse.

—He still standing there?

—Who?

—Pace.

Larry gave a sideways glance and scratched his shoulder at the same time, trying to make it look natural.

—Yeah. And it's too bad. I was just about to call break.

—Nothing stopping you.

Larry placed the next cedar shingle in line, moved it a fraction, and Rene popped two nails in with the gun while Larry grabbed another.

—Suppose he'll be doing that the whole time?

—Maybe. Jay said he was going to be "overseeing the final stages of completion".

Larry said the last bit in a deep rasp with his hand over his mouth, doing an impression that anyone alive in 1977, or since, couldn't help but recognise.

—Vader didn't say that line.

—What?

—It was some chick. One of the rebel commanders.

—You sure?

—Watched it three times last year. They have the whole series in the prison library.

—That what they call paying your debt to society these days?

—It's not all good. They only have microwave popcorn and it ain't that Redenbacker stuff neither. Fucking no name, with the simulated butter flavour. God, almost puked every time I opened the bag.

René pressed the trigger on the nail gun but nothing came out and he held it up to Larry.

—Reload.

Larry took it from him and stepped to the box of nails coiled together like ammunition.

—He's still looking. Probably wants me to move the truck. Looks like a turd in a tea shop sitting there.

—So you going to move it?

—Not if I can help it.

Inserting the cartridge into the gun, Larry threaded the nails into the chamber and locked them down. René held his hand out for it but Larry walked past him and knelt down at the roof.

—You set, I'll nail.

—That a promotion?

—Maybe.

—Do I get a raise?

—I don't know, when was your last?

—Eight O'clock.

—Better wait till noon.

They finished the next two rows in silence then Larry stood up and gave them an eyeball.

—We should chalk it.

—It's straight.

—Still.

Larry handed the end of the line to René. He took it to the edge and held it tight while Larry went to the far side and pinged it.

—It's straight.

—Told you.

Larry wound the chalk line up and René went about making it look like he was going to start the next row.

—That's break.

Mr. Pace was still in front of the house when they climbed down but he wasn't looking at the boathouse anymore, he was pacing back and forth and waving his hands in the air again.

—Oh, hey. I heard the damndest thing on the radio. Two pit bulls killed a kid.

René turned off the compressor then sat on the tailgate and broke an apple in half. He scrutinised the inside, maybe looking for worms or maybe just taking a moment like Larry did before he touched flame to the end of his smoke.

—You say something?

—A couple of pit bulls killed a kid. I heard it on the radio.

—In town?

—Uh huh.

—Morgan has two pit bulls.

—I was thinking that.

—Useless prick. It was only a matter of time before he clawed his way into a real mess.

—If it was him.

—It was.

—How do you know?

—I got a feeling.

—That an Indian thing?

—It's a been-around-pricks-long-enough-to-know thing. He's the
reason I was living at the falls, I tell you that.
—No.
René pitched the half core into the bushes and bit into the other
piece of apple.
—Him and Darren got into a fucking thing, and Darren took off to
who-the-hell-knows-where. Probably to his girlfriend's.
—The real one or the imaginary one?
—I don't know. Both, I guess. I came home one day, the front door
was kicked in. All my stuff was gone.
—Shit.
—Not that I had anything you know, but...
—Yeah.
—Son of a bitch. If I was still smoking, I'd have kicked his ass into
next week.
—Still could.
—Don't tempt me.
—We could drop by after work.
—Yeah. Except he's probably in jail by now.
René dropped the remains of the apple at his feet and ground it
into the dirt.
—He's looking this way again.
—Guess that's break.
Larry took a last drag off his smoke and pinched the end until the
cherry dropped off. The butt he pressed into his pocket.
—Ah shit. He's getting in his car. Give me a hand with the com-
pressor.
Taking either side, they lowered the compressor to the ground.
—Better grab a couple boxes of nails and the extra hose.
—What about the lunches?
—I'll get 'em.
The Jaguar eased to a stop twenty feet from the back of the pick-up
as Larry mounted the driver's seat. There was enough room for the
car to squeeze by but it'd be close and Mr. Pace didn't look like the
type to take the chance. Keying the ignition, Larry turned, felt the
engine catch, then released and pressed the gas. The truck made it a
foot before stalling.
—Goddamn.
Larry slow counted, muttering piece of shit to himself all the way
to twenty, then turned the key again and pumped the gas. The motor

sputtered then let out a roar. Shifting into gear, he eased the truck along the winding path and tried not to look in the rear view mirror. The gate was already opening as it came into view and Larry angled around the big black walnut, taking a sharp right into the gap between the trees that almost hid the empty lot. He parked as close to the entrance as he could then collected the coolers holding his and René's lunches and stepped onto the crushed limestone scouring the ground. He heard the crunch of the Jaguar's wheels an instant before he saw it appear between the two cedars bracketing the entranceway. He slung the coolers through one arm, making a play at looking in the truck's bed, already knowing that there wasn't anything else they'd need. The Jaguar circled the lot and pulled up alongside him. Mr. Pace was talking into space again, the ear piece hidden on the far side of his head.

—I told her I'd make it up to her. Anyway, I got to go. Give me fifteen minutes. Right. Okay.

There was a set of a golf clubs propped in the back seat and Larry guessed they had something to do with what he was talking about. They looked brand new and it made him recall a story he'd read about some rich guy who never wore the same pair of socks twice. After he was finished with them, he just threw them out or gave them away; he couldn't remember which. Hell, maybe he auctioned them off. Wasn't that what rich people did with stuff they didn't want anymore?

—Good morning. Is it Larry?

—Yes, sir.

Larry looked up from the clubs, trying not to make eye contact, the same thing Carl told him to do if he ever chanced upon a bear.

—Hell of a day.

—So far.

—The roof's coming along.

Larry nodded.

—What happened to the guy that was with you last time?

—Roy? He popped a disc a couple of weeks ago.

—Who's your new man?

—René.

Slipping his Blackberry from its holder on the dash, Mr. Pace used a stylus to tap the screen a few times.

—René?

—Yeah. It's got one of those slashes above the second e.

—Last name.

—Right, uh, Descartes.

Mr. Pace's hand froze on the stylus and he glanced up at Larry.

—You're kidding me?

—No, sir.

A few more taps and he slipped the device back into its holder. The thought skirted through Larry's mind that the machine was working away at the problem its owner had given it, chewing it over, and at any moment it would beep, notifying him that it had reached a verdict. Such a little thing and yet... Larry didn't know how to put it into words but it made him uneasy staring at the black sheen of its casing and wondering what it was thinking.

—Keep up the good work.

—Will do.

In the twenty-some years since he'd left Carl to bounce around Muskoka as his own man, figuring out when most people's days started had became a diversion to bridge the gaps between job sites. After living with Heather for a few months it'd become clear that most of her days started during what she called The Chicken Shit Summer. Cal's days started when, for better or worse, he followed Lucy out of Vancouver with enough money from a dead uncle to buy the Gryphon outright. Lucy's started at the same time (which Heather said was romantic and Larry thought was a heavy burden for any relationship to bear). Every one of Roy's days, Larry gathered, began on the evening he attended his first AA meeting. Only Morgan's days started the moment he woke up, and that was only because he couldn't remember what had happened before.

On the first night René spent at their house, drinking and playing euchre, Larry had come up with a few leads (René was raised by his grandparents, off rez, and answered a question Heather asked him about being an Indian by saying he wasn't an Indian anymore, he was a roofer, which had made Larry laugh and blow beer through his nose). Then, just after midnight, he sat back at the table after spinning up a Zeppelin bootleg in honour of Cal, who always rang in the midnight hour with something by "The Lords Of All Things Fine And Good". It was a new round, René had won the previous three, and Heather was dealing. She was two beers past her limit of four and had settled into the goofy mood that Larry knew would last until she'd opened her seventh bottle then would abruptly change into something entirely different. Larry figured he had an hour until he'd have to drag her off to their bedroom and didn't say anything as she dealt all of René's cards face up. René left them where they sat until she was finished then picked up his hand, carrying the joke by keeping the cards open to the table.

—You'll probably still win.

Heather sneered at her cards and called pass, even though it was Larry's turn to do so, then reached for the dummy hand not giving anyone a chance to grab it first. Larry made it hearts and led with the ace of spades.

—It's just practise, is all. Played three hours a day for the past eighteen months.

—And why's that?

—I was in jail.

Heather's cards sagged in her hands and she levelled a drunken glare at him that might have looked funny if Larry didn't know how quickly it could drag her into the something entirely different.

—What?

—I was in jail.

—I heard you the first time. What the fuck you in jail for?

The F-bomb, as Heather called it, set the alarm bells ringing and Larry reached his hand over and put it on her knee.

—What the fuck you doing? You think I fucking care if he was in fucking jail. Well I fucking don't. I was just being curious. That's all. Fuck. Get your fucking hand off my fucking knee.

Larry did as he was told and Heather turned back to René.

—You going to tell me or what?

—I hurt a woman.

—On purpose?

—That's what they said.

—And what do you said? Say. What do you say?

—I guess I say it didn't happen like that.

—Well, how the fuck did it happen? Did you hit her?

—No.

—You fucking shoot her?

—No.

—Throw something at her?

—No. I stepped out of the way.

—Huh?

—She was coming at me. I stepped out of the way. She tripped. Hit her head on a desk.

—What'd you do?

—I called an ambulance. She was bleeding pretty bad.

—No before. What'd you do to make her come at you?

—It must have been something.

—But you forget.

—I guess I do.

Heather shook her head trying to figure out if he was being smart, and Larry tugged on the card he'd had two minutes to think about playing.

—We playing or not?

—Whose turn is it?

—Mine.

—Well, what the fuck you waiting for?

Larry played the right bower hoping Heather had the left (he could see René had the ace).

—What's trump?

—Hearts.

—Bah!

Heather threw down the jack of diamonds and René tossed in the ace. Larry laid his queen and king.

—That's two points.

—You're sleeping alone tonight. Just so you fucking know.

Larry smiled, scooping up the cards. As he shuffled to the beat of Whole Lotta Love, he counted up from the time he'd found René at the falls and thought, pleased, that six hours was a new record.

The moving truck rumbled past while Larry and René were eating their lunch. Larry didn't wave at it this time and neither did the guys in the cab. Finishing his mustard and cheese sandwich, he stuffed the crust into the Ziploc bag and reached for his pack of smokes. He took out one of the three joints tucked into the foil lining.

—What'd he want?

—Who?

—Pace. Saw him pull in after you.

—You could see that from here?

—Almost.

Larry wet the joint and stuck it in his mouth, squinting to see if he could find his truck between the cracks in the trees.

—So what he say?

—Nothing. Just wanted to tell us we were doing a good job. Happy that we're ahead of schedule, that sort of thing.

René coaxed the peel off his sixth or seventh apple of the day with a utility knife. He got halfway before the peel broke off. He took up the end of the spiral and stuck it in his mouth, chewing it slowly as he finished peeling the rest.

—You said something about a raise.

—I was thinking maybe a nickel.

—Rather have a dime.

—I know that feeling.

Larry held the joint out to René but he shook his head, the same way he'd been shaking his head ever since the night they'd met that couple at the falls, whatever their names were. Larry took a couple clipped tokes then squeezed the glowing ember between his wetted thumb and forefinger and tucked the rest under the foil lining his cigarette pack. René stood up and stretched his back hard enough to make it crack.

—God it's hot. Feel like a swim?

—You think she'd mind?

—No more than if we'd asked her.

Both looked down at Mrs. Pace reading a book in a lawn chair on the dock beside the boathouse, a flimsy wrap doing little to cover what her bikini didn't.

—Fuck it.

René kicked off his boots, stripped his socks, shirt and jeans, the latter revealing black boxer shorts, then paused a moment on the peak of the roof like a gymnast before a routine. Filling his lungs with air he took off at a run and five feet from the edge he leapt, tucking his legs into his arms and lowering his head to form a cannonball. He dropped out of sight and the resulting splash was enough of an exclamation to get Larry on his feet. Prying his shirt off, he crept to the edge of roof and looked down at René treading water. The drop was twenty feet, twice the height he was used to jumping from at High Falls, and Larry couldn't remember if he'd worn a pair of briefs without a hole in them.

—You coming in?

—I guess not.

With a quick thrust of his head, René hurled the hair off his face then ducked under the water, kicking hard. Larry watched as he swam under the boathouse's garage-sized doors then walked back to the peak slipping his shirt back on. He took a smoke from his pack, lit it and sat waiting for René. He was down to the filter when he heard the ladder creak under weight. He touched it out on the exposed particle board and stuffed it in his pocket as René climbed onto the roof and hurried towards his pile of clothes.

—Took your sweet Mary time.

—Mrs. Pace says she needs to borrow my services.

—And what'd you say?

—I said I wasn't the boss.

—She say how long?

—No.

Larry sat trying to think his way through the haze of marijuana.

—You want me to fill the compressor first?

—Nah, I'll do it.

René buttoned his pants and slung his shirt over his shoulder but didn't waste time with his socks, instead slipping his bare feet into his boots. Larry waited until he'd clomped over to the ladder and he could hear it jostling under René's haste before he got up to follow him down. From the bottom rung, he watched René disappear through the front door of the Pace's summer residence then turned to the matter of gas for the compressor. A quick scan of the area told him he'd left the can in the back of the truck.

The two minute walk to the parking lot gave him plenty of time to thoroughly consider how Mrs. Pace had given René's ass a once over as she followed him into the house. He stepped past his truck and stood at the edge of the parking lot, his eyes fixed on the north corner of the cottage where he was almost certain that the Pace's bedroom was located. All manner of scenarios presented themselves as he tried to think of what he might expect to see if he were to, say, creep up to the window and sneak a peek inside. Most showed as little imagination as the fuckfilms he'd treated himself to before Heather came along and, the pressure of an erection inflating against his pants, he chided himself for harbouring such adolescent thoughts.

It's the weed, he reminded himself as he rounded the northern most corner of the cottage, breathing heavier than he should from such a short skirt through the trees. Go back to the truck, pick-up the gas and get to work. You're acting like an idiot.

Larry nodded to himself then turned and reached up for the window ledge two feet above his head. He took a quick gulp of air and, hoisting himself up, hung suspended at eye level with the window, certain that either the ledge would break or that Mrs. Pace would see him and he'd be done for anyway.

My problem with women, René had told Larry just after they'd finished the Quemby's eavestrough and were driving back to town, is that I've never had a problem with women.

—I ain't great looking and god knows I ain't got a head worth spitting in but, before I quit smoking, I never spent a night alone that I didn't want to.

Hearing men brag about their sexual prowess was as common in the trades as were jokes about Chinese drivers but there was little doubt that what René had said was true. Larry had witnessed it first hand with the "landscape artist', which is what she called herself on the minivan parked in the Quemby's driveway when they got there just after ten. When René and Larry had carried the two ten foot pieces of copper eavestrough from the back of Larry's truck to the front of the cottage they'd found her kneeling in the flowerbed exactly below where the eavestrough had to go. She was in her late-forties but years of living on a diet of fresh air and questions about whether she was a model had kept her looking as fresh as a flower pressed in a book. She had dirty blond hair, straight down to the small of her back, and freckles almost the same colour as the tan covering both shoulders. She was wearing a blue tank top, short enough that when she stretched you could see the green gemstone piercing her belly but long enough that when she crouched you couldn't see the folds of skin bunched over the waist of her cut-off jean shorts. Two perfectly placed holes below both rear pockets left little doubt about the colour (black) and the fabric (lace) of her underwear.

Her first glance at the two of them had sideswiped René with a smile that made it hard to be Larry for the rest of the morning, and the little refreshers she gave him whenever she moved to dig a new hole or swatted a mosquito feeding on her arm had Larry thinking of dropping a copper bracket on her to give her a reason to look his way. René, for his part, didn't seem to notice and went about doing whatever Larry told him to do with a quiet sort of confidence, a welcome change from two years of listening to Roy's nonstop suggestions, grumbles and outright complaints.

They finished the job by one and were walking back to the truck. She was sitting on the driveway side of the deck that circled three sides of the house, blossoming into a patio with umbrellas and gas heaters around the front, and eating a salad of fluffy, exotic looking leaves that she obviously hadn't brought with her. Mr. Quemby was leaning over the table, his hands alternately smoothing the bump in his shirt where his gut bulged over his belt and fidgeting with the sunglasses hanging from his breast pocket. In a low voice he was telling her that his wife was going to town for the afternoon but that he'd be there if there was anything she needed. Seeing Larry and René, he straightened and excused himself, scuttling towards the patio with the speed of a cockroach caught in the light. The woman brightened at the sight of René and set her fork down so she could give him her full attention as he walked back to the truck.

—What the hell's that about?

—What?

Larry didn't get a chance to clarify as he spotted her walking towards René's side of the truck, plucking at the frayed ends of her shorts as she navigated the hard packed gravel driveway in a pair of Crocs. Tossing his tool belt into the truck bed, Larry angled a smoke from his pack and leaned against the driver's side door. The "landscape artist' introduced herself to René as Cheryl, or maybe Carol, and had a few equally muffled words with him. Larry tried, as far as his pride would allow, not to listen to what she was saying but did pick up a few strays such as, "I'm finished at 4:30" and "Why don't you drop by for a beer". Whatever René told her was lost to the wind but a quick glance told Larry that he didn't seem to mind the way her hand settled on his arm. She waved goodbye from the lawn as Larry turned his truck around and he waved back, René's hands busy as they were with tearing up the business card she'd given him.

—I guess that means you're not dropping by.

René stuffed the shards of paper into the ashtray and told Larry about his problem with women. Larry drove in silence for a while trying to think of the last time a woman had come on to him but gave up when he couldn't think of one before the pockmarked dirt road switched to a crumbling asphalt one.

—Why do you think that is?

—Huh?

—I mean why do they choose you?

—I thought a lot about that over the past two years, hell maybe it was the only thing I thought about, and it always comes down the same thing: trouble. They're looking for trouble and back when I smoked, I was more than happy to give it to them.

If Mrs. Pace was looking for trouble she was doing a good job of hiding it. She was wearing the black pants again and a green blouse that struck Larry as familiar enough to make him think she'd worn it earlier as well. From his vantage point, peering down from his Peeping Tom perch, he could see René holding a large painting, maybe six feet by six feet, against the far wall while Mrs. Pace gave him directions. Larry couldn't hear what she was saying, the glass was triple-paned and the walls were eighteen inches thick, but René kept moving the painting left and right and up and down then holding it still while she walked around the room, checking each position from various angles. Before Larry's arms gave out, he watched her look for something in the walk-in closet then step out empty-handed, a ploy that let her come upon the painting as if by chance. Feigning surprise, she nodded to herself, satisfied, and walked over to René. Careful not to touch his exposed arms, betraying not so much as a quiver under the painting's weight, she leaned across him and traced one pencil mark on the wall beside the frame and another below.

Cursing himself for being a damned fool, Larry hurried back to the boathouse, glancing about furtively for anyone who might have witnessed such a shameful display. There were a few boats out on the lake. Larry thought it a safe bet that no one on board could've seen him, unless they had a pair of high powered binoculars and just happened, at 12:53, to be looking at the Pace's summer residence. He stood at the end of the dock and scanned for a glint of light to tell him whether someone on one of the half-dozen boats he could see was spying. Light glinted off all the boats and after a few minutes he gave up trying to figure if any were from binoculars, high-powered or not. He turned back to the cottage. René was walking up the driveway and Mrs. Pace was looking at him from the bottom of the stone steps that led to the front door.

—She said she might need my services later this afternoon. Wanted me to check with the boss.

Larry waved at her. She turned and trotted back up the steps as René pulled on the ripcord on the compressor.

—It's empty.

—What?

—The compressor.

—I'll get it.

—Gas is in the truck.

René frowned and started off towards the parking lot, the heels of his untied boots dragging on the cedar chips. He'd just reached the black walnut tree when he stopped, waited for Mr. Pace's Jaguar to pass, then plunged through the gap between the cedars and out of sight. Larry, hanging on the first rung of the ladder, glanced at his watch. It'd been two hours and change since Mr. Pace had left. Maybe enough time for nine holes but certainly not eighteen, and he would have had to skip drinks afterwards...

The Jaguar rolled to a stop in front of the boathouse. Mr. Pace was yelling at someone to get his ass out here, pronto, and it didn't take much of a leap for Larry to know he was talking to Jay. The passenger door opened and Larry looked to the man getting out, wondering how he could have missed seeing such a giant specimen until now. He was a foot taller than Larry and his nipples, as sharp as tacks, poked against his green golf shirt. He circled the car and stood by its front with his hands hanging by his pockets until Mr. Pace slammed the driver's door shut then he crossed his arms in front of his chest.

—I found out about your boy.

Holding up his Blackberry Mr. Pace read off the screen:

—On May 29th René Descartes was released from the Fenbrook Correctional Facility after serving eighteen months of a two year sentence for hitting his girlfriend in the back of the head with a beer bottle.

Larry's eyes drifted to René ambling down the driveway, the gas can swinging loosely at his side.

—The attending physician removed seven pieces of glass from the base of the victim's skull. Even though it was his first offense, Judge William Carter gave him the maximum sentence allowable, citing Mr. Descartes refusal to take responsibility for his actions.

René had stopped walking and, removing his boot, dumped it upside down then slipped it back on. He bent on one knee and tied the laces and it was only then that he looked over. Larry nodded and he pulled his laces tight into a bow, his head shaking ever so slightly.

A door slamming jerked Larry back to Mr. Pace sitting in the driver's seat, protected by 370 horses and almost as many pounds of protein supplements.

—I want you off my property.

The morning after René's first night in the basement, Larry woke up with little memory of what had happened except a vague recollection that René was a damn good euchre player and had a bladder that could hold beer like a camel's hump. For ten minutes he sat swooning on the toilet, waiting for something to happen and hoping it wouldn't, then shuffled to the kitchen table and stared past the poached eggs on toast Heather'd slopped in front of him. Later, after Heather had removed Larry's uneaten breakfast and started the dishwasher, René came up from the basement, declining her offer of breakfast by holding up the apple in his hand. Heather brought him a cup of coffee and sat keeping her own mug company with a pack of smokes, an ashtray and a Bic lighter. Nobody spoke for as long as it took Heather to reduce her cigarette to a crushed and smouldering stub. She then fixed René with a look that had Larry twitching in his seat.

—We've been together, Larry and I have, for seven years and three months now. There's a few extra days tossed in there but I try not to worry too much about those.

Heather let out a little laugh. It was how she always started this particular story, with the years and months adjusted, and hearing it again was already driving Larry to thoughts of going outside, maybe to mow the lawn or to hang himself from the maple tree in the backyard.

—If anyone had told me, the first time I saw him, that he'd be the man for me, I'd have seriously questioned their sanity. Not that I was a catch, mind you, far from it. Just a younger version of what you got right here, for better or worse. But the first time I saw him, you see, he was dancing with a woman old enough to be his mother, and I mean they were dancing. She had her hands in his back pockets and she was riding his leg; god, when I think about it. And boy was he drunk. So drunk I bet he thought he was dancing with the prom queen. That what you think, Larry?

Rooting through the fridge for want of a more elaborate escape, Larry's hand found the one bottle of beer that had somehow escaped last night's slaughter.

—Come twelve-thirty, which was when The Albion closed on weekdays, the stragglers met on the sidewalk, as was the custom, so they could pool their change for a cab home or maybe just get a good look at the person they'd ended up with under the glow of the streetlights. Easier to have second thoughts, especially if you're a woman, when there was a crowd around. You ever been to The Albion?

—A few times.

—So you know what I'm talking about.

—Sure.

—Of course it's closed now, which is probably a good thing, but back then it was a real haven for end-of-the-liners, the destitute and professional drunks. Really, it was the only place they had. It's why I went there; I'm not ashamed to admit it. On any given night I'd see specimens that'd make me feel like a princess. I walked out of there feeling tall, let me tell you, and I always hung around to see who'd be that last sorry son-of-a-bitch left standing there trying to convince himself that he wasn't too far gone to drive. There was always one and on that night it was our Good King Larry here.

Larry slipped back to his seat and Heather patted his arm. He cracked the beer and the momentary urge to put the cap on his head in place of a crown was drowned by the icy goodness of the first sip.

—His dance partner had given him the slip, she probably had a husband back home passed out in front of the news. He kept glancing around, looking for her I presume, although, and this isn't just speculation, he'd of had about as much chance of cinching the deal with her as he would have had playing pool with a wet noodle. Between the staggering, and the stopping to pee on the tracks, and the looking behind him every ten seconds, it must have taken him five minutes to get to his truck. It was parked in the lot across the street, the one reserved for train passengers that had enough space for maybe seventy-five cars even though there's never more than four or five people getting on or off at the station. You've seen it, right?

—The parking lot?

—No, the train station. Little building, looks like a square mushroom because of its roof?

—Yeah, I've seen it.

—Well, it's where I used to go and smoke whenever I was at The Albion. There's a bench on the far side, so I was out of sight of the drunks and they weren't always pestering me for a cigarette. I was sitting there watching Larry trying to get his keys out his pocket, he was having a helluva time with them, and that's when I saw the police cruiser coming around the corner on The Albion Expressway. That's what we call the street that runs behind the town; I can never remember its real name. It turns into James Street-

—Hiram.

—Hiram, are you sure?

—I used to live there.

—I thought Hiram was one block up.

—That's James.

—Hmmm. Anyway, I saw the cop coming around the corner and right away I knew he'd seen Larry because he slowed down. He'd already gone past the entrance to the parking lot, it's right at the corner so he had to turn around in the lot beside The Albion. Larry finally got his door open and was just getting inside the truck when the cop pulled up behind him. God, he was so wasted that even then he didn't see how screwed he was. He started up the truck and, I kid you not, backed straight towards the cruiser, would have hit it too, if the cop hadn't blown his horn. I could tell he was pissed off the moment he got out of his car because of the way he slammed the door and took a moment to compose himself before marching up to the truck. He gets up to the window and raps three times. Larry unrolls the window and he would have been finished, that very second, if God herself had not intervened on his behalf.

Pausing a moment, Heather took up a piece of crust, dipped it in her coffee cup then popped it into her mouth, chewing it to air before continuing.

—Now God, being a woman, isn't into all that flash you read about in The Bible, the parting of the seas, the raising of the dead and all the rest of the stuff that was written by men. God being a woman knows that miracles happen every day and that it's people that make them. On that night, and I know this sounds borderline or worse, she chose me to be a vessel for one of her miracles. I don't know how else to explain it, because no sooner had I stood up than I was standing right behind the police officer. I could smell the booze on Larry's breath, the underlying rot of tooth decay and even the faint odour of a Big Mac, the remains of which I'd see in the dabs of secret sauce flaking at the corners of his mouth when he was finally passed out in bed. What I'm trying to say is that I smelled and saw and thought and felt with a clarity that I never had before and haven't since. And I knew just what to do. Really it was nothing; all I had to do was open my mouth and she spoke through me. She said,

—God Larry, what the hell are you doing? Sorry about this officer. I told him to start the truck, it takes an awful long time to heat up, and then I told him to wait for me in the passenger seat because I'm driving. God, men huh?

The police officer, who turned out to be a woman - the only female cop then assigned to Bracebridge at the time – smiled like she understood. It was only a little smile and then her lips were all business again.

—You been drinking ma'am?

God had I ever. Two pints by my lonesome and a pitcher with a woman at the table next to me that only had enough for half. Of course I didn't tell her that. Instead I said,

—No, ma'am. Larry's turn this week. Mine's next.

She stared at me hard and usually I'd have wilted under that kind of look but that night I just stared right back, a twinkle in my eye to let her know that I'd be dealing with my man plenty once we got home.

Drive safe, she said, then got back into her cruiser leaving me and Larry standing in the empty lot and only the Lord Almighty above as witness.

Heather tapped a cigarette on her plastic case. When Larry went right on sipping at his beer, she shot him a warning frown then followed it up with a sharp pinch to his forearm. He had the bottle to his lips and most of what sprayed out of his mouth found its way back inside.

—Amen!

Nodding, Heather lit the cigarette and watched the trail of smoke drift to the ceiling.

—Amen is right.

—Where to now, Boss?

Larry, standing at the ditch beside the truck, shook himself and zipped. A reserve spurt of pee trickled down his leg and he patted at his pants to dampen the flow then took another toke off the joint and pitched the roach into the algae encrusted pool at his feet. Circling to the driver's side door, he popped it open, spat onto the asphalt, and dragged himself inside. The ignition caught on the first crank and he eased the truck onto the road, thinking that straight had served him well in the past.

—How's that sound?

—What?

—Straight.

René, his arm resting on the open window and the wind flapping the hair around his face, made no signal one way or the other.

—Straight it is.

He hadn't told René why they'd suddenly packed up in the middle of the job. Until he'd opened his mouth just then, he hadn't spoken a word beyond, "We're leaving", from the time Mr. Pace had left the Not-So-Jolly-Green-Giant to watch over them as they trundled their gear, in two trips, to the parking lot. It struck him now, with straight offering him endless possibilities to veer and swerve and play race driver with the wheel, that he should just lay it all out for René, tell him the truth about what Mr. Pace had said, but every time he tried to think of how to start he couldn't get past the seven pieces of glass that the attending physician had removed from the base of her skull.

—It's a good question.

—What?

—I was thinking of dropping by Morgan's. To see, you know. About his dogs.

—You're driving.

The road forked ahead. Both ways led to Bracebridge, a fact that seemed significant to Larry for no reason he could put into words. Left followed the 4 over to the 35, from there it was ten minutes to town, while right led you along the 25, a meandering path that touched upon a half a dozen small lakes and also Rosseau and Muskoka, where most of Larry's summer work had been for the past five years. Larry took the latter, turning off the main road fast enough to make the ditch wince. He then settled his foot on the gas until the speedometer was pushing eighty and pressed the cruise control ON button. Tucking his feet up against the seat, he watched the hood devour the gravel road in one great streaming gulp and tried not blink.

When he was growing up, Larry's mom had a weakness for many things, among them scratch and win lottery tickets, homemade peach schnapps, Cameo menthol slims, liquorice allsorts and door-to-door salesmen. Because of the latter, most Sundays from the time he was eight until he was ten Larry put on a clean pair of jeans and a white collared shirt and sat next to her in their Mercury Lynx as she drove to a store on the other side of Timmins that sold expensive vacuums from Monday to Saturday. They helped the owner of the store, a skinny man with a greying beard named Mr. Wilkinson, move all the vacuums into the back room and set up five rows of folding chairs, seven in each. His mom made coffee and set out a tray of assorted No Name cookies and then went in the backroom with Mr. Wilkinson for a few minutes leaving Larry to peel apart chocolate wafers so he could scrape off the filling inside with his teeth. What his mom and Mr. Wilkinson did in the backroom he never saw. They left the door open a crack and he could have easily looked in on them but the thought never occurred to him, just as it never occurred to him to eat the strawberry jam filled cookies either.

At a quarter to ten the Darlings would arrive. They were an elderly couple with a middle-aged son who was what Larry's mom called simple and who had two bulging fish eyes behind thick glasses and the softest hands of anyone Larry had ever met. Mr. Wilkinson appeared from the backroom the moment they knocked on the glass and unlocked the door with the big ring of keys he kept on his belt. After that, people, middle-aged women mostly, would come in spurts and Mr. Wilkinson would greet each person with a handshake and a smile and Larry's mom would join him at the door and nobody would talk to each other until the last person was seated, just after ten. This was always Clara Boyle, whom everyone called Miss Boyle (a name which was funny to Larry because she had a red stain on her face and he thought that was what a boil looked like until his mom told him it was a birthmark and that a boil was something else entirely). Miss Boyle was incredibly fat and, Larry thought, even more simple than Len Darling (although Larry's mother used the world special when talking about her). She always sat in the middle chair in the middle row and after she was settled, Mr. Wilkinson locked the door. Even if someone showed up later, he wouldn't open it and the whole congregation would ignore the person standing outside until after they were done, when he or she, but most often she, would be let in to have coffee and cookies with everyone else.

Every week Larry sat in the front row beside his mom, his hands folded in his lap, and listened to Mr. Wilkinson talk from a chair perched on a platform that, from Monday to Saturday, held The Whirl-Itzer, the most expensive vacuum in the store. Mostly he talked about things he'd read in the newspaper and showed the congregation clippings to prove he wasn't making it up. Sometimes the stories were about people who did funny things for money or about strange animals that were discovered at the bottom of the ocean, but mostly they were about disasters like a landslide that had killed two hundred people in Mexico or a typhoon that had wiped out an island in the South Pacific. After he finished reading his clippings, he asked everyone to close their eyes and everyone sat around with their eyes closed until one of two things happened: Mr. Wilkinson told everyone to open their eyes or Miss Boyle started wailing. She did this every three or four weeks for as long as Larry and his mom went to the store but no matter how many times he heard the strained wheeze, like air leaking out of a balloon, grow into a moan then erupt into a full-fledged scream that lasted sometimes for five minutes and a few times longer than a half hour, it terrified him. He would sit trembling, his eyes squeezed shut, telling himself, as his mother had told him, that it was just the voice of God and that as long as his thoughts were pure he had nothing to fear. He would fight not to grab his mother's hand so that she wouldn't know how scared he was and that his thoughts weren't pure as he waited for Miss Boyle's voice to ebb or for her to start coughing or pass out so he could open his eyes.

On the last Sunday they went to the store, it was raining and cold. The door was locked and the store was dark. There were still posters advertising different vacuum cleaners taped to the window and the hours sign still hung from a suction cup. Larry's mom rapped on the glass then, cupping her hands to create a spy hole in the reflection, peered into the store. After a few seconds she pulled her face back and told Larry to wait there then hurried around the side of the building. Larry could already feel ice water soaking his underwear but he did as he was told, all the while telling himself that the car was open and was probably still warm from the drive across town. He stood in the rain, staring at the store, getting wetter and colder but feeling happy because, even without using his hands to make a spy hole, he could see that the store had been stripped clean.

When his mother returned she went straight to the car. She started it and backed halfway out of the parking space then stopped and honked the horn. By the time Larry had sloshed through the water filling the parking lot and was sitting in the car beside her he was shivering and turning an ashen shade of grey. His mother shifted into drive, forgetting to remind him to put on his seatbelt, and she drove home, the silence between them broken only when they'd navigated the pitted, puddle strewn mix of gravel and mud that was their driveway and had pulled to a stop in front of their house. Larry's mother let out a long staggered breath that seemed to deflate her, making her look like an old sack of skin and bones.

—They were nuts anyway.

She sat with her hands on the wheel, the engine running, and Larry sat beside her, wanting to put his hand on her knee and tell her that it was okay but was worried that he'd stutter and she'd know he was afraid.

The drive from Port Carling to Bracebridge is twenty-five kilometres and takes fifteen to twenty minutes, depending on the traffic and how willing you are to bet there isn't a moose or a cop hiding around the next corner. Larry set the cruise on eighty, a snail's crawl compared to doing the same on the race track curves that made up the 25. He wasn't worried about hitting a moose or running into a cop; he just liked the drive. It was as Muskoka as you were likely to find without a boat and when Larry was shuttling along the 118 on his way to a job or scooting over to Bala to buy smokes at the reserve he always took a few extra minutes to remind himself how lucky he'd been when his truck broke down outside of Parry Sound, stranding him three hours from Toronto.

Everywhere along the road there was evidence of who was really in charge, no matter how many golf courses strung out on swamp fed wells and pesticides or resorts clamouring for space on lakes drunk with sewage and diesel fuel there were. You could see it in the cracks severing the great walls of granite blasted into canyons to make way for the road that bled water all summer long and crumbled fast enough to make you wonder when they'd come crashing down. It was in the fire watch signs every few kilometres with their arrows pointing into the red from June through November and it was in the shards of plastic and bits of fibreglass smashed into every chunk of rock too close to the road to be ignored.

An SUV honked as it passed and Larry waved at the shiny red Patriot with tinted windows that hid the driver. Looking in the rear view mirror, he counted twelve more vehicles in the line stretched to the bottom of the hill leading to the most impressive rock cut Larry knew of and thought that it wasn't bad, as he hadn't even reached Milford Bay yet. The speedometer dipped towards seventy-five on the steep grade and the truck downshifted, letting out a groan as the needle inched back to eighty. In the passenger seat René lay slumped against the door and Larry thought about what would happen if he himself closed his eyes, listening for the sound of wheels on gravel screaming that he had two seconds to live.

Another honk rose with alarming speed and an oncoming car pitched onto the shoulder to avoid the souped-up black Mazda zipping by the truck. Larry clenched the wheel tight and his right foot instinctively hit the brake pedal.

—Goddammit.

René opened his eyes, blinked a few times then yawned and reached for one of three apples left in the bag at his feet.

—That son of a bitch almost killed us.

The Mazda was already dipping down the hill two hundred metres away, and Larry's foot found the gas pedal without thinking about it. He pressed it down hard, knowing that he had no way of catching the bastard. The two lanes of broken asphalt leading into Milford Bay was called Butter Egg Road and it zipped by so fast that Larry forgot to mention that it was his favourite name for a road, even though he'd been thinking about it since they'd stopped for fresh cut fries at the chip wagon off Brackenrig. The pick-up crested the hill in time to see a streak of black merge with the cover of trees around the next corner. He released his foot, letting the truck coast down the slope, the speedometer holding at ninety-five, and tried to remember what the Mazda's make was. Something with an X and a Z. About as much help as thinking about what he'd do if he ever saw the driver again.

On the same Sunday that Heather told René about the divine intervention that had brought her together with Larry, Larry told René the story about his mom and Mr. Wilkinson, the vacuum cleaner salesmen. The three of them had driven to High Falls and found it busier than Larry had ever seen it (most of the bodies clogging the falls coming from the resort in the kayaks and pedal boats tethered to three mooring hooks drilled into the rock just above the water line). While Heather soaked her feet and read, René and Larry swam out to the sand bar, Larry holding his pack of cigarettes above his head until they were on dry land. Hidden by the tall grass that covered the far end of the island they smoked the joint Larry had rolled in his bathroom. Larry chuckled to himself until René asked him what was so funny. He had a hard time getting past the bit where the voice of God spoke through Miss Boyle, he was laughing so hard, and he left out the part about being too scared to leave his mom sitting in the car but, he thought, he did a pretty good job of making it sound ridiculous which was what he was after.

—So you don't think it was a miracle when Heather saved you from a DUI that night?

Larry took a deep breath, trying to keep the laughter from bubbling over again, and when he couldn't he nodded vigorously and pointed to his nose.

A kayak glided past them a few feet from shore. The teenage girl piloting the craft gave a start when she saw she'd almost run over Larry's feet stretched into the shallow water warmed by the sand. She smiled, her eyes lowered, and muttered sorry as she back paddled. Looking away, Larry squinted as if catching sight of the hard nubs pressing against both sides of her bathing suit had momentarily blinded him.

—I'm going for a jump. You coming?

On his feet, René rotated his arms in tight swirls, loosening his shoulders.

—Hell no.

René dove in and swam towards the cliff. Larry stood and watched him climb to the jumping ledge fifty feet up, marvelling at just how high it looked from this close. René pulled himself up the last few feet and was gone over the top for only a few seconds before he appeared in mid-flight, plummeting towards the water. Larry slipped into the river and pushed off from the sandbar, angling in the direction of Heather on the far side of the falls. She was hunched over her book, her feet dangling off the ledge submerged to the ankles. He crossed the current spewing from the falls then flipped onto his back and scanned the water for René. He found him back at the cliff, pulling himself onto a ledge that sloped upwards at a sharp angle. The kayak bobbed a few feet away, the girl inside holding the paddle crossways on the hull as she craned her head back to watch René's ascent. René jerked his neck, tossing his hair out his face, and said something to her then drew himself up the rock face, his hands pressed into a crack small enough to make him look like Spiderman.

—You save me any?

Larry pulled himself up onto the ledge beside Heather and lay on his back.

—You'd have to ask René. It's his stuff.

—Right. What was so funny? I heard you laughing all the way over here.

—I was telling him about that nudist.

—Mitch.

—Yeah. Hard to believe.

—Hmm.

—You ready to go?

—A few minutes.

Larry heard the splash and sat up. René's head popped up to the surface and he took two strokes towards the girl in the kayak before diving under. She glanced one way then the other trying to figure out where he was, her movements growing frantic. She slashed at the water with her paddle and yelled for René to show himself. When he did, twenty feet away at the base of the falls, she called for him to wait and dug her paddle in, propelling herself eagerly towards where he was dragging himself onto the rock.

Before the 118 drops into Bracebridge, it passes a Santa's head with an arrow below it pointing down Golden Beach Road, a half kilometre's worth of farmer's field with a billboard sized "For Sale' sign on it, the Highlands Golf and Country Club, the Bracebridge Veterinary Clinic, a natural gas depot and the Bracebridge Villa Retirement Residence. The latter maintains the shape of the oversized motel that used to sell itself as a ski resort because of the five hundred foot hill behind it. The posts for the chair lift still dot the slope and in the winter there are always a few teenagers willing to brave the No Trespassing signs wired to the cow fence surrounding it for the chance of getting a good run. Though now, more often than not, they're riding snowboards which were almost unheard of the last time anyone paid to use the hill. Another farmer's field, vacant except for a rusting eighteen wheel trailer with For Rent spray-painted on its side in clumsy letters, spans the distance to an old farmstead overlooking the valley. The house's owner still brags to his grandchildren, when they visit him at The Villa, that he used to own everything he could see from the front porch. They in turn nod and smile, saying nothing of the heavy drapes their mom had to put over their bedroom windows to keep out the light from the parking lot below. Mostly, he used the land for pasture, although he'd still planted hay and alfalfa until the early eighties before he sold it and the Canadian Tire jumped across the highway, filling the largest building in the mall that also boasts a Mark's Work Warehouse, the Muskoka Office Depot, a Dollarama and a few stores that rest fallow as if in silent memorial to the fields they had replaced. Across Wellington Street, the Tim Horton's is an island unto itself in the parking lot of a smaller mall and occupies space that used to support a brick farm house and a barn that provided the milk that was delivered on Monday and Thursday to every home in town.

(These fragments of local history had been passed to Larry by way of a driver for Norstar, the largest vinyl siding company between

Barrie and North Bay. He was in his sixties with a greying red beard and always wore a smile that was looking for an excuse to laugh. Whenever they met, which was just as likely at the Tim's as at a site, he greeted Larry by name then gave his own when Larry's scrunched brow made it obvious he couldn't remember his. If they were at a site, he'd offer Larry a cup of coffee from the thermos he filled with two extra large triple triples every time he passed through town, and in exchange Larry'd take a few minutes to listen to one of the stories that made the truck driver twitch uncontrollably and talk out loud to himself when no one was listening. If Larry ran into him at the Tim's, where he always sat in the same corner booth so he could keep an eye on both doors, he'd motion Larry over and tell him the same story over and over again; the one about how he bought the rights to tearing down the milk barn.

—And like a damn fool I built my house out of it. God, when I think of how much that barn board'd be worth now, it being all the rage with them big city interior design types. Enough to build the house all over and I sure as shit wouldn't need to be using left over scrap wood neither.)

The valley that Larry saw as he slowed to within five clicks of the mandatory fifty kilometres an hour speed limit was almost exactly the way it was when he'd first come to town: big box stores on either side with enough fast food restaurants in between to make sure you didn't starve to death while you were bringing your bags out to the car.

Traffic was backed halfway up the hill and the line didn't start moving when the light at the intersection changed to green. There were a few honks from the cars in front and Larry could see that more than one of them was inching towards the shoulder, debating whether they should make a break for the Sleep Inn hotel's driveway so they could cut into the mall parking lot and maybe save thirty seconds on their way to get a Blizzard at the Dairy Queen. None could commit, owing to the cop in the middle of the road with his hand in the air, stopping traffic.

—Must have been an accident.

Larry scanned the intersection but couldn't see any evidence of one.

—It's Santa.

—Huh?

René pointed at the Safeway's parking lot where he was sitting on a sleigh made out of plywood and tinsel and tethered to a wagon pulled by two work horses, not big enough to be Clydesdales but still impressive in a non-reindeer kind of way. The horses shook their heads against the heat and exhaust fumes and pawed at the pavement, anxious to get moving. Their driver, dressed as an elf, held the reigns tight, waiting for a break in the flow of cars and trucks skirting through the three way stop in front of the grocery store. Finally a gap appeared and the driver slapped the reigns over the horses' backs. They heaved forward and, as the sleigh drew around the corner, it clipped the curb giving Santa a jolt and he held fast to the sides of his chair all the way passed the cop and into the parking lot across the street where a thin string of waving children lined the sidewalk.

A trace of bells jingling made it through the pick-up's open windows. It wasn't enough to put Larry in a festive mood but it did ease some of the pressure he'd felt building in his belly ever since he'd past Golden Beach Road and Bracebridge had become as certain as snow in December. Heather would be at The Riverside for another three hours, meaning he wouldn't run into her and have to explain why he wasn't still up on Lake Rosseau. His stomach could feel her presence nearby though and kept sending out little warning jolts to remind him that the countdown was on and when it reached zero...

Larry trailed into the parking lot behind the parade of cars following Santa's sleigh as it wound its way to the clump of amusement park rides wedged between Canadian Tire and Harvey's. He turned into the first row looking for a space and, when he couldn't see one, he waited for a minivan to back out then stole its space from a car that had been there longer but had the bad luck of coming from the wrong direction. He shut off the engine and ignored the car now pulled up behind him, its driver trying to decide if it was worth the trouble. A violent squeal of tires alerted him to the car racing down the lane behind him. He sat hunkered over the steering wheel long enough to make sure it wasn't circling around then slipped his pack of smokes from his pocket and snuck a look at René. His hand was hanging outside the open window, his fingers drumming idly on the truck's door, and he looked bored or amused or angry, Larry couldn't tell which. It was the same expression he'd worn around for two days after they'd met that couple at the falls, whatever their names were. It made Larry think of one those old rear projection TV's that you had to stand right in front of to see a picture and even if you only stood a couple of feet off centre all you could see were flickers of colour, their substance lost in a grey dark enough to make it seem black.

Opening his door, Larry stuck the cigarette in his mouth and made a play at looking for his lighter.

—You feel like going on a ride?

Some days are so clear they shine like a razor cutting into the most stormy and hateful of nights. The day they met that couple at the falls, whatever their names were, was one of them, and when the stormy and hateful parts came later, Larry forced himself to remember that feeling, hoping that somehow in the remembering he would find the path that would lead him back.

He'd awoke just after seven to feel Heather's fingers probing beneath the band of his boxer shorts. He was barely hard inside her touch when she told him to go roll something then gave him a short, hard squeeze to make sure he knew she meant now. They smoked the joint naked on top of the covers then she turned her back to him and he rubbed his thigh against the wetness soaking the valley between her stomach and back. After she came, he turned her over, propped her legs on his shoulders and slow-fucked her until he was limp. While they lingered over cigarettes, Heather ran her fingers in a loop through his pubic hair, brushing her knuckles, as if by accident, against his cock and Larry made a game of jerking it upwards every time, hardening a little with each thrust. With their butts smouldering in the ashtray on the night stand, Heather climbed on top of him. She bit his left nipple hard enough to make Larry think he'd have to hit her to make her stop then, laughing, she leaned back and rocked her hips until Larry's legs were too numb to feel the sweat and sex soaking the sheets beneath him.

It was the first time they'd had sex since René had moved in and the first time they'd done it in the morning in Larry couldn't remember how long. In the shower afterwards, he told himself it was Heather's way of saying she was okay with how things had worked out.

He was towelling off when Heather knocked on the door before opening it a crack to tell him that René was up.

—Were we that loud?

—I guess so.

Heather cast her eyes down, not really embarrassed but wanting him to think she was. Shimmying in behind him, she turned on the taps to run a shower.

Dressed for a day off in track pants and the tattered Slayer muscle shirt that he'd taken to hiding in the back of his closet after he'd found it pressed against the inside of a garbage bag, Larry tracked René to the kitchen where he was making breakfast. He sat at the table and moved his plate aside so he could slide a full platter of chocolate chip and banana pancakes into its place. He clinked his knife and fork together to get René's attention at the stove. René responded by yawning and stretching his arms out.

—Trouble sleeping last night?

—Nope, just this morning.

Larry grinned and poured syrup thick enough to drown anything that had escaped the frying pan. He was mopping the last of it up with a finger when Heather joined them. She was dressed in a pair of cargo shorts and the green tank top she'd told Larry she was too fat to wear anymore. René slopped a fresh pancake on her plate, ignoring her protests that she just wanted a coffee, and Larry and René sat watching her eat every last bit of it.

—God, I can't remember the last time you had a Thursday off. It's nice.

Heather stood to clear her plate from the table but didn't make it an inch off her seat before René snatched it from her.

—Don't look at me, it's all him. Christ, if Roy hadn't thrown his back out, we'd still be doing that Bunkie we finished Monday and forget about the Kemp's garage. It'd been August before we got to that. Now I got time to do the siding on Gerald's place and maybe the chimney for Stan too. He's a goddamned gold mine, is what he is.

—When do you start at the boathouse on Rosseau?

—Jay says the framing should be done by next Friday. Said after that we'd have the whole weekend up there by ourselves. Should get the roof pret' near done, the rest'll take another ten, eleven days.

—You said it'd be three weeks.

—They're not paying us by the hour, so there's no reason to drag it out. We'll have to go back and do the trim after they put the windows in, but meantime we can get to a couple of shingle jobs I wasn't planning on doing until the fall. Then we got Leonard's barn and...

As he ran through the jobs filling his calendar until the end of November, half of them for Jay and the other half repeat customers, leaks and quick fix-its, Heather and René listened attentively, their fingers hooked through the handles of their mugs.

—God, even factoring in the raises I haven't thought of giving him yet I'm on track to clear fifteen, maybe eighteen grand over last year.

—Enough to take a vacation?

—All of February, how's that sound? Except of course it's the shortest month so maybe we'll have to bite into March too.

—Hawaii.

—What about Australia?

—I've always wanted to see Spain.

—Hell yes. Anywhere it's hot and the drinks are served cold-

—in hollowed out pineapples with pink umbrellas-

—and three shots of rum because two just wouldn't be enough.

—We should celebrate.

—Yeah.

—We could-

—get a bottle of rum-

—and a pineapple-

—and a half dozen steaks to wash it down.

—With corn-

—and grilled zucchini.

—Well, what are we waiting for?

Enthusiasm and a hastily rolled joint carried them to town, up and down the aisles of the grocery and liquor stores, and only began to wane with thoughts of a pick-me-upper when Larry pulled into High Falls on their way back. A couple in their fifties were unloading two kayaks from the roof of a Land Rover but otherwise the parking lot was empty. Larry slipped the truck into the picnic spot closest to the falls. He opened the door a crack, poured half of his 500ml bottle of Coke onto the ground then reached under his seat for the litre of Captain Morgan's dark to top it off. He screwed the cap on tight, snagged his smokes, and hurried to catch up with Heather and René, waiting for him by the bridge.

The falls themselves were deserted. Even the beach at the resort across the river was quiet except for a toddler playing in the sand while his mother read a book under the shade of a brightly coloured umbrella. Just inside the gap between the stand of cedars and the rock face that lead to the falls René stripped to his boxers and took a running dive off the ten foot rock. Larry peeled off his shirt and doffed his shoes and was about to follow when the meanest looking dog he'd ever seen appeared in the crevice leading down to the water, snarling and barking as it strode forward with a look of utter hate blackening its eyes. Heather screamed and clutched Larry's arm and Larry glanced about for a rock or a stick he could use if the dog got any closer.

—Ruff!

A bearded man in his late twenties, skinny except for the Wonder Bread-sized paunch curled over his shorts, poked his head out from the rock ledge and shouted for the dog to cut it out.

—Don't know why he does that. Really he's the friendliest dog you ever met. He was the runt of the litter. I guess he thinks he has something to prove.

The dog sat down and his owner scratched him behind his floppy ears. With his tongue lolling out and a goofy grin now spread across his face, Larry was having a hard time remembering why he'd seemed so fierce a moment ago.

—Go on then, say hi.

Ears flapping and a string of drool trailing like kite string behind him, the dog bounded over to Larry, took a sniff of his outstretched hand then rolled onto his back, offering up his belly. Heather's hand loosened in his and Larry bent down to give him a scratch.

—He's a Boxer, right?

—Yeah. Come on, Ruff, you old suck.

The bearded man patted his leg and the dog flipped onto his feet then trotted back to his master. Larry took a quick gulp of air and four strides later launched himself into the water. When he came back up, Heather was lowering herself the last few feet onto the flat outcropping of rock that formed the shoreline. The dog squeezed past her then raced towards the water and jumped. He swam towards Larry with a frantic thrashing of his front legs, barely able to keep his head above the water.

—Watch out for his nails, or he'll mark you good.

The bearded man, standing on the ten foot rock, turned to show Larry three eight inch red lines gouged into his back, and Larry play-fully batted the dog's face away when he got too close.

—Go on, now.

Obediently the dog turned tail and swam towards a woman sitting in Heather's usual spot, her feet suspended in the shallow pool of water where the rock dipped below the surface. She looked about the same age as the bearded man and had short, bleach blond hair with dark roots showing. Both ears were lined with silver rings and her jeans were rolled up to the knees with a grey sports bra showing off her fit, tanned body.

—He's trying to save you.

—Huh?

—Aren't you boy? You big goof.

The dog stuck his nose against the woman's cheek, gave her a sniff then a lick and the woman pushed his head away, scowling. The dog turned back to Larry, panting heavily, and there was no mistaking the pride of ownership in his simple gaze. The bearded man splashed into the water a few feet away and Larry kicked off, swimming for shore.

—He really going to jump from up there?

The woman stared over at René disappearing behind the ledge at the top of the cliff.

—Sure, why not? Used to do it all the time when I was growing up.

The bearded man, treading water, squinted against the sunlight reflecting off the river.

—Well, I think he's crazy.

Heather, leaning against the rock face, turned her head away as René catapulted himself off the ledge and into the fifty feet of open air separating him from the water.

—Must be a guy thing.

The woman waited until René had hit the water then reached for a metal container shaped like a foreign-looking pack of cigarettes. She popped the lid and took out a rez rolly, the same ones Heather smoked.

—Ruff!

The bearded man slapped the water and the dog, drinking from the water's edge, cocked his head at him.

—Come on, boy.

The dog took a step into the water then stopped, making a play at being timid. The bearded man swam towards him and the dog barked, bent low with his front legs stretched out in front and his ears pulled back. Lunging out at him, the bearded man grabbed the dog by his paws and dragged him towards the water, and all the while the dog yelped and clawed at the rock, carrying on like he was being dragged to his death. Finally, his back legs plunged into the water and his head dropped below the surface. He was gone for less than a second then came up sputtering water and swivelling his head left to right until he spotted the bearded man and set out after him. The bearded man backstroked towards the center of the river with the dog following him about twenty feet out. Then, as if an invisible line had been crossed, the dog swam in a loop and headed back towards the falls. He spotted René, just crossing the current, and took a bead directly for him. René gave no sign that he saw him coming but, five feet from the dog, he dove and swam underwater. Coming up at the shore with the force of a seal, he grabbed onto the ledge three feet above the water. He hung there for a moment before heaving himself up and sat on the platform with his feet dangling down just out of reach of the dog's outstretched nose.

—You in on this?

Larry held up the joint he'd just plucked from Heather's plastic cigarette case. René shook his head then lay back on the rock and closed his eyes against the noon sun. Larry lit it then passed it to Heather who had pried herself away from the wall and was sitting on a sheath of stone as high as a bench. She took the joint, forced two clipped drags and held it out to Larry. He inhaled half of it in one long drawl then passed it to the woman. She held it for a moment then took a quick puff, her lips, Larry noted, not touching the filter. She handed it back to Larry, who passed the time waiting for the bearded man to reach the shore by blowing smoke in carefully measured streams through his nose. The bearded man didn't hesitate when handed the joint and inhaled a staccato burst, bringing it to within a hair of the filter. He passed it back and Larry speared a final drag, more for show than because there was any left, then popped it into his mouth.

He could feel the sun's heat on the curls of reddish hair that softened the valley between the mounds on either side of his chest and trailed down to his belly, mingling with the darker strands converging from under his shorts. Dipping his hand into the water, he brushed the coolness over his chest then shook his fingers out and leaned back, squinting against the brightness imbedded in the river. A tease of burning tobacco turned him to the woman who was passing her metal case to the bearded man, a smoke perched at the corner of her mouth, making her look at once comical and earnest, like an old-time starlet who wanted to be taken seriously.

—You mind?

The bearded man held out the cigarette case to Larry. He put one in his mouth and leaned forward to let the bearded man light it.

—You're not from around here.

—Huh?

—You a tourist?

—Kind of. I guess. We tourists, you think?

The woman shrugged.

—I used to live here, so I guess I'm a local.

—How long you been away?

—Ten years.

—You thinking of staying?

—The summer anyway. After that...

The bearded man's eyes strayed to the woman, drifting blissfully into the afternoon with smoke sails.

—So, d'you go to school here?

—BPS, grades five to eight, then BMLSS.

—When did you graduate?

—91.

—Same year as my brother.

—Who's that?

—Michael Asche. You know him?

—Sure, a dozen different ways.

—What do you mean?

—Scouts, soccer, basketball...We had a few classes together. He used to go with Sandra, what was her name?

—Allen.

—Right. They were...

The bearded man shook his head and swatted at a fly.

—They were what?

—Not part of my crowd. He was a good guy though. Always thought so.

—Still is.

—He live in town?

—He teaches at the new high school. Algebra and what's that other math? The hard one.

—Calculus?

—Right. He just adopted a baby from China. A girl. She's the cutest little thing.

—He okay?

—Huh?

Larry cocked his head toward the dog paddling beneath the ledge where René lay. Only his eyes and nose were still above the surface and he was taking on water in stuttered gasps.

—God, Ruff.

The bearded man swam over to him and grabbed him by the collar. He dragged him to the submerged ramp and pushed him onto shore. The dog stooped over, his barrel shaped chest heaving, and puked up a thin gruel of water and dog kibbles.

—That'll learn ya.

The dog turned towards his master, grinning as the woman swished water up over the mess, washing it into the river.

—Shit, the steaks.

—What?

—They're in the truck.

—They'll be fine.

—They'll be half cooked by now.

—I guess we ought to get a move on then.

Larry called over to René then swept his eyes past the woman, on her hands and knees trying to get the last of the dog's sick from within a crack.

—We got six of them.

Heather was at the crevice, shimmying her way up.

—What?

—Steaks.

—So?

Larry shrugged and Heather looked past him at the man in the water.

—We got a couple of extra steaks in the truck.

—And some corn.

—You're welcome to join us.

A teenaged elf with rosy cheeks and smudged freckles stopped in front of Larry and René, holding out a bottle of anti-septic gel. Larry told him no thanks and craned to look down the line for any sign of movement.

—You can't see Santa unless you disinfect your hands.

—Santa? Isn't this the line for the candy apples?

The elf rolled his eyes and pointed at the front of the line where Larry now saw that what had looked like a bulge, a bottleneck he'd thought, was actually a second, smaller line leading to the concession stand. Larry skirted to the end of it and rocked back and forth with his hands in his pockets, imitating an anxious child.

—God, I love candy apples. You want one?

René shook his head, but when Larry got to the window of the van he ordered two anyway. He held both up, his eyes darting from one to the other.

—You sure you don't want one?

—I don't want a candy apple.

—Hey, a wheel of fortune.

Larry asked the attendant, a pudgy high school kid with a front of hair like a hurricane, to hold his candy apples while he dug for his wallet. He placed a twenty on the counter and said he wanted it in toonies. The pudgy kid counted out six then scrounged in his money drawer for a roll. While he peeled it open, Larry scraped the last of the candy coating off the first stick with his teeth.

—Two on the king.

The pudgy kid repeated the bet back in a bored monotone then spun the wheel.

—We have a winner.

Larry doubled up, lost, then cycled through the symbols, betting twice on spades, queens, double zeroes, clubs, diamonds, hearts, jacks, and kings again. His stack reduced to two coins, he bet them both on black, made four dollars, bet two red, made another two then pushed them all onto black only to have a heart come up.

—Shit.

Clamping the second candy apple's stick between his teeth, he pulled out one of two twenties from his wallet and checked on René standing behind him. His lips, slightly parted, revealed clenched teeth and his nostrils flared under assault from the typhoon blowing from his lungs. Larry followed his narrowed eyes to the closest of two teenage boys shooting bb's at small paper targets in the next booth. Flecks of what looked like pink insulation clung to the stubs of hair dotting his otherwise bare head and suspender straps hung loose from his black cargo pants, dangling to the heel of his combat boots. His finger twitched, releasing short, controlled bursts from the machinegun draped over his crooked arm. Chunks of red tore loose from the target. When his ammo was spent, there was nothing left of the target but two corners with a thin strip connecting them. The attendant, a teenage Sherlock Holmes with a hat and pipe to go with the magnifying glass he produced from his pocket, inspected what was left of the target. Then, ringing the bell hanging from the tent post, he followed the skinhead's pointed finger to the display of stuffed animals. He plucked a pink Care Bear from a hook and set it on the counter. After a few words to the punk beside him, the punk unclipped an oversized safety pin from the row stuck to his jacket and handed it over. The skinhead opened it wide and jammed the pointed end between the stuffed bear's eyes then secured it to one of his belt loops. Walking away from the stall, his knuckles knocked against it, each touch drawing attention to its cute and fuzziness, and Larry placed his hand on René's shoulder, restraining him, although he hadn't made a move to pursue.

The bearded man and the woman rode in the back of the truck with Larry and René. The boxer stood with his chest pressed against the bed wall, the wind flapping his ears and pushing his jowls back to expose inch long canines. When they got to Heather and Larry's he leapt over the side of the truck and tore in circles around the back yard, the bearded man chasing him until both were breathing hard.

The dog trailing behind, the bearded man walked to the porch where Larry and René sat on the far side of the picnic table. He sat backwards beside the woman on the near side and the dog knelt at his feet, his head in his lap. The woman lit a cigarette and offered him one from her case. Heather came out of the house with four beers and a glass half-filled with ice and the rest with rum and coke from the bottle Larry'd mixed earlier. She set the beers on the table and took a sip from her glass then put it on the barbecue and lit a smoke.

—You were playing with the dog so I didn't ask. I figured you for a beer drinker.

—Beer's good.

—We also have rum and coke. Or rum and pineapple juice.

—Beer's fine.

The five all took their first sip more or less at the same time and sat quietly letting it sink in.

—I never caught your names.

The bearded man introduced himself then the woman and by the time Heather had returned the favour, Larry'd already forgotten what he'd said.

—You said you're coming back. Where you coming back from?

—All over. Vancouver.

—Montreal.

—Germany.

—Barcelona.

—Wow.

—Nova Scotia for the last year.

—Ten months.

—I've always wanted to go to Barcelona. It's funny because we were just talking about it, weren't we Larry?

—Huh?

—Spain.

—Yeah.

—It was amazing. We saw real life gypsies.

—No shit.

—A whole caravan of them were parked on the street in these big moving trucks they'd converted into, like, apartments. There was maybe a half-dozen of them. The women were inside watching TV and doing the laundry or cooking or whatever. The men and the children, the older ones anyway, were out scavenging. We ran into a group of them heading back, this was just as it was getting dark and we were lost, and...

Larry leaned back, his arms lounging on the deck's rail behind him. He sipped patiently at his beer, waiting for the bearded man to finish. Every time it looked like he was winding down he'd think of something else and he'd spin off on another thread, and pretty soon it was looking like the story would never end.

—Her father had died in Barcelona. He drank himself to death. That's why we were there. No one found his body for fourteen days. When we showed up at his apartment there was a trail of blood leading from the bedroom to the living room, like he'd filled up with gas and exploded or the rats had got to him.

Heather sniffled and wiped her eyes with the back of her hand then plucked an ice cube from her glass and let it melt in her palm.

—Kind of reminds me of what happened when Mike and Annika went to Ghana to give away all these shoes they'd collected. When they opened the door to their room at the mission, there was a dead goat hanging from the rafters. It was all a misunderstanding, of course but...

Larry kept himself busy by rolling a joint using three papers and an extra strip of glue he tore off a fourth. By the time it had gone the circle and was back in his hand Heather was inside for some reason he hoped involved pineapple juice heavily seasoned with Captain

Morgan's. She came out carrying the first of the scrap books that she'd fashioned out of the hundreds of photos her brother Mike had emailed her.

Larry collected the empty bottles from the table and held one of them up to René. He nodded, a weak smile telling Larry that he thought as much of the conversation as he did. Heather spread the book on the table between the bearded man and the woman as Larry sidled past, making for the kitchen. He deposited the empties in the box beside the recycling bin and took the eight beers left inside and wedged them in the fridge wherever he could find space then took four cold ones out. The coke bottle with the fifty-fifty split in it was sitting on the counter with the cap off. There was only a couple inches left in the bottom. He finished it off in two gulps and made a mental note to keep the rest of the rum in the truck where it wasn't likely to do any harm.

On the porch Heather was deep into her brother Mike's wedding, and it only took a quick listen to know she was already a good way to gone. Larry parcelled out the beers and slumped onto one of the matching benches he'd built on either side of the steps the summer after he and Heather had pooled their money for a down payment then signed on the dotted line, with only their lawyer as witness. It was as close to a wedding as they were likely to have and, in honour of the blessed event, he'd carved his name into one of the benches and hers into the other so that every time they left the house they'd see their union etched there before them. Heather'd said it was as good as any ring and, most often, Larry believed that she meant it.

—Where's mine?

Heather was looking straight at him, trying to keep her good mood but he could tell it was failing her around the eyes and at the corners of her mouth.

—Your glass is still half full.

—With ice water.

She held it up as proof. Groaning, Larry leaned back and, taking the rail in both hands, he sling-shot himself towards the front door.

—Where you going?

—To get you a drink.

—Rum's in the truck.

—Right.

Larry hit his thigh with a balled up fist and spun his leg around, imitating a woodcutter in one of those fancy Swiss clocks, then switched his imaginary axe to his other shoulder before marching towards the stairs. Heather was already back at the wedding, the bearded man and the woman studious beside her, and he gave a glance at René. Both of his hands were closed around the bottle of beer in front of him. The cap was still on and he bore a look that, had he been a soldier in a war movie, would've been called a thousand yard stare.

Unable to think of a reason that would've made René look that way, Larry conceded that he was probably just spacing out; exactly what Larry would have been doing if he hadn't gone to get drinks and had an excuse to sit on the far side of the porch where he didn't have to listen to Heather going on about her brother like he was the second coming. Whatever the reason, he was looking the same when Larry returned from the truck with the Captain Morgan's and hadn't changed when he came back out of the kitchen with Heather's drink (heavy on the pineapple). He didn't so much as twitch for the whole time Larry sat on his bench drinking the rest of his beer except to grit his teeth in exactly the same way Larry did the one time he tried to quit smoking before deciding he'd rather die young if it meant he could stop thinking about having a cigarette for five freaking minutes.

No, there was no doubt about it, there was something bugging René and...Dammit, the fucking book. It was the fucking book. Why didn't I pick up on it when Heather first came out with it? (One guess, Mr. Three-Papers'll-Show-Them-How-We-Roll-In-Muskoka). God. God. God. Idiot. The fucking book. Of all things. And it would have been so easy to keep René from seeing it; a jerk of the head towards the yard to get him to follow him to the horse-shoe pit, or a nod towards the house to get him to help with some snacks to go with the drinks, or, god, just about anything to get him to do anything else but sit there feigning interest as Heather opened the book to the first page where there was an invitation to Mike and Annika's wedding, which she'd skirt by so she could get to the next page: the-atom-bomb-going-off-in-the-lower-atmosphere-and-spreading-its-corrosive-radiation-all-over-the-poor-unsuspecting-people-below page. The one with Mike on one side and Annika on the other, both dressed in traditional Mohawk ceremonial costumes? outfits? suits? Whatever they were, they were both made of out tanned leather with simple designs stitched into each of their breasts, his of the moon, hers of the sun. Both of them had feathers clipped into their hair, and they smiled like it was the end of the world and they were alone and happy because they'd just inherited a planet that they could do whatever they wanted with. It was taken on their wedding day, before they were married on Annika's reserve by a shaman or a medicine man or a witch doctor, whatever they called them, and Heather, no doubt, had told the bearded man and the woman, with René too close not to hear, that Mike had requested these photos be taken because, he said (tears boo hooing in all the ladies' eyes), he wanted it to be the last time they were ever apart. And, true to his word, if you flip, flip, flip, you'll never find a picture in the whole book that isn't one of them together: saying their vows in front of the river, waving goodbye from the international terminal at Pearson Airport, handing out shoes, playing horsey with African kids, eating rice from bowls, praying, kissing, living, laughing, drowning a world of despair in a tidal wave of their love and not for a second looking away from the other because that was the promise they made on pages three through five before the shaman/medicine man/witch doctor gave them his blessing on page six and everyone ate the barbecued venison on pages seven through twelve.

—Huh?

Heather had just said something and she and the bearded man were looking at Larry.

—I said can you start the barbecue?

—Right.

—For the steaks.

—Yeah.

—Never mind.

—What?

—I'll get it. Why don't you go play some horseshoes? You like horseshoes?

The bearded man nodded.

—You need any help?

—Can you mix the salad?

—Sure.

Heather led the woman into the kitchen and the screen door slammed shut behind them with the finality of a screen door slamming shut.

—So.

—Yeah.

—Horseshoes.

—Right.

Larry slapped his legs then rose and looked out over the yard at the horseshoe pitch, the spikes barely visibly above the grass.

—You need another drink?

—Okay.

—Beer or rum?

—Yeah.

—Which one?

—Oh. The rum. With some pineapple.

—Juice?

—Yeah.

When Larry came back with the drinks, he went with the tide and poured himself a rum and pineapple juice too, the bearded man was at the bottom of the porch steps wrestling with a stick in the dog's mouth and René was still sitting at the picnic table staring past his unopened beer.

—I hope you like ice.

—Perfect.

The bearded man took a healthy drink and made too much of smacking his lips for it to be genuine.

—Tasty.

Larry took a small measure of his, letting it slosh around his tongue before sucking it back.

—Let's do it.

Midway through the first game it became clear that the dog was having more fun chasing the horseshoes than the people were throwing them but by then the steaks were flavouring the air and it didn't take much resolve to see the game through to its end. The tenth end found them slinging their horseshoes with the quiet determination of professional ditch diggers, working too long beside each other to have anything new to say and only looking up to see how far the sun'd got towards quitting time.

—Ringer!

The bearded man raised both arms in lacklustre victory and the dog barked. A moment later, Heather called to say that the steaks were ready. The dog took off for the porch with the man jogging behind and Larry flung the horseshoe in his hand like a discus thrower. He watched it part two trees and disappear into the forest. On his way back to the house he glanced at the one hanging on a nail over the garage door. It was too rusty to have much luck left in it. Still, he reasoned, next time he wanted to play it'd fly just as well as the ones he'd got from Canadian Tire.

Larry drove past 240 Hiram Street, saw what he needed to see, then took a right onto Anne, another right onto James and parked at the edge of the lot behind the pharmacy.

—You coming?

René shifted in his seat and gave a brief glance at Larry.

—Where?

—Morgan's.

—Why the hell would I want to go to Morgan's?

—To get your stuff back.

—My stuff? It's nothing but a couple of blankets, a broken tape deck and some clothes, not even enough to fill a garbage bag.

—So you're not coming then?

René shook his head and Larry paused, hand on the door latch, to make sure it was his final answer.

—Back in five.

Larry grabbed a flat screwdriver from his toolbox in the back then scurried across the street and ducked into the driveway of the doctor's office behind Morgan's backyard. He'd used what Morgan called the secret way many times, mostly to take a piss after smoking one on Morgan's porch, but also whenever Morgan thought the "heat was on' and he stopped answering the side door, conducting business instead through a window in the basement which, he said, was out of sight to anyone who didn't have satellite capabilities.

He navigated the backyard, keeping low, weeding his way through the piles of dog shit, enough for five dogs much less two, and crouched at the basement window. Inside there was a screen covered with wisps of dust like deserted spider webs. It took a couple of whacks with the palm of his hand to get the blade of the screwdriver wedged into the seam. He pushed on the handle and the aluminum trim bent back too easily to give him any leverage - the sharp end popping loose immediately and scraping an exclamation point into the paint - but the opening it made let him see the crack where the sliding part of the window met the frame. A tiny ridge ran along it, put there to prevent someone from getting something into the crack and boosting it open. A second, smaller screwdriver would have helped, one that he could use to pry past the ridge and open the crack a hair so as to give the bigger one enough space to latch onto. He had one in his truck that would have done the job but it might as well have been on the moon for all the good it was doing him. He placed the dull blade of the one he had against the ridge and gave the other end a few hard whacks with his palm. When he pushed against the screwdriver it slipped again, this time gouging a swirl in the paint that looked like a question mark and he rolled back on his haunches to ponder what it meant.

How they got onto the topic of witches, Larry couldn't say. The last thing he remembered talking about was the price of houses in town (too high). That was when they were outside, before dusk brought a storm of mosquitoes so sudden that they'd abandoned their plates, dirtied with bits of gristle and picked over cobs of corn, and had fled to the kitchen table. Their relief was short lived as the dog was riddled with the insects so fattened that when the bearded man ran his hand over the pink skin of his belly everyone cringed at how much blood there was. After he'd cleaned the dog with a rag from the sink, they'd gone round the table recounting their favourite stories about mosquitoes and black flies. Larry tried to think of something to say but couldn't and finally remarked that they really didn't bother him that much.

By then the pineapple juice was gone and the ice cubes were melted, the tray having been left on the counter, if Heather could be trusted, by none other than Larry. Larry and the bearded man switched back to beer while Heather and the woman finished off the rum with some store brand diet cola that was flat from being in the fridge too long but was at least cold for the first couple of sips before the heat got the better of it. René had disappeared for a while, to the bathroom or downstairs Larry didn't see, but now he was back at the table, hiding behind a row of beer bottles that surely he couldn't have drank all by himself, Larry would have noticed that, but there it was: a wall of bottles all but concealing René's face, his body slumped so far down in his chair he was almost sitting on the floor. One eye was all Larry could see of him, peeking through a gap between the necks, and in it he was certain he could detect a trace of irony. He took it for a sign that maybe he was wrong about the fucking book when really René was just shy around strangers, or dogs, or strangers with dogs. Or that the bearded man had said something stupid, unheard by Larry, and René had sealed himself off from the group to keep himself from slugging the dumb shit who obviously didn't know when to keep his mouth shut.

Point in question, what he was saying when Larry returned from putting a Best of Muddy Waters CD on the stereo:

—Nah, nah, nah. Witches don't dance around naked in the woods trying to summon the devil. That's just Hollywood make-believe. Those who practise Wicca have rituals like everyone else, and maybe they involve dancing, and maybe sometimes they dance in the woods but that's like saying Christianity promotes cannibalism because its most important ritual involves devouring the flesh and blood of its saviour.

—Bullshit!

It was more a squeal than a yell. Heather was half out of her chair and was leaning across the table about to smack the dumb out of the dumb shit when she knocked over René's wall. Three of the bottles toppled onto the floor. Glass smashed and the bearded man froze, his mouth open about to say something that, if spoken, Larry was certain would have had him grappling Heather to the floor while the bearded man and the woman ran for the door.

The dog whimpered and his owners looked down at him. Larry knew what had happened even though from where he sat he couldn't see the dog holding his paw up, a trickle of blood dripping from between two of his toes.

—He must have stepped on a piece of glass.

—Oh shit, I'm sorry. I'm so sorry. I didn't mean-

—Don't worry about it. It was an accident.

Heather circled the table, steadying herself on Larry's chair for the three steps it took her to get to the corner where the bearded man had pulled the dog to get him away from ground zero. For the next few minutes, Heather and the bearded man tended to the dog while the woman swept up the mess, René cleared the table and Larry rolled up the last of the weed. With the dog's paw wrapped in gauze and medical tape from the first-aid kit in Larry's truck, the bearded man told Heather that they should be leaving. Heather wouldn't hear of it, insisting that the wound needed time to clot before the dog was made to walk home. Fetching another beer from the fridge, she twisted it open and handed it to the bearded man, and Larry lit up the joint.

—So where do you live anyways?

Smoke from four cigarettes had settled over the kitchen in place of conversation. On his way back from the stereo to switch the Muddy Waters with the mixed CD he'd cobbled off the internet for Heather's

35th birthday, the question had slid out, greased by Nina Simone's desperate boast that she was feelin' good.

—My parents own the kennel on Kirk Line, just off the highway. We're staying there for the summer.

—The WellandGood?

—Yeah.

—Jack Welland's your dad?

—Stepdad.

—I did some work for him a few years back. Fixed a leak in his roof. Not the kennel, the house. How's it holding up?

—He hasn't complained.

—That, uh, guy still living upstairs?

—Gil?

—I think that was his name.

—Sure. Parents say they'll have to move to get rid of him.

—I ever tell you about him?

Heather shook her head although Larry knew he'd told her about him at least twice and was really asking René, trying to lure him back into the fold.

—It was the strangest damn thing. I was working around back. Leak was at the joint where someone, the previous owner I guess, had built an addition. They hadn't put any flashing around it, just tar paper and shingles so the wood was all rotten on either side. It was a two day job, half a day if I'd had René there, but back then I was on my own...

It was surprising, given that a minute ago he was barely able to muster a grunt much less a complete sentence, how easily it came back to him. It was one of only three or four stories he told that seemed to keep an audience from drifting before he was through to the end, and telling it fresh to René alongside someone who knew the guy invigorated it. Not far into it he was adding little things that had never happened but seemed like they could have, like how he should have known something was off because Jack Welland kept pestering him about getting Gil to help him out when Larry had already told him it was a one man job. And how Jack had called up to Gil, and when Gil stuck his head out of his window, he asked him if he had his work boots on, and Gil, who seemed normal enough even if he was a little on the delicate side, answered that he did. Then why don't you get your arse down here and do something useful for a change, Jack yelled like he was dealing with a teenager and not someone pushing fifty. Gil answered that he'd love to except that he was expecting guests, and that made Jack nod and smile like he knew what was coming but didn't want to ruin the surprise.

—His first guest arrived as I was sitting down to eat my lunch. The window was still open and I heard him call down that he'd be right there. There was a pause like he was doing a last bit of cleaning and then I heard his feet clomping on the stairs; he really was wearing work boots. A few moments later he led the guest up and they chattered away like two old ladies, I don't know, planning a church bazaar or something. I didn't catch much of what they said except that one of them, I think it was his guest, kept saying amen like it was a period at the end of each of his sentences. The second guest came shortly after and Gil called for him to come on up. He sounded sick, he kept coughing and wheezing and Gil offered to make him a tea then insisted when the man said he was okay. I got the feeling that maybe the two guests didn't like each other much because they were real quiet until Gil returned, and then it was as before, with the three of them jabbering, and the two guests in a contest to see who could say amen louder and more frequently than the other. Then, all of a sudden, Gil shushed them and ran down the stairs to the door. His third guest was a woman, and I took her to be elderly on account of she talked so quietly and Gil spoke to her a little louder and more clearly than he spoke to his other guests. Mostly he was saying how nice she looked and how rosy her cheeks were, that sort of thing. And he asked about her cats, I remember that. So anyway, I finished my lunch and was about to go back to work when I heard Gil screaming, Fuck you, you dirty old hag. I'll rip your fucking head off. You cunt. You filthy, fucking cunt. I mean, I couldn't believe it right. I mean it sounded like, I really thought he was going to do it. That he was going to rip her, you know, fucking head off, so I run to the window and I look inside and there was Gil sitting on the couch, alone, his hands folded neatly in his lap, four cups of tea on the table in front of him. I stood there, I was stunned, and after a minute or so he got up, set the tea cups on a tray and took them into the kitchen.

—That's Gil, all right.

Both the bearded man and the woman nodded their heads, smiling, while Heather rocked back and forth on her chair in imminent danger of falling off. Only René was still, his hands folded over his chest, his eyes dropping, looking beat and, Larry realised later, well past drunk.

—I see him in town once in awhile. Riding his bike around and–

—Talking to the boys.

—Sorry?

The bearded man laughed and scratched at the back of his head.

—Yeah, he sure likes the boys. I swear every time I go to the 7-11, he's out in the parking lot and he's got one of them cornered.

—What do you mean? Kids?

—Yeah kids, teenagers whoever. As long as they're cute and–

—You think that's fucking funny?

René slammed both fists down on the table, knocking over all four empties marking space between two full ashtrays. The bottles rolled off the table and the dull thud of them hitting the floor was drowned out by the dog growling. On his feet now, his ears were pulled back tight to his head and one tooth stuck out from behind his quivering lips. He was staring right at René, his eyes the same colour of hate they'd been when they first saw him at the falls. René ignored him, glaring at the bearded man with a look so barren of bluff that Larry had the sudden insight that no one was going to make it out of there alive.

The woman leapt from her chair and grabbed the dog by the collar, dragging him backwards towards the door. That only made him bark and snarl louder, his nails scratching at the floor, and there was no doubt in Larry's mind that if she let him loose he'd go straight for René and there'd be one less dog in the world, and maybe the smell of the dog's blood on his hands would prove too much for René and he'd come at the bearded man, still frozen in the chair, smiling like he wasn't about to breathe his last. Larry would try to get between them but René'd toss him aside like a vampire drunk on the scent of a virgin, and then René's hands would be around the bearded man's throat. Larry'd go for the cutlery drawer, not thinking about what was to come, just grabbing, and the butcher knife would be in his hand, the one that wasn't sharp enough to cut meat anymore but whose size made it perfect for slicing watermelon. He'd turn back to René knowing what had to be done from the purple blistering the bearded man's cheeks and the woman's screams and the weight of the blade in his hand.

After the defeat at the window, and it was a defeat as surely as this was a day of defeats, Larry took his time getting back to the truck. He lingered over a joint in the secret way then lit a cigarette and smoked it down to the nub, thought about smoking another but settled for bouncing up and down on a squeaky bit of ground on the way out. He was half expecting the truck to be empty when he got back, René taking the opportunity to get while the getting was good, but there he was, his arm hanging out, fingers drumming on the side of the door.

Larry turned out of the pharmacy parking lot then coasted down James Street looking for something in front of the houses to tell him which one the three year-old had lived in but there was nothing that suggested grief beyond one with a sagging roof, the green shingles peeling upwards like flower petals towards the sun, and one with a black Neon propped on cement blocks in its driveway. At the end of the street Larry signalled right then turned left and drove around the corner, past the hospital and down the hill, thumping over the railroad tracks midway. He knew where he was going but not why he was taking the long way to get there except that Anne Street dead-ended at the river and he'd been meaning to see how close the water was to the road, what with all the rain they'd had in the spring. There were enough trees along the bank to block his view until he was through the three way stop where the road turned towards Wilson's Falls. On his left he saw that the river, sunk ten feet below the street, had barely enough current to move the leaves, drifting in flocks, left over from the previous autumn.

The houses on the other side all had yards hollowed out by the yearly flood and rustic wraparound porches sagging at the corners. The house at the end of the block seemed to have mascara running down from dead eyes and it was only on second look that Larry saw it'd been gutted by fire. The last person out, a fire inspector maybe or a kid from the neighbourhood, hadn't bothered to close the front door and two squirrels were chasing each other through it. A moment later they appeared at a second floor window then skirted along the porch's overhang, jumped to a tree, raced down to the lawn and started the loop all over.

His tongue was sticking to the roof of his mouth when The Albion came into sight on the far side of the tracks. He thought, not for the first time, it was a shame it had closed because nothing made a bad day better than watching the five o'clock show with a crowd, to the man, who didn't want to go home either. He parked behind the Royal Bank and got out of the truck without giving a second thought to whether René was coming with him. He heard footsteps behind him as he emerged onto Manitoba Street and didn't check to see if something was coming before stepping between two parked cars. His feet kicked into a jog, an odd bit of self-preservation that didn't account for the gap in traffic, and he had to rein them in once he reached the far side, not wanting it to look like he was making a break for it. That was the worst thing he could do. Carl'd been very specific about that when he was talking about bears, which he often did, maybe to fill the time and maybe because he'd never seen one up close, Germany not having any bears left when he was a kid or maybe never having had any to begin with, Larry couldn't remember. He'd read about them though, Carl did, in the wilderness survival guides he'd bought to prepare himself for life in the new world as if there weren't grocery stores and fast food restaurants and Wal-Marts, just an endless expanse of wilderness full of bears and wolves and cougars — Yeah cougars, Carl had something to say about them too. He'd said the thing about cougars, the thing you had to know about cougars was, that if you saw a cougar it meant you were already dead. If you saw one it was only because it was ripping out your throat or slicing into your soft underbelly to get at the juicy stuff inside. Maybe you'd live to see it take its first bite, long enough to wish it had gone for your jugular so you didn't have to watch it devouring your liver.

Halfway up Chancery Lane, stooped over against the slope, he reached for the hand rail, feeling more tired than he could remember feeling in years. He willed his legs to keep moving, and looked up at the crest, thinking: why, all of the sudden, these thoughts of violence mixed up with Carl, who was just a crazy old fool? Do I really think René is dangerous, and that Heather is right, and that it's only a matter of time before I'll wake up from a dream where I'm drowning to find that I can't breathe because my throat's been cut and René's holding me by the hair, the paring knife, the one we use to slice tomatoes, is already sawing at my hair.

—Ray!

Larry pushed past Milky's outstretched hand like it was a turnstile, spinning the old man, making him clutch for the porch rail, his fit of fuck yous and cocksuckers lost to a sudden violent cough and the click of the Gryphon's door easing shut.

The bearded man and the woman said their good-byes and see you arounds as they dragged their dog down the porch steps. They proffered smiles and waves before the pitch beyond the garage gobbled them up, leaving Larry and Heather alone with only the house behind them. They smoked, not talking, then Heather got up and clambered through the front door. A few breaths later, deep with the rasp of too many cigarettes, Larry followed. The kitchen was dark and empty. A glow was coming through the window over the sink that looked to be the moon although Larry knew it was from the street light where the road met the highway. He shuffled around the table, his feet playing with the idea of emptying the ashtrays or at least tracking the bottle he sent clattering against the cupboard but drawing him instead to the basement stairs. It was midnight in a mineshaft down there and Larry fought to regain control of his legs, driving them towards the bedroom, his hands slapping against his thighs to keep them in line.

The noise started not long after: a low moan leaking through the floor with the rhythmic pulse of a machine warming up. Sweating under a flimsy sheet, it was easy to pretend it came from something outside the house, the wind or the four lanes of the 11 clouded behind a fringe of trees but still known by the stink of diesel and the odd siren, and Larry lay in bed trying to place it, like he'd done with an altogether different sound on the second night he'd spent with Heather in the house down the road.

It had been late then too. They were stretched out naked on their backs with their heads making a triangle on the only pillow he owned. The window was open behind them, holes in the screen fixed with scotch tape giving mosquitoes the resolve to find the ones Larry had missed. The noise came through on a breath of wind, too hot and sticky to be called a breeze. It sounded like someone crinkling paper three rooms away but bit by bit the faint crackle grew into a rattle, a roar, a thousand whispers and something Larry had no words for. His imagination danced along the edges of it, trying to make sense out of the tangle, his body begging for sleep but his mind clinging to the mystery.

—What the hell is that?

Heather stirred beside him and Larry shook his head.

—Sounds like a goddamn stampede.

And she was right. A herd of moose heading their way, pounding the woods into pulp, scouring the ground with their fright and making it known to the world. Both listened, tense, as the herd drew near. When its thunder reached its peak it suddenly dissolved, the bulls and cows scattering, leaving a musk hanging on the air that might just have been the sex between them, and all that remained of it was a fine mist exploding from the screen, its coolness hazing the bed and Heather and Larry on top.

—It was just the rain.

—Yeah.

—On the leaves. Must have heard it coming from miles away.

—Wow.

—You ever heard anything like it?

—No.

They lay there until they were soaking wet from the spray, sharing the joy of discovery and marvelling that something as simple as rain could still fool them.

Seven years later, on a night that could have been its twin, Larry gave up trying to pretend there was any mystery to where the noise was coming from. It was an ungodly sound, a braying moan that could have been the devil laughing or God herself sobbing oceans; an angry clash that turned people to salt in the old times and split the walls of non-believers. It was a noise man was not meant to make (and certainly not in someone else's basement with only the thinnest wedge of land between night and day). Larry lay motionless as if any movement would disturb the delicate balance that kept the it a noise and not, say, a bloody axe pumping at the bed until it was a butcher shop's display case of severed limbs and guts. Heather dug her nails into his arm, making him press his eyes shut against the sting, all the while muttering a string of nonsense indecipherable to even himself-

adaytoendalldaysanddaysanddaysanddaysonedayat
atimeadaytorememeberadaytorejoiceadayadayaday

-to keep from thinking of one particular day, a day like any other, just another day, a day that René woke into every morning.

At his table in the back, Larry couldn't see the front door but he knew Rene was there from the skittish glances Cal threw at it in between snatches of conversation with a table of silver haired mixed pairs fresh from the court. Tennis balls and heart monitors mingled on their table with half-eaten plates of steak and kidney pie, the french fries untouched except for a taste; wine glasses with spritzers still tingling and expensive sunglasses lost without the sun.

Larry turned to the only other person in the bar, a frail looking man with blonde wisps where there should have been hair and a doughy softness to his cheeks taking up four chairs between an out-stretched leg, a black shoulder bag and a straw hat. His fingers were bent over a laptop, his eyes squinting at the keyboard as if he'd suddenly gone blind and couldn't understand why the letters were so hard to find.

A sharp pain exploded just below Larry's knee and he looked to Cal who'd just kicked him hard enough to make him want to kick back.

—He with you?

—Who?

—The guy at the door.

—Yeah.

—I hope he likes his horse piss flat.

—Huh?

—Something's wrong with the taps.

—Then make it a couple of Keith's.

—Keith's? Well, maybe there's hope for you yet.

Cal swerved towards René on his way back to the bar. Shortly after René tracked Larry to his corner and sat hunched forwards with his arms crossed on the table. Cal brought over the beers and set one in front of each of them. René pushed his over to Larry's side and ordered a Coke with no ice. While Cal was getting it for him he tapped his fingers on the tabletop, not watching Larry drink the first beer in two easy swallows.

—You want to tell me what Pace said?

—Seven.

—What?

Larry tilted the second beer and, by the time he'd drank half of it, Cal was back with René's Coke. He stood at the side of the table between them, his head moving back and forth like he was watching a ball bounce even though neither was talking.

—Where's Lucy?

—Her mother called. Big emergency with Nana.

—It's Saturday.

—Tell me about it. She said she'd be back before it got busy.

—You want me to take a look at the taps?

—You think it'll help?

Larry shrugged.

—When's the guy coming?

  Monday.

—Then I guess it couldn't hurt.

Larry took his beer and followed Cal to the taps. He drained his bottle staring at the six of them then set it on the bar and picked up a pint glass, filling the bottom inch from the tap marked HP. The beer fizzed but couldn't muster a head and Larry drank it down.

—It's flat.

—So how much do I owe you?

Larry poured a spurt from the Guinness tap and braced himself for the bitter taste.

—They're all flat, like I said.

Larry dumped what was left of the dark liquid into the sink.

—When was the last time you cleaned the lines?

—That was the first thing I did.

—The CO2 hose might be blocked.

—I checked. It's fine.

—Pressure's good?

—It's good.

—You got a wrench?

Cal shook his head and wandered off towards the kitchen, in no hurry to have Larry taking apart his taps. The bell over the door dinged and a middle-aged couple with matching denim and sag walked in. Pouring himself another half glass of HP, Larry sipped at it and stared at the back of René's head until Cal returned with a bright red toolbox, too small to be of any real use.

—You really think you can fix it?

—Don't see why not.

—There a lot of taps on the roofs of those big cottages?

—Summer residences.

—Whatever.

—You know R.J.'s?

—On the 11?

—Yeah.

—I did the remodel a few years back. Taps were pretty much the same.

—Pretty much?

—The same.

The bell over the door dinged again.

—Getting busy.

—Yeah.

—Your friend hungry?

—I expect.

—He like nachos?

—Everyone likes nachos.

Over the next two hours, The Gryphon filled and emptied and looked like it was going to fill again before the flow tapered off leaving all but the corner tables empty. René had two more Cokes to go with his nachos and didn't move an inch from his chair. Lucy called at four-thirty to say she was at the hospital and just after five a waitress Larry had never seen showed up to fill in. She was in her mid-twenties with hair the colour of lava and wore a see-through black blouse chosen to show off the tattoos on her back and the athletic tone to her front. She didn't smile at Larry or ask his name but she didn't linger at René's table either, so Larry didn't take it personally. By the time the hour hand on the Kilkenny clock over the bar reached half past six, Larry'd run out of ideas on how to resolve the problem with the taps and settled into a regime of sampling that he hoped would provide a new direction.

—So what's the verdict?

—Still flat.

—Hasn't kept you from drinking it.

—Ah well, you know.

—Yeah.

—So I was thinking...

The two of them turned towards the waitress, sitting at the far end of the bar counting her tips. Larry'd learned her name was Chloe but not much else.

—I worked at a place in Toronto that had the same problem. They tried everything they could to figure out what was wrong.

Chloe dumped a handful of change from her pouch and chased a few errant loons into the spill trough.

—So?

—Nothing worked.

—That's a great story. Very inform-

—Until, you didn't let me get to the until.

—Sorry.

—Until, and this was after they'd started talking about sabotage and poltergeists, I mean the guy who ran the place was getting so desperate-

—Until...

—Right. It was the dishwasher.

—The dishwasher sabotaged the taps?

—No, I mean the dishwasher. The machine, you know. You see, this brewer was dropping off a few kegs and they told him about the problem. I don't remember exactly what he said, something about a chemical reaction between detergent and C02 that makes beer go flat. He told them to check the dishwasher. Turned out, the jets were all clogged up with calcium so it wasn't rinsing the soap off the glasses and-

—And you're just mentioning this now.

—Well, he was having so much fun.

Cal levelled a scrunched-up face at Larry that froze the glass a hair from his lips.

—You want me to, uh-

Cal wheeled around before Larry could finish and strode towards the kitchen. Dumping the rest of his beer in the spill trough, Larry ran his thumb along the inside of it and sure enough it did feel a little soapy. He rinsed it out, felt it again, still soapy, then used the bar rag to scour the inside and rinsed it under hot water for the count of twenty. Shaking out the damp clinging to its curve he tilted it under the HP tap and drew a pint. A head rose to tell him he was onto something, and his first sip confirmed it. He was smacking his lips when Cal returned from the kitchen holding a rack full of pint glasses. Larry held the beer up to Cal, giving the thumbs up with the other hand, and Cal draped a rag over his outstretched arm.

—What's that for?

—You going to pay for all that beer you drank?

—It was flat. And it tasted like soap.

—Then it's to clean the glasses with.

—What about the dishwasher?

—The blades are soaking in vinegar.

—No, I mean the dishwasher. The kid you got back there.

—Off at eight. He's a minor. It's the law.

—That ain't a law.

—Well, it should be.

Unable to conjure a glib reply, Larry set to work on the glasses. The rack beside him became a stack of three then five and he was just about through with them when a siege of baseball players from the Fatman's League, "Over Forty or Over Two-Forty" stitched on the breast of their jerseys, left him with another four.

—God.

—I didn't take you for a praying man.

—That's it, I'm done.

—You plan on finishing the beer you just poured.

—I got money, you know?

—Your money's not good here. Not tonight.

—You're a hard man, Calvin Webster.

—I never said any different.

—Shit.

—What's with your friend anyway? He hasn't moved an inch since he sat down.

—Tell me about it.

Larry finished the rack he was working on and called break to no one in particular then slipped outside and lit a cigarette to go with his fresh pint. Milky wandered off to piss against a wall and didn't return, so he smoked a second cigarette as he waited for the Fatman's League to stream past.

Back in the bar René was still doing his statue routine and Larry headed for the bathroom. One foot caught on a two-seater, knocking its wine glasses and appetiser plate onto the floor. He bent down for the broken shards, his hand steadying himself on the table, but couldn't do it without falling over. Calling for a clean-up in aisle four, he lumbered down the hall and through the door marked Gents.

It took forever to relieve himself and even longer to wash his hands and straighten his hair in the mirror. Emerging into the bar, it felt like midnight but the clock wasn't even showing nine. He leaned against the wall, sober enough to register that someone had cleaned up the broken glass, then swivelled his head towards René's table. A woman was sitting in Larry's seat, leaning forward with one hand on René's arm and whispering something that Larry couldn't hear. She was ugly, her face was pockmarked and her nose squashed over cracked lips, but that her ugliness had a recognisable pattern was a few blinks in coming. It was, what's her name? The woman Heather was always going on about. The one who said she knew Lucy from a past life but probably just meant the time Lucy called the cops on her when she showed up naked at her Nana's house. The one that stank like the sewer but that Lucy gave free bowls of soup to because she felt sorry for her, and also because she believed in past lives and lived by the motto, 'You never know...' " The same woman, it was all coming back to him now, Larry'd seen at Morgan's the last time he was there, slouched on the couch watching TV, the matted bush of her privates exposed beneath a loosely tied bathrobe. That woman was sitting in Larry's chair, her fingers casually picking at the hairs on René's unmoving arm and smiling at him in the same way the old hag smiled at Snow White when the dwarves were out working in the mines, just before handing over the apple.

Pushing himself off from the wall gave Larry enough carry to get him to the table in a straight line, and grabbing the back of René's chair gave him enough support to keep him upright.

—It'd just be for a couple of nights. I'll make it worth your while.

The woman smiled through brown stained teeth and Larry swallowed to keep from throwing up.

—What the fuck are you doing?

—I'm talking to my friend. What the fuck are you doing?

—What the fuck's she doing?

—Take it easy, man.

—Get the fuck out of here.

—Don't you fucking touch me.

The woman took a swipe at Larry, her nails raking skin from his cheek, and Larry raised his arm back to give her a taste but couldn't move it an inch beyond that.

—Time to leave, Corrie.

Cal let go of Larry's arm and stepped between him and the woman. Her eyes softened and for a moment she looked almost human.

—I'm just talking to my friend.

—Let's go.

—No.

—Now.

—No!

Cal grabbed her by the arm and pulled her towards the door. Corrie let out a scream and swung at him, the fingernails of her free hand clawing for his eyes. He snatched it by the wrist, not much bigger than a twig, and squeezed hard enough to make her forget about kicking him.

—Get your fucking hands off me.

—Chloe!

Chloe was at the door opening it when Cal got there, dragging Corrie along behind. She made a stab at getting her foot against the frame but Cal jerked her hard and then they were outside with the door slamming shut behind them. A few moments later, Cal returned and locked the door then stood looking at Larry, like he was trying to summon the strength to eject him too.

206

—We need to get the fuck out of here.

Grabbing Larry, René pulled him backwards through the darkened kitchen. Then there were stairs stumbling him up and a stretch he thought was flat but that had him on his ass anyway. René helped him up and didn't let go of him until they were at the truck.

—Compressor's gone and so's the nail gun.

—What?

—Never mind. Get in.

Larry sat in the passenger seat and tugged on the seatbelt stuck in the door but couldn't get it loose.

—Fuckin' thing.

—I'm going to need the keys.

Larry unclipped them from a belt loop. Halfway across the bridge leading out of town, red and blues swirled in the rear view mirror.

—Shit, my seatbelt.

—What?

—It's stuck in the door.

—You're wearing it.

—What the fuck?

—Just let me handle this, okay.

—God, do I ever have to take a piss.

—Just keep your mouth shut.

Rene pulled off to the right and unrolled his window. The officer bent low to it and took a long look inside.

—This your truck?

—No sir, it's his.

—You been drinking?

—No, sir, that would be a violation of my parole.

—I'm going to need you to come with me.

René followed the officer back to his car and Larry tried to look through the back window but the lights were as bright as the sun. He closed his eyes and the next thing he knew, the world was spinning. He opened his eyes again and found that it really was, but only for moment. The ramp led the truck off the highway and Larry gulped back the sick he could feel rising up his throat.

—Pull over.

—We're almost home.

I'm going to be sick.

—It's your truck.

The headlights flashed over the dull grey sheen of his mailbox and he hung onto the door, afraid to move. Rene eased the truck into the driveway then sat there stiff as stone, his hands still on the steering wheel.

—I wasn't trying to save you. Just so's you know.

René shook his head and maybe he was laughing or gritting his teeth, or maybe he was just waiting for Larry to get out so he could back the truck onto the road and be gone because that's exactly what he did, leaving Larry staring after him until the truck's tail lights were just spots burned into his eyes. He stood wavering in the space where Heather's car should have been but wasn't, and he wondered what would happen if he'd just laid down. Would she stop if she saw him and, if she didn't, would she scream or cry or plead with him to be all right? In the end, he decided it wasn't worth the risk and turned towards the porch, thinking that if he made it to his bench it would be a damn miracle.

The End

About the Author

John Jantunen has never been jailed for his political views, fought in a war, or hallucinated giant lizards. He does, however, share the same convictions about writing with many authors who have. Namely, that only by engaging with the world can one create good literature, that memory is a writer's most valuable tool, and that one's imagination should only be used as a last resort. Prior to settling in Guelph, Ontario, with his family John travelled extensively across Canada, living and working in almost every region of the country, and has translated these experiences into two novels, numerous short stories and a dozen screenplays.